A Polish Book of Monsters

A Polish Book of Monsters

Five Dark Tales from Contemporary Poland

———————————

Edited and translated by Michael Kandel

PIASA Books
New York

Published by PIASA Books,
The Polish Institute of Arts and Sciences of America,
208 East 30th St., New York, NY 10016

Library of Congress Cataloging-in-Publication Data

A Polish book of monsters : five dark tales from contemporary
Poland / edited and translated by Michael Kandel.
p. cm.
ISBN 978-0-940962-70-5 (alk. paper)
1. Fantasy fiction, Polish—Translations into English.
2. Science fiction, Polish—Translations into English.
3. Polish fiction—20th century—Translations into English.
I. Kandel, Michael. II. Title.

PG7445.E8P65 2010
891.8'530876208—dc22   2010050583

www.polishbooks.org
Printed in the United States of America

Contents

Introduction

Most Americans who have heard of Stanisław Lem, the Polish science fiction writer and essayist, probably know his name only from the film adaptations of his novel *Solaris* (Soderbergh's in 2002, Tarkovsky's in 1971). Fewer have read one or two of his books. Far fewer people in the United States—who aren't Polish or connected by family to Poles—have any idea of the nation behind him: of Polish history, tradition, culture, of the many generations of Polish writers.

Translation is one way to address this terra incognita problem, to build a communicating bridge across the Atlantic, from Polish reader in Wrocław to American reader in Saint Louis. Thirty and forty years ago, it was my privilege to participate in such bridge building on behalf of Lem, translating several of his books into English. Lem may not have made the best-seller lists here, but he is definitely on our literary map now. He is in the American literary bloodstream. His works, written mainly from the 1960s to the 1980s, are recommended on the Internet by a wide variety of readers and groups. A young author like Jonathan

Lethem, who knows no Polish, said in an interview that he was influenced by Lem.

Lem died in 2006. He had stopped writing fiction for about twenty years but still commented in occasional articles on Poland, the world, and the human condition. His website (http://english.lem.pl/), basically run by his son, is informative and charming (with the whimsical cartoon illustrations by Daniel Mróz) but really gives no sense of the author's stature as both writer and thinker.

In 1997, I was invited to attend a small conference of Polish science fiction and fantasy writers in Warsaw. I went and met many of the genre's stars. In the days and weeks that followed, I began reading their work. I was entertained, fascinated, moved. So now, again, I am in the role of the translator who says to his countrymen, "Look at what I found."

The five Polish writers of this collection range in age from thirty to sixty. Their day jobs are in the fields of science, business, and publishing. Some of their hobbies are mountain climbing, comics, and computers. Their religious beliefs and nonbeliefs are equally varied. All have won awards for their work; all have devoted readers.

For the general American reader, I offer, as context, a brief background about Poland, Polish literature, and Polish fantasy and science fiction. I also share a few thoughts on monsters, obviously the connecting thread among these stories, particularly on how Polish monsters differ from the American varieties.

About Poland

Most countries have a golden age in their past, a period of political ascendancy, military success, perhaps even empire. Poland's height, the Commonwealth, was in the sixteenth century. (The last hurrah perhaps was when Jan Sobieski stopped the Turkish-Tartar invasion of Europe at Vienna in 1683.) Poland ruled over not only Poles but also Lithuanians, Ukrainians, White Russians, and assorted Germans. Its warrior aristocracy was proud and independent, a bit like the nobility of England, with whom they liked to compare themselves.

Their independence led to weak kings, lack of organization and centralization, factions making selfish and destructive deals with foreign powers. Also, no mountain range or body of water served as a buffer against neighboring armies. By the end of the eighteenth century, Poland was a place of political entropy, political vacuum. A final, and moral, grasp for glory was Poland's progressive Constitution of May 3, 1791, which occupied the stage of enlightened liberalism briefly with the American and French constitutions. Then, for the first time in history, a nation ceased to exist without a weapon raised (a simplification for dramatic effect: there was some fighting in the few years before the end). Poland was partitioned; Prussia, Austria, and Russia divided it up among themselves in 1795. Poland had no existence again as a state until after World War I.

During that long nationlessness, poets and novelists strove to preserve Polish identity at home and abroad; soldiers fought in other lands, also hoping to make a future Poland possible; and young men periodically sacrificed themselves in uprisings (in 1830, 1848, and 1863) that were crushed. Poles became known for their visionary idealism, also for their valor in the face of an overwhelming enemy. They became known, in other words, for impracticality—for a splendid if suicidal recklessness, for the grand and gentlemanly gesture. They played a Don Quixote role, feeling both despair and pride.

If one feature in the nineteenth-century construction of Polishness was patriotism, another was irony—which is understandable, given that patriotism time and again proved futile. Equally present was an obsession with betrayal (treachery, treason), which often accompanies frustrated patriotism, as if some principle of human balance regularly pairs opposing qualities in a culture.

In every story of this collection, you will find both courage and betrayal, and that mix is very Polish.

The twentieth century played back the patterns formed earlier, but cynicism grew deeper. Then the dreadful Jewish story—before World War II, Poland had the largest Jewish community in Europe—added a new discomfort, a sense of shame in some, a touchiness in others. Jews had really never been part of Poland, even if some of Poland's cities (e.g., Łódź) were predominantly Jewish. Polish Jews were a country within a country, having separate laws, culture, language, and religion. When few living Jews were left after Hitler, Jewish ghosts, whether seen or denied, became a troubling part of the Polish psyche.

Poland fought with the Allies against Hitler but "in reward" (Polish sarcasm) had to spend the next fifty years behind the Iron Curtain, under the Soviet thumb.

About Polish Literature

Polish literature has been strong in poetry and drama. It began in the sixteenth century but blossomed into world-class writing in the 1830s—a blossoming that seems to occur in most Slavic nations, if sometimes in different decades, under the sign of Romanticism.

One name from Polish Romanticism should be mentioned, that of the poet Adam Mickiewicz. Unfortunately poetry is, as the famous definition tells us, that which is lost in translation, so I believe Mickiewicz is fated to remain only a name to most of the world. Foremost among his masterpieces is *Pan Tadeusz*, an epic poem (novel in verse) that expresses Polish patriotism, irony, and the ever sore point of treason. His epic's attempt to restore a lost world succeeds, every time the book is opened, by the in-exhaustible magic of great art.

Polish poetry and drama in the twentieth century were first-rate and avant-garde. Both the writing and the staging of plays were sophisticated and groundbreaking; this tradition probably accounts for the better known—globally known—achievements of Polish filmmaking. Absurdism and dark humor are Polish specialties. For a sampler of modern Polish literature, I'd recommend Zbigniew Herbert's poetry, Sławomir Mrożek's plays, Witold Gombrowicz's prose; all three authors appear in respectable, readable English. Polish absurdism tends to be more political than philosophical, though of course those two things are not mutually exclusive. Since political realities have been a survival issue for Poles over two hundred years, it is no surprise that politics is central to Polish literature.

Polish Fantasy and Science Fiction

One could argue that science fiction begins in Poland in the early twentieth century (with Żuławski, Grabiński), but Lem really fills that sky suddenly, like a nova.

Stanisław Lem (born 1921) is, by any measure, a giant of the genre, of political-philosophical satire, and of the futurological essay. For a sampler, I'd recommend his novel *Fiasco* (science fiction) and his *Star Diaries of Ijon Tichy* (satirical stories). Lem's genius as an essayist is not yet demonstrable in English. His great *Summa technologiae*, written in the mid-1960s, is now being translated for a university press, but I am not sure that even with the best intentions and efforts of the translators the depth of his thought and the power and wit of his prose will make it across the gap of years, cultures, and languages.

Janusz Zajdel, born 1938, was a nuclear physicist who wrote science fiction novels. I think of him as a bridge between Lem and today's generation of writers in fantasy and science fiction. He tells a good story, has many of the virtues of a commercial writer, but does not provide easy solutions to complex problems. Zajdel's sociological science fiction of the 1980s depicts rigidly and inhumanly controlled societies that allude to Poland under Soviet rule. His *Limes inferior* (1982), set in a futuristic city that resembles Chicago, portrays a gritty hero who fights a totalitarian system only to learn, in the end, that the system is merciful, in place to keep the human race from the knowledge that it is doomed.

It is partly thanks to both Lem and Zajdel that so many writers in Poland today do not provide happy endings to their fantasy and science fiction tales. Zajdel died in 1985 (from lung cancer: he worked with radiation and also smoked heavily), and a literary award in his name was created that year. Presented at the annual Polcon, Poland's most important science fiction convention, the award goes to novels and short stories. At the ceremony, the trophy is presented by Zajdel's widow.

Poles are surprisingly cognizant of American and British fantasy and science fiction—of our best sellers and classics both. The premier genre magazine *Nowa Fantastyka* (New Fantasy and Science Fiction) offers not only translations of stories written in English but also intelligent reviews and discussions of many American and British science fiction novels. One reason for this strong English-Polish link is that there are several excellent Polish translators; another reason is that far more Poles read English now than did a generation ago. A favorite American writer, practically an icon in Poland, is Philip K. Dick. Poles understand and relate to the aura of death and defeat in Dick's work, the hidden conspiracies, the bitter humor of the victim.

Poles also looked east: Russian science fiction (the Strugatsky Brothers, Kir Bulychev) was widely read. So from the beginning Polish readers have had a broader perspective on the genre than American readers.

(A note for those unfamiliar with this genre: despite fantasy's differences from science fiction, both have been placed under the same rubric. Although many people prefer one to the other, many also enjoy reading—and writing—both. After Tolkien's incredible success in the 1960s [which led to a fantasy boom in Poland in the early 1980s], publishers and booksellers made fantasy a kind of subgenre of the science fiction category.)

Turning to the authors of the stories in this collection, in the order they appear:

Marek Huberath, born 1954, is a physicist yet writes not on science and technology but on themes philosophical and moral: how people become beasts or remain human in extreme circumstances. His hobby is mountain climbing. He told me once that he feels at peace only when he has empty air under his feet. A traditionalist, Huberath is protective of women in a way that with no exaggeration could be called knightly. (In general, chivalry toward women is high among Polish virtues.) His realistic treatment of suffering and ethical problems has a punch that reminds me of the work of Aleksandr Solzhenitsyn.

Andrzej Sapkowski, born 1948 in Łódź, began his writing career with "Spellmaker." This first work, submitted in a short story competition, appeared in 1986 and began a cycle of fantasy adventures—starring Geralt, a kind of magician samurai for hire who goes from village to village slaying or neutralizing monsters—that became extremely popular in Poland and the Czech Republic. These adventures have also been translated into Russian, German, and Spanish. The high-budget Polish fantasy film *Wiedźmin* (in English, *Hexer*), based on them, came out in 2001. More recently, a video game was based on them.

Tomasz Kołodziejczak, born 1967, is an editor in Warsaw for the international company Egmont; he edits

Donald Duck Magazine, quite successful in Poland, and Polish comic book collections of various kinds. He is an active organizer in the science fiction world, interviewing for TV and radio, putting together conventions, discussing, collecting. His novels and stories reflect the human tragedies of a Poland caught between Stalin and Hitler during World War II. Military encounters and martyrdoms recur in his fiction.

Andrzej Zimniak was born 1946 in Warsaw, when that city was mostly a field of rubble. Although he is a much-published chemist, his science fiction tends to be psychological rather than technological. His story "Cage Full of Angels" was nominated for a Janusz Zajdel Award in 1995. In his spare time Zimniak dives in the sea and hikes in the mountains.

Jacek Dukaj, born 1974, caused a stir by his youth: his bravura "Golden Gallery" came out when he was eighteen. Dukaj has been applauded for his unusual abundance of science fiction ideas and for his ability to convey alien worlds and minds. His stories and novels have won numerous awards in Poland. An animation by Tomasz Bagiński of his novella "The Cathedral" was nominated for an Academy Award in 2003. He is well versed in American science fiction; some of his favorite authors are Gene Wolfe, Greg Bear, and Greg Egan.

These five do not exhaust the field. But it seems pointless to list names if there is no possibility yet for an

English reader to attach them to texts in passable English.[1] Someday perhaps another translator will introduce more Polish authors of fantasy and science fiction to the anglophone public.

Polish Monsters

Slavic fairy tales feature monsters that Americans are more or less acquainted with, with the exception maybe of the aggressive witch: she comes after perfectly innocent people and does violence to them, with no connection to Satan or hell. The *poludenica* (south Slavic), for example, will grab you in broad daylight; the word for her derives from "noon." A Slovak witch will attack you in an open field. Some younger Americans know Baba Yaga (Russian), who lives in a hut on chicken legs and flies in a mortar, from a version of her in the comic book *Hell-Boy*.

This book of monster stories was put together not in reference to Slavic folklore. My notion, rather, is that monsters are representations of evil and that the Polish take on evil differs from ours.

Monsters in American movies—Frankenstein, Dracula, the Wolf Man, the Mummy, zombies, Freddy, Jason, Hannibal Lecter—are partly human, partly not. The "partly not" is the operative pivot. A monster's humanity—and therefore anguish—may be an element, but it must not get in the way of the main purpose: to make us gasp and scream. Thus American monsters lurk, stalk, suck blood, maim, and kill. They are villains. In the horror genre of publishing, their role is to deliver the commodity of fear. It is not unknown but unusual for a work of American fiction to tell a story from the monster's point of view (e.g., John Gardner's *Grendel*). Whereas you will find that in three of these five Polish stories, the monster is also the protagonist.

What is monstrous to Poles? The question leads to paradox and puzzle. For example, is a monster one who exists outside of and endangers a social system, like Zimniak's hoodlum with vampiric powers, or is a monster one who keeps that system going, like Dukaj's magic general? Is a monster's physical deformity associated with humanity, as in Huberath's postapocalyptic future, or with inhumanity, as in Sapkowski's fantastic adventure or Kołodziejczak's war among different species from different worlds?

Consider two heroes from Polish nineteenth-century literature, one tragic, one tragic and comic at the same time. Mickiewicz's poet-prophet-patriot Konrad, in "The Great Improvisation" (in the play *Forefathers' Eve, Part III*), speaks to God on behalf of Poland's misfortune—and in so doing, in his anger, teeters at the brink of blasphemy and eternal damnation. In a twentieth-century play (*Tango*), Mrożek suggests a link between Konrad's improvisation and fascism. The impassioned plea for justice, the reaching for salvation, has a dark side, a satanic possibility.

INTRODUCTION

In Henryk Sienkiewicz's *With Fire and Sword*, a historical novel set in the mid-seventeenth century, Longinus Podbipięta, a Lithuanian, is a bit like the lovable, gaunt Knight of the Mournful Countenance. He has taken a vow of chastity: he may not pursue the object of his affections until he has cut off three enemy heads in battle with a single blow of his enormous Crusader's sword. His opportunity finally comes at a siege, when three Tartars climb a defending wall, where Podbipięta stands, and show their heads together. Soon after, the hero is killed, and in both book and film his death by arrows is Christlike. Bolesław Prus, an author contemporary with Sienkiewicz but no Romantic, remarked that Podbipięta, for all his praying, was no Christian but a killing machine, a human guillotine.

Both heroes are champions of the good and of the nation, but the Polish mind, even in the throes of patriotism, observes that the line between good and evil, between human and monstrous, can be perilously thin.

Polish monsters, internal, are therefore always very near.

Note

1. Here are fifteen more writers nevertheless, given alphabetically and with a few remarks. My list is neither complete nor particularly fair—as I am no authority in this field:

INTRODUCTION

Ewa Białołęcka: young adult fantasy, not unlike
Andre Norton; emphasis on feelings

Anna Brzezińska: fantasy realistically conceived
(medieval) and set in a brutal world; irony,
humor

Eugeniusz Dębski: all genres; a prolific veteran

Jacek Inglot: his *Quietus* an alternate history of a
Christianity that arises in Japan, not Rome

Mirosław Jabłoński: sociological science fiction, also
postmodern hijinks

Jacek Komuda: magical Polish history; resonance
with Henryk Siekiewicz (*Quo Vadis?*)

Feliks Kres: military fantasy; naturalism, an original
world builder

Konrad Lewandowski: idea-generated science fiction;
philosophy, satire

Marek Oramus: literary science fiction (sociological,
political, psychological), sometimes with sharp
humor

Andrzej Pilipiuk: humorous fantasy, his most famous
character an alcoholic exorcist in the sticks

Adam Wiśniewski-Snerg: science fiction; an obsessed,
alienated individualist—not unlike Philip K.
Dick, except crazier

Marcin Wolski: satirical science fiction, postmodern
history (not unlike that of Umberto Eco)

INTRODUCTION

Maciej Żerdziński: a psychological creator of sick
worlds

Andrzej Ziemiański: entertainment fantasy, very
popular

Rafał Ziemkiewicz: solid psychological-political
science fiction deeply set in the real world

A Polish Book of Monsters

Yoo Retoont, Sneogg. Ay Noo

Marek S. Huberath

I

On the floor, several bright spots formed a row. Snorg liked to watch them move slowly across the dull tiles. The spots of light were different from the glow that suffused the Room. He had discovered some time ago that the source of this light was the small windows near the ceiling. He liked to lie on the floor so the spots would warm him. He wanted to do this now. He tried to move his arms but managed only to fall helplessly off the bed.

"Dags . . . ," he hissed between clenched teeth. He couldn't move his numb jaw.

"Dags . . . ," he repeated with an effort.

One of the Dagses turned his head from the viewscreen—in reaction probably to the thud of the body instead of to Snorg's voice. Moosy was humming some tune the whole time, making little yawps for the words. The Dags with a few quick jerks pulled his way to Snorg and slapped him in the face, hard. Both Dagses had strong arms. They didn't use their undeveloped legs much.

"Pa . . . pa . . . ," stammered the Dags, making rhythmic motions with his shoulders to say that Snorg would be able to move his arms in a minute. He started hooking the tangle of wires to Snorg. The other Dags also came, pulling himself, and gave Snorg's hair a yank. The yank hurt, but pain was what Snorg wanted.

"My head . . . head . . ." A pounding in his skull. "Good . . . good."

The second Dags then poked a finger in Snorg's eye. Snorg twisted his head away and roared. The first Dags beat at the second Dags, until the second Dags rolled away. Snorg's eye brimmed with tears, so he couldn't see if the first Dags was attaching all the electrodes right. But he didn't worry, because the Dags usually did. He imagined the Dags attaching the wires of the machine, imagined him cocking his head comically as he worked. Both Dagses had eyes set so wide apart, they had to cock their heads. It was amusing.

"Tavegner! . . . Want to hear a story?" That was Piecky's smooth, resonant voice. Snorg admired the way Piecky talked. He could make out every word, although his lack of external ears limited his hearing. Piecky was answered by a loud gurgle. Tavegner still couldn't move. He announced his presence only by gurgling. Had he stood up, he would have been the tallest of them, taller than Tib or Aspe. Tib was the only one who stood, so she was the tallest.

"I might be taller than Tib, if I could stand," Snorg thought.

He was pleased that today he had feeling in his entire head. The pain was a service provided him daily by the Dagses.

"Piecky, shut up!" shouted Moosy. "You can tell him the story later . . . I'm singing now."

Snorg's hands were numb, like pieces of wood, but they moved according to his will. He tore himself free of the tangle of wires and tubes. He pinched his arm. There was no feeling.

"At least I can move it," he thought. He inspected the cuts and bruises on his body. Most were healing. But he had two new cuts from his last fall off the bed. Cuts were Snorg's curse: a moment of inattention, and he could blunder into something and break his skin without knowing it. He was constantly afraid that he wouldn't notice a cut in time and it would get infected. He crawled to the viewscreen. Tib stood nearby, rigid, while one of the Dagses was trying to pull her clothes off from the bottom.

"Who dresses her?" Snorg wondered. Every day the Dagses did the same thing, and every day, in the morning, Tib was dressed again.

Finally Tib's gray gown fell to the floor, and the Dags started to climb up her leg.

Snorg watched to see. What happened was what always happened: the little Dags got nowhere. When he was high enough, Tib simply scissored her legs shut. The Dags, resigned, went and squatted in front of the viewscreen and stared open-mouthed at it.

"She's not that stupid," thought Snorg. "She always closes her legs in time . . ."

Tib was a woman—only lately had Snorg realized this. She looked very much like the women the viewscreen showed during the lessons.

"Her hips maybe are a little narrow, and she's too tall, but everything else is in place . . ." Until now he had thought of her as furniture, a motionless decoration of the Room. She seemed even taller from the floor. Someday he would like to talk to her. Tib was the only person in the Room he had been unable to communicate with. Even Tavegner, who lay like a mound of meat and couldn't utter a word, had interesting things to tell. You conversed with him by the trick of having yes be one gurgle and no two. Tavegner filled almost half the Room, and for a long time everyone thought he was like Tib. It was Piecky who figured out how to talk with him. Before that, the Dagses discovered that Tavegner responded to jabs, because they liked to lounge on his immense, soft, warm body. Clever Piecky worked out the way for Tavegner to gurgle yes for the letter of the alphabet he wanted and to gurgle twice to end a word. Everyone would gather around to listen. Snorg would bring the box that held Piecky, and the Dagses would drag Moosy. All together they would spell out letter by letter.

"I am Tavegner," Tavegner said. Then he told them a number of things. He told them he liked it when the Dagses lounged on him, he thanked Piecky, and he asked them to move him a little so he could see the viewscreen better. But lately Tavegner had become lazy: he preferred to be given simple yes-or-no questions.

Snorg moved himself to Piecky.

"Piecky, are you a man or a woman?" he asked and began to unwrap the sheet.

"Stop that, damn it, Snorg . . . It doesn't matter what I am." Piecky's small body twisted, but Snorg unwrapped it all the way. Then he wrapped it up again.

"You don't have anything," he said.

"What did you think, stupid?" Piecky sneered. "The Dagses would have found out long ago if I had . . ."

Piecky's head was beautiful. It was larger even than Snorg's and formed better even than the heads of the people on the viewscreen.

"You have a beautiful head, Piecky," said Snorg, to put him in a better humor. Piecky actually blushed at that.

"I know," he replied. "And yours is ugly, but normally formed, all in all, except for the ears . . . I'm the brains here and will be around long after they've put you all away."

"What are you talking about?" asked Snorg

"Nothing . . . I need the sucker now."

Snorg pulled out the wall tube for excrement, plugged it into Piecky, and left him. The viewscreen was

5

showing trees, a lot of trees. They were pretty, colorful, and moved gracefully. Snorg had never seen trees but dreamed of sleeping in one. He imagined branches arranged around him to make a soft, warm bed. The viewscreen always showed pretty things: spreading landscapes, people shaped correctly. He learned a lot of useful information.

Snorg felt regret that he wasn't pretty like the people he saw on the viewscreen who engaged in all kinds of complicated activities. From the perspective of the floor and his physical shortcomings, those people seemed perfection. It was his fault he was the way he was instead of like them, though he didn't know why it was his fault. Watching the viewscreen, he forgot everything. With his eyes he absorbed the scenes and facts that flowed from it. He saw things that had never been in the Room, things that would have remained unknown to him forever without the viewscreen.

A woman appeared. She stood unmoving. She was a model to demonstrate what bodily proportions a correctly formed woman should possess. Near the viewscreen, Tib stood unmoving and watched with glassy eyes. Snorg compared her with the woman on the viewscreen. Tib was bald, not a hair on her, which made her head very different from the head of the woman on the viewscreen, but when Snorg tried to picture hair on Tib's head, the comparison wasn't so bad. Tib had delicate ears, which stood out a little and were translucent. Snorg envied her those ears. On the viewscreen, lines appeared, showing the correct proportions. Snorg crawled to Tib to measure her proportions with a string. Not only did she have both arms of equal length, and both legs equal, but also her arms were shorter than her legs, and even in the smallest details Tib's build agreed with the build of the model. To measure her head in proportion to the rest of her body, he got up on his knees and stretched his arms as high as he could. Everything was right. He beheld Tib with admiration.

"Her body is completely correct," he thought, and then realized that he had managed to lift himself up on his numb knees. He immediately fell.

The hum in his ears told him that with the fall he had lost consciousness. When the hum went away, Snorg heard Piecky yelling to Moosy.

"Relax! Stop fighting! . . . When he's done, he'll go," Piecky was saying.

Moosy sobbed. "I can't stand . . . He's disgusting, an animal . . . Stop! Leave me alone . . ."

Snorg lifted his head: one of the Dagses had climbed into the box with Moosy.

"This is becoming unendurable," he thought. "We can't defend ourselves against them . . . and we can't live with them."

The Dags stopped its hoarse panting and plopped to the floor.

2

Piecky was going to tell a story. The Dagses held up his arm for the gesturing, though he could make only the most limited motions with it. He scratched his face with his hand.

"That's great, that's wonderful," he said over and over. "You people don't know how to make use of your bodies."

A few slaps by the Dagses brought him around.

He began to tell the story.

"It was a lovely dream." Piecky closed his eyes. "I was floating in air . . . It was heavenly . . . I had these black, flat wings on my sides, the kind we see sometimes on the viewscreen . . . The air moved with me. It was wonderfully cool," he said more softly, as if to himself. "Moosy was flying beside me. Her wings were bright green. She had four wings and flapped them so nicely, I was sorry I was only Piecky . . ."

From the corner came a gurgle.

"Tavegner asks you to speak up," said Snorg, and the next hollow gurgle confirmed that.

"All right. I'll talk louder," Piecky said, as if shaking himself awake. "The Room became smaller and smaller," he continued, "and everything around me got greener and greener. Both the Dagses were flying below us, going in the same direction we were . . . and it was wonderful, because the sky we were flying toward was an enormous viewscreen, and as you got nearer, you could see the pixels. I could move in any direction . . ."

From the corner where Moosy's box was came a quiet sob. Snorg pulled himself toward her.

"Do you need anything?" he asked.

"I wanted to call you, because if one of the Dagses comes, he'll do the thing I hate again. Put me next to Piecky, could you?" she asked.

"Did his story move you?" Snorg asked Moosy, regarding her. Unlike Piecky, she had all her limbs, though they were shriveled.

"It's not Piecky, it's Tavegner," she said through her tears. "The last time Piecky told a story, Tavegner asked to speak by letters . . . and he said . . ."

Snorg nodded.

"He said he wanted to go into the grinder instead of Piecky . . ."

"Grinder?" Snorg didn't understand.

"Piecky learned about it a long time ago," Moosy explained. "He analyzes everything they say on the viewscreen. They pick the best of us . . . those who are formed the best, and the rest—go into the grinder."

"You mean, the thing they show on the viewscreen and call war?"

She nodded yes. "Put me next to Piecky," she said. "Every time he finishes telling his beautiful dream, he's so feeble . . ."

Making a tremendous effort, Snorg lifted Moosy from her box and put her in the crib Piecky lay in, after

9

which he had to slide back to the floor in a hurry, because Tib was soiling herself. He attached the sucker to her. When she was finished, he grasped her hips with all his strength and pulled himself to his knees.

"Don't do it that way, all right . . . ?" he said, looking up at her. Tib looked down and saw his face twisted with effort. Her ears stuck out a little, and the light shone through them. To him they seemed extraordinarily beautiful. He clenched his numb jaw and took Tib by the shoulders. He felt that she was helping him, not pulling away but trying to stand straight to support him. She continued staring at his face. Between her parted lips, white teeth were visible.

Rising, Snorg felt large, gigantic . . . He stood. For the first time he stood on his paralyzed legs. Now he was looking at her not from below but from above . . . looking at Tib, who was as high as the sky.

Everyone stopped talking.

He decided to take a step. He felt power . . . Suddenly he saw that one of his feet was moving toward her . . .

"Tib! I'm walking . . ." It was meant to be a shout, but it came out as a snort or sob. Suddenly the Room swayed, and Snorg fell flat on his back with a crash.

3

The Room had two other occupants, whom Snorg never met, because they both used the same machine he did.

While he was active, they slept. They were Aspe and Dulf. Aspe resembled Tavegner in shape, though she wasn't his equal in size. Piecky said she was intelligent and nasty. She couldn't speak, but communication with her presented no problem. She never detached her artificial arms and loved to play odd tricks on Piecky or Tavegner. Snorg hoped to talk with her someday, and with Dulf, who lay curled in a fetal position and whose incredibly wrinkled skin made you think he was ancient, though he was the same age they all were, that is, just after puberty.

Tib stopped fouling the Room, she learned to go to Snorg when she felt the need. Snorg, seeing her, usually was able to get the sucker. Tib began to respond to him: sometimes she would walk to the part of the Room where he was lying and stand by him, looking at him. She was much more active than she had been before.

"I underestimated you, Snorg," Piecky said once. "You're okay . . . You were able to make contact with Baldy." Baldy was what he called Tib. "I couldn't, though I tried plenty . . . You've changed, Snorg. Before, you looked like an animal that's beaten all the time. Now one can see thought in your face."

"Animal" meant primitive, mindless, and strong. Occasionally the viewscreen showed pictures of real animals that were long extinct. Snorg was pleased by Piecky's compliment and understood why Piecky had given it. From that day Snorg practiced to strengthen his fortitude and will. After the moment when an exertion of will forced his unfeeling legs to make the first step, will became for him the most important thing. He could take many steps now, though often it ended with a dangerous fall. He stood by leaning on Tib's body, but he walked by himself, and she only helped him a little. Sometimes, when he woke, he could move his arms without the help of the Dagses, and without the machine.

"You can see the will in my face," he told Piecky.

Piecky, lying down, lifted his head and looked.

"You're right," he said. "The lines have hardened, the corners of your mouth turn down. But you better hurry, Snorg. I have the feeling we won't be together long . . ."

What Piecky relied on was his brain. He would spend hours at the keyboard of a viewscreen and, if one of the Dagses didn't unscrew his artificial hand as a joke, he would tap at the keys continually. Learning was his passion, and being with the machine. Snorg knew that you could make Piecky happy by setting him down at the keyboard and letting him sit there for hours.

4

Snorg decided to teach Tib to speak. Piecky advised him to press her hand to his throat so she could feel the vibrations of his vocal cords. For this purpose, in order to stand, Snorg grabbed her by the hips. But he did it too suddenly, and Tib fell. It was the first time he saw her on the floor. One of the Dagses, seizing the opportunity, quickly got between her legs, which had been thrown apart. Snorg swung, and the little one, from the blow, went rolling across the floor. There was blood.

"Snorg! Stop!" cried Piecky. "You'll hurt him."

"It's my blood," said Snorg, inspecting his hand. "I cut my hand on him."

Tib had pulled herself together and sat up. The Dagses didn't approach her, watching Snorg carefully.

"Maybe it's good you did that," said Piecky. "I would have, if I could, for Moosy . . . They do with her what they want, whenever they want."

Snorg took Tib's hand and placed the palm on his throat.

"Tib," he said, pointing at her.

She watched him in silence.

"Tib," he repeated.

She looked frightened.

He passed his hand along her face, touched a pink ear, and was surprised: Tib's ear had no opening.

"Piecky!" he shouted. "You're a genius! You were right. She's deaf. Only by touch . . ."

Over and over, with extreme care to be correct, he pronounced her name. He had complete control of his mouth now. After one of the times, her lips moved, and she gave a muffled, hollow noise: "Ghbb . . ." She got to her feet and repeated it several times.

"Ghbb . . . ghbbr." She said it louder and louder, walking across the Room.

"She'll wake Dulf," Piecky said.

Snorg gestured for her to come. She came and sat. Again he started saying her name.

"You know, this morning I saw the Dagses doing it to each other," said Moosy. Morning meant the time when the rays of sun came through the windows at the ceiling and made spots on the floor.

"They took turns being on top," she said.

"That never happens during the day," Piecky stated.

"Are they ashamed in front of us?"

"The Dagses?!" Piecky burst into laughter. "With those low foreheads? . . . They must be cretins."

5

Tib learned quickly. Soon she could say her name, Snorg's, Piecky's, and several other words. Piecky was of the opinion that her sight was not good either and that most information came to her through touch. He wasn't sure, however, whether this was physiological or whether Tib's brain was simply unable to process all the data entering through her eyes.

Dulf began to wake up more frequently. He never changed his position on the floor, though he blinked and even spoke. His speech was comical: he stammered and couldn't find words. Snorg wanted to know how Dulf managed without a machine, but Dulf didn't know the meaning of the word "will," so there was nothing to discuss between them. The Dagses once tried to straighten Dulf on the floor, but it turned out that his body was actually in a ball. Piecky said that was impossible, the only explanation was that Dulf was twins grown together and he had a little brother on his belly.

"Have you noticed, Snorg," Piecky remarked, lifting his artificial hand from the keyboard, "how quickly we've been changing? Before, I thought everything was fixed for us: you crawled, Tib stood like a post, Dulf spoke only when you slept. And now?"

Snorg was interested. "What do you mean, Piecky?"

"A big change awaits us, a very big change. Remember how it was at the beginning?"

Snorg nodded.

"Each one of us had a viewscreen in front of his nose. The viewscreens taught us everything, showed us what the world was like and how it should be . . . We were surrounded with wires, which got our muscles going, our organs, the whole body . . . and kept us alive."

"I still use the machine sometimes, but I seem to recall, through a fog, that it was that way with all of us," said Snorg.

"Through a fog, exactly!" Piecky became excited. "They pump drugs into us, give us powders. We forget . . .

Though maybe they want what we forget to remain deep inside us . . . in the unconscious."

Snorg saw that Piecky didn't look well: his beautiful face was tired, the skin was dark around his eyes, and he was very pale.

"You spend too much time in front of the viewscreen. You're looking worse and worse . . . ," Snorg said.

Suddenly one of the Dagses became interested in Piecky. The Dags apparently wanted to carry him to another place, though for the moment he only stroked Piecky's cheek gently and tugged at his hair.

Piecky gave Snorg a knowing look.

"You see?" He smiled. "They understand some things after all. I only became aware of this recently. I don't know why they both want to pass themselves off as cretins . . ."

The Dags gave Piecky a slap and angrily left for another part of the Room. Piecky's grin broadened.

"You think I'm entertaining myself, Snorg? . . . That all Piecky needs is to be put in front of the viewscreen and have his hand screwed on, and he's happy?"

The look on Snorg's face said nothing.

"Snoegg," said Tib. She could now take the sucker from the wall herself and didn't foul the Room anymore, but she wasn't able to put the tube away. Snorg helped her and returned to Piecky.

Piecky told him, "Thanks to the viewscreen, I've learned a lot of things. Did you know, Snorg, that there exist many rooms like ours? . . . The people that live in them, they're like us. Some more defective, some less. One can see those rooms, because there are not only viewscreens everywhere but also cameras . . . We are being constantly observed. My guess is that the lenses are near the ceiling, but it's hard to see them. In one of the rooms, a dark-blue room, lives a Piecky just like me . . . His name is Scorp. We've introduced ourselves. He looks at me on the viewscreen, and I look at him. He too has an artificial hand . . ."

"Maybe," Snorg suggested, "we don't deserve to live the way the people shown on the viewscreen do, who are correctly formed."

Piecky became furious.

"So you've swallowed that crap! And you feel guilty." He twisted so violently, it loosened the straps of his hand. Snorg had to tighten them.

Piecky's eyes roved, glittered. "They feed us guilt," he spat. "I don't know why they're doing it, but I'll find out . . . Just as I found out a lot more from those goddamn viewscreens than I was supposed to . . ."

Snorg was awed by the strength that pulsed from Piecky. "And I thought will was my specialty," he mused.

Piecky must have read the expression on his face as doubt, because he went on:

17

"Think about it, Snorg. Every program they show us, every fact . . . it's all about how a human being should be. The arms, such a way, the legs, such a way, the correct way . . . And we? And I, what am I? A tatter of a man . . . And that's supposed to be my fault? Do you understand?! Why do they keep drumming that into us?"

Snorg said nothing. This proved how extremely wise Piecky was. One could learn from him, learn how to look at the world differently. But Tib sat down beside Snorg and began to snuggle her face in his. The touch of her delicate skin, Snorg loved that more than anything.

"I'm afraid I won't have time to learn everything. Time's running out," Piecky concluded under his breath, seeing that Snorg was no longer listening.

6

"Pieckyy! . . . ," called Moosy.

"Don't, he's sleeping," said Snorg.

"Then come here and look at Aspe," she insisted. "She's not breathing."

Getting up by himself took Snorg several seconds of excruciating effort. Aspe, it turned out, was lying as she usually did—a little twisted, her withered hands tucked underneath her large, flat face.

Snorg examined her.

"She's sleeping, the way she always does."

18

"You're wrong, Snorg. Look again."

Turning Aspe's face toward the ceiling was beyond Snorg's strength. Fortunately the meddlesome Dagses were nearby. The three together were able to move her. Her body was cold and stiff.

"Damn, you're right . . . It must have happened some time ago," he said in a hollow voice. "And I never exchanged a word with her. She was always asleep . . . Should we wake Piecky?"

"No. He'll find out anyway," Moosy said. "I don't understand her death. It doesn't go with what Piecky told us."

Snorg sat with his face in his hands. Hearing a low, incoherent noise behind him, he turned. It was Tavegner crying. Tears, one after the other, were streaming down his red cheeks.

"Turn me over on my back," Moosy asked Snorg. "The skin on my stomach burns. I must have bed sores."

"On your stomach, you're safer from the Dagses," he said.

"When they want it, it's no problem for them to turn me over."

Aspe's body disappeared while everyone slept, so no one knew how it was done.

Seeing Piecky sitting haggard at the keyboard, Snorg decided to tell him what Moosy had said. He put Piecky in a more comfortable position, sat beside him, and told him.

"Aspe's death doesn't contradict what I've con-cluded," Piecky answered. "The laws that govern us operate statistically. It's simple: first they tested us thoroughly and selected those who were viable, or possibly the others died . . . Then they discarded those who couldn't learn, the com-plete cretins. The rest they taught intensively, using various means . . ."

Snorg watched the capering Dagses, then looked at Piecky, who returned the look with a smile.

"Exactly," Piecky went on. "Aspe died because the tests they ran weren't perfect. Unless continued survival is itself a test."

"What comes next?" asked Snorg.

Piecky's shrug was with his whole body: he had no idea.

"Nothing good, I'm sure . . . In any case, nothing good for me." He hesitated. "You see, Snorg, I was able to penetrate the information system that serves us. I saw other rooms, many of them. In each one, the people are our age, or younger. The very young ones sit in front of viewscreens and fill themselves with information. The ones our age do what we are doing now: living, observing, conversing . . . I haven't yet found a room with people who are older than us . . . There's a kind of information barrier. The system doesn't answer questions about that . . . But it will end soon, this. I feel it, Snorg."

7

A strong light hit Snorg in the eyes. For a while he couldn't focus. Then he became aware that he was no longer in the Room. He was lying on something hard, in a place that seemed vast. He felt terribly alone, because none of his companions was with him. At the other end of the place sat an unknown man. He was very old, but Snorg realized that the man was simply older than those Snorg had been living with. The man, seeing that Snorg was awake, approached him and extended a hand.

"My name is Bablyoyannis Knoboblou," he said.

Slowly, with an effort of will, Snorg rose from his bedding.

"Congratulations, Snorg. On this day you become a person. You were the best . . ."

Snorg reached and shook the man's hand, curious to see what the hand felt like.

"I have here the report of Central"—the man took a few sheets of paper from the desk—"and the decision of the Committee, which is made up of persons . . . You will receive an identity card and can choose a name."

Snorg didn't understand.

The man gave the impression of a kindly clerk who was performing a pleasant yet routine duty.

"Your results," Bablyoyannis continued, running an eye over the papers he held. "A 132. Not bad. On my test, I scored 154," he said with a smile of pride. "That Piecky one got dangerously close to you, with 126 points, but his lack of limbs, genitals . . . It's hard to make up for that with intelligence alone . . . Better that someone like you was chosen and not one of those stumps."

Snorg thought, "I'd like to crack your head." He said, "Piecky is my friend," and felt the old numbness in his jaw.

"It's better not to have friends until you become a person," observed Bablyoyannis. "Do you want to know how the others did? Moosy—84, Tib—72, Dulf—30 . . . The rest, close to zero. The Dagses scored 18 each, and that ox, Tavegner, 12."

Snorg heard the scorn in Bablyoyannis's voice and felt a growing hatred for the man.

"What happens to me now?" he asked. The numbness in his face wouldn't go away.

"As a person, you have a choice. You will enter the normal life of the society. A short period of training . . . and then you can either continue studying or take a job. From today, you receive an account with the sum of 400 money, as does everyone who becomes a person. Personally I would advise you not to have cosmetic surgery until you obtain a steady source of income. Ears are not really that important . . ." He gave Snorg a confidential look. "In time, you'll be able to save up. There's always a large selection of parts."

Snorg felt cold sweat trickling down his back: he could see Tib before him.

"What happens to the others?" he finally managed to ask.

"Ah. Yes . . . You have the right to know." Bablyoyannis was trying to be patient. "There are always many more individuals born than individuals who attain personhood. We harvest them for material. Among them, you can find a perfectly good pair of ears, or eyes, or a liver . . . Though some don't even possess that. A type like Tavegner is probably good only for tissue cultures . . ."

"That's inhuman," Snorg said, couldn't help saying, through clenched teeth.

"Inhuman?!" Bablyoyannis turned red. "No. The war, that was inhuman. Today a hundred percent of the population is born with physical defects, and three-quarters with mental defects. Reproduction, as a rule, is possible only by test tube. Save your indignation for our ancestors."

Apparently Snorg didn't seem convinced, because Bablyoyannis went on:

"The birth rate has been maximized, to increase the probability of obtaining normal individuals." He looked hard at Snorg. "As for the others . . . They're the cheapest way for us to produce the organs we need. Because even the chosen aren't perfect, are they, Snorg? . . . I've been working in this department for seven years now," Bablyoyannis said, "and I can assure you that this path is the only one that's right."

"You're not perfect either, Bablyoyannis. You drag your left leg, and your face is partially paralyzed," said Snorg.

"I know. It shows." Bablyoyannis was prepared for that remark. "But I work hard, and I've been saving almost all my money . . . for an operation."

8

Tibsnorg Pieckymoosy began work in the Central Archive of Biological Materials. At the same time, he continued his education. The salary he made was good, but after a pro rata deduction to pay for the care he had received until now, not much remained. Expenditure for food and the rent for a dark little room consumed the rest of his money, so that his paycheck was only symbolic. The food, synthetic, was eaten in a cafeteria. It was an improvement over the IV. In the cafeteria he kept seeing the same people, which was boring, but by his calculations he couldn't afford a better eating place, one where he would be able to come at different hours. He exchanged few words with the people he met in the cafeteria. They were all older than he. Some came in wheelchairs, but most could walk. He looked at them carefully: not one was completely normal. Each had deformities.

Tibsnorg was lucky: had he scored lower than 120 on his test, he wouldn't have been allowed to continue his education. But he also kept working, because he feared the memories that came with free time. He would pay for all his operations himself, but he didn't forget who had first helped him stand on his legs and conquer his nerveless body. Also, as a person, he had the right to know the truth, to know— despite the pictures on the viewscreen showing pretty landscapes, people formed correctly, and animals that had once lived—what the world really looked like now. Every five days, after work, he was allowed to go up to the surface and from an observation tower view his surroundings.

It was a grayish brown waste. Massive gray trucks continually moved across it, carrying loads from different mines. The trucks, he knew, were operated by people who could not have children, because the radiation background on the plain was too high. One of these drivers ate at Tibsnorg's cafeteria. He looked completely normal and made three times more money than anyone else there, and yet Tibsnorg would not have traded places with him.

The tests Tibsnorg had done on himself, with his first saved money, showed that he was fertile, though probably only passively, that is, through the collection and storing of his sperm. In a short time he mastered his job, a computer job, and was promoted. His new position was administering the decisions made by the division of Central that chose material to harvest from among the living specimens. Central's decisions were clear, logical, and in general didn't need correction. A bonus was given for discovering mistakes in them, and Tibsnorg paid close attention to his work. The material was harvested both for the general public hospital and for individuals who at their own cost wanted to reduce their defectiveness. There was plenty of work: several dozen requests came in every day, and with them the decisions, which all had to be read, considered, processed. Soon Tibsnorg established a procedure and began to have free time, which he used to familiarize himself with the computer and learn various facts.

He remembered Piecky's words, that because information was a privilege, one had to make the best use of it. He learned that the decision whether someone would be a person or not was usually based on a simple sum of scores on tests. There was therefore a fairly large margin of error. He also learned that he had become a person thanks only to Bablyoyannis's intervention. Bablyoyannis had changed Central's decision to give Piecky personhood. The number of points Piecky had earned for mental ability had in fact exceeded what Snorg accumulated for physical function, correctness of form, and intelligence. When Tibsnorg read on the viewscreen that Tib had received exactly a zero, he uttered an obscenity.

He had always been intrigued by the light of day that fell into the Room. Now he learned that it was only a lamp in the visible and somewhat in the ultraviolet spectrum, a lamp that was turned on and off periodically. The Room was located far beneath the earth. On the surface, he saw the sun only once—a bright-gray disk shining through a thick mist. The sun was better now than it had been; in the time when the earth was covered constantly with snow, the sun never pierced the clouds.

9

Tibsnorg became better acquainted with the classification system for biological material. Tib, Piecky, and the others had been given serial numbers, from AT044567743 to AT044567749, and no longer possessed names. It soon happened that from number 44567746—from Moosy—an eye, nose, and one kidney were harvested for cosmetic use. Tibsnorg submitted a memo in opposition to the selection of AT044567746, but it was ignored, no doubt outvoted by others who were experts. He was very upset by this, still feeling a tie with Moosy and the others.

Next was the Dags numbered 44567748. The surgery was fatal: from the Dags was taken the esophagus and stomach, liver, intestines, both hands, and penis (though not the testicles). What was left could not live, so the skin, muscles, and bones of the arms were put in a tissue culture bank, and number 44567748 was removed from the database.

The value of each organ was calculated on the basis of what it had cost to maintain the individual. It was easiest to make such a calculation when the individual's number was removed, because in that case one simply divided the cost of maintenance of the biological material among the recipients of the organs harvested, by organ (using the proper coefficient). When the organs were not harvested together, the method of calculation applied became complicated and unclear, and Tibsnorg suspected that only the computer system could keep track of it.

He wondered what number he would have been given, if not for Bablyoyannis. Would it have come after Tib's?

At the cafeteria, he no longer sat alone. He began talking with the driver who worked on the trucks that carried loads from the metal mines. The man called himself Abraham Dringenboom, and he was tall, thickset, and extremely proud of his name, which had been dug out of some library of history. Dringenboom had a deep, powerful voice and spoke very loud, which made Tibsnorg uncomfortable, because ordinarily the cafeteria was silent. It seemed to him that everyone was watching them, though that made little sense, seeing as no one was interested in them. Besides, many of the diners had poor hearing or couldn't hear at all.

"Tibsnorg Pieckymoosy . . . ," boomed Dringenboom. "A strange name. Why did you choose it?"

"It's many names," Tibsnorg replied quietly. "There are many in me."

"Hmm," muttered Dringenboom. "So you made it up . . . It's not wise to get too close to the others in your

Room . . . You know, today they said that the average lifespan of a person now is as much as twenty-four years." He was changing the subject. "I think it's too good to believe. I think they're fiddling with the medical statistics a little, so we won't feel bad."

"How do they arrive at that figure?" asked Tibsnorg, interested. "Is it for all individuals born or only for persons?"

"Are you kidding? For persons, of course. Less than a tenth is born alive."

Tibsnorg scrutinized Dringenboom. The driver seemed completely normal. True, he wore a gray tunic and trousers, so his body was not visible, but apart from the harelip that had been operated on, the scar from it mostly hidden by a graying stubble, nothing indicated any departure from the norm.

As if reading his thoughts, Dringenboom said, "My entire trunk was covered with warts on long, disgusting stalks. I had them removed. But the biggest problem is between my legs." Dringenboom grimaced. "But don't feel sorry for me, Tibsnorg. I'll buy myself the proper equipment and make five living kids with it. I've already put 1620 money away," he added, seeing Tibsnorg's disbelief.

That much money was inconceivable: Tibsnorg could save only 22.24 money from each ten-day period. For the sum of 1620 one could buy all of Tib—that is, of course, as biological material. More and more often her slender,

29

graceful figure appeared before him, surrounded by a storm of colorful hair. His dreams were invariably about the Room. In and out of those dreams moved familiar shapes, but Tib was always present.

Tibsnorg rented a better room, one that had a window. Rooms at the surface were a rarity, so he was surprised that his new room—though a little smaller and with two viewscreens instead of three—cost only eight money more than the previous one. He understood the reason when he learned how high the radiation background was in rooms at the surface. But the view was worth it. He would spend hours looking at the opaque, leaden clouds that hung over the bare dun hills. The edge of the glacier wasn't visible, because his window was too low. The glacier could be seen only from the observation tower, and only on clear days or with good binoculars.

The scene, though it wasn't lovely like the ones on the viewscreen, drew him with irresistible force. That was probably why he applied for the position of driver of an outside transporter. Another motive was the high salary, which would allow him to save a considerable sum in a relatively short time.

At the transport bureau he was told to go to an official in a wheelchair. The man didn't come much above the desk, but there was something in his eyes that advised caution. When Tibsnorg presented the application, the man looked him over.

"Are you neuter or sexed?"

"Neuter," Tibsnorg lied, aware that being neuter was a condition for the job. The official nodded and with a disproportionately small hand entered something on the keyboard. He regarded the screen, and the lines of his face hardened. Even before he spoke, it was clear that the interview was over.

Dringenboom almost struck Tibsnorg when he heard what had happened. In a fury, he pulled from the pocket of his worksuit his indicator—a small, pink piece of plastic.

"Look at that, idiot!" he said, pointing a thick finger at the plastic. When he was agitated, he couldn't control the shaking of his hands. His finger wobbled over the pink rectangle. "When that turns red, I can throw out my calendar . . ." His eyes flashed in his deeply tanned face. He made so much money, he could tan his skin. "Are you in such a hurry to get into the ground?!" he snarled.

"You can afford a sun lamp," said Tibsnorg quietly.

"And what, stupid, is that worth? . . . You can have woman by the bunch . . . even if you're missing everything between your legs but balls. The balls are what's important . . . the rest of it, the meat, doesn't cost more than 600, 800 money."

"I'm all right physically," Tibsnorg blurted. "It's my nervous system that's not complete."

"That's even cheaper . . . I'm telling you, you won't be able to drive the women away. They'll pull you apart. You should live, not die, my friend . . ."

Tibsnorg thought of telling him about Tib, but changed his mind, and the conversation ended there.

Abe Dringenboom was the only person Tibsnorg saw regularly. With random acquaintances at the table Tibsnorg exchanged only a few words. In contrast with his life in the Room, he led a solitary existence. He didn't seek out people; he lived with his memories. The women he met in the cafeteria or passed in the corridors couldn't compare with Tib: either they were ugly or their deformities were too evident. He began to wear, according to the rules, the red stripe that signified that he was not neuter, but that made no change whatever in his behavior. Perhaps he grew a little curt with the women, who now began to approach him. Possibly, had he worn the two red stripes that indicated full function, the pulling apart that Dringenboom warned about would have happened, but with one stripe Tibsnorg was left in peace.

Several days later, Dringenboom brought unpleasant news.

"I have cancer," he said in a dull voice, looking at the soup in the bowl in front of him. The soup was vile-tasting and slimy but contained all the necessary nutrients.

"So? Half the population has cancer," said Tibsnorg with a shrug.

"Mine's in phase C," said Dringenboom.

"You have 1620 money, you'll be all right," said Tibsnorg.

"It's 1648," corrected Dringenboom. "But it's too little, it's worth shit . . . I have the kind that spreads quickly. To cure it, I'd need at least one and a half thousand, and then there'd be nothing left for a dick."

Tibsnorg was annoyed. "Why did they let it get to phase C? That's advanced. You could sue the medical division," he said.

"It's my fault," muttered Dringenboom. "I didn't go for the tests, because they cost and I wanted to save up before my indicator went completely red."

"But you can get free medical care, like every person."

"No thanks." Dringenboom's eyes were lusterless, and in his voice you could hear the lisp from his harelip operation. "They'll leave me my brain, eyes, and part of my nervous system, and the rest they'll take out and burn because of all the metastases. Then they'll make me part of a control unit for a shoveler in a mine or for a conveyer belt . . ."

"I think they could cure you in another way than by replacing the diseased organs. But they don't do that for economic reasons. The demand for organs would fall if they did that . . ." Saying this, Tibsnorg began to calculate: 1648 money could buy all of Tib. And Dringenboom would be dead soon in any case. His indicator was already very dark. How many organs could Dringenboom buy? Twelve? Fourteen? Tibsnorg thought, "He'll lose his body in the end anyway, and for him that's worse than death. How can I get his money?"

Dringenboom looked at Tibsnorg, saying nothing.

Dringenboom changed after that. He became reticent and less sure of himself. When Tibsnorg told him about Tib, he shook his head wearily and said it was ridiculous, Tibsnorg should pick a woman for himself among persons and not go looking among biological material. To purchase an entire Tib he would probably have to save for a lifetime, and long before that happened, others would buy different parts of her body.

But Dringenboom agreed to take Tibsnorg for a ride on his huge truck. He carried loads from a fairly distant open mine. The run went through hills covered with wind-driven gray dust.

"All it takes is a dozen breaths of that," Dringenboom said, baring his teeth between his assymetrical lips.

Tibsnorg looked at him with fear.

"But the dust has to get past a pretty good filter," laughed Dringenboom, "so instead it takes a few hundred thousand breaths."

The open mine was the ruins of an ancient city, from which the metal was being reclaimed. A giant shovel dug into the twisted walls of a former residence or factory. Dringenboom waited on line for the metal. Finally a portion of reinforced concrete, rubble, and dust was emptied into his truck.

"I make four, five runs a day . . . Central always tells me the path to take that has the lowest radiation level. Be-

cause the path changes, according to how the wind blows
or how the rain or snow falls."

He pointed at the tiny screen.

"The radiation level is constantly updated. Today
it's low, but sometimes the screen makes an awful racket . .
. On such days we get a bonus of two or three money."

On the way back he let Tibsnorg drive a little. It
was a matter only of how to give the commands, since the
truck was computer-controlled.

"If anything goes wrong, the autopilot brings it
home," said Dringenboom. "Like if you pass out. The load
can't be lost."

On one of the hills stood a solitary little building
half buried in dust. It was all in one piece, even to the roof,
door, and glass in the windows.

"I'd like to live in that house," said Dringenboom,
"and not in the city."

"Live on the surface?"

"Your room is on the surface, Tibsnorg. One can do
it, with enough shielding . . ."

II

At last the day came that had to come. The day that Tibsnorg had imagined in many different variations, but
never thought that when it came, it would find him so unprepared.

He was working, as usual, at the viewscreen. He had saved up 48 money plus 320 of deferred credit. The screen presented the next order requiring a decision. A neat row of green letters and numbers informed him, with precision, that for AT044567744 it was proposed that the arms, legs, and trunk with neck be removed for one female recipient, the head for another. The brain would be terminated, and of course the code would be removed from the register.

"The woman must have had to work hard and long to afford such a body," he thought bitterly. "And the other woman, she must have liked the slender face and blue eyes in the catalogue, liked them tremendously, to put up with deafness. Unless she saved enough to buy another pair of ears . . ."

"Shit, shit . . . ," he muttered, chewing his fingers.

He had known all along that this would happen, yet now he hesitated. He had thought he could save more money for this moment. But he had to act quickly, in this situation that was not the one he had imagined.

"Shit," he said over and over.

He asked the system for time to think, explained that he was considering the possibility of only one recipient's acquiring specimen AT044567744, as that would be more profitable. His request would delay the decision a little. He disconnected the cameras, got up from his desk, and left. His stride was efficient, swift. Exertion of will at every step had become a habit with him.

It was not far to the warehouse of biological material. He had already learned from the system in which room
she was being kept. The system had also given him all the
entry passwords. The sleepy guard at the massive metal
door did not challenge him. Tibsnorg was covered with
sweat. The elevator went with terrifying slowness. At last—
the right level. An endless corridor with identical doors. He
felt constant doubt about what he was doing. What he in-
tended to do was unheard of. He came to door ATo44567.
It opened automatically. Along the walls of the next corridor were stations that held biological material—dozens of
individuals of different sizes and different degrees of deformity. All were without clothes; all were in a web of wires,
electrodes. At first he counted nervously, then saw that
there were numbers over each station. A long time passed
before he reached her. She stood with open eyes. Their eyes
met. She knew him. Disconnecting the wires took a few
moments. It took longer to undo the straps that constrained her arms and legs.

She immediately pressed herself, her face, to him.
"Yoo retoont, Sneogg. Ay noo," she said softly.
"Hurry, Tib, hurry." He took her by the hand.
He knew that her muscles would be in good con-
dition from electric stimulation. No one wanted to buy an
atrophied limb.
"Piecky," she said, pointing to a small shape in a cluster
of wires. Together they freed Piecky, who immediately woke.

"Leave it, Snorg," he said. "This is absurd."

Snorg took him in one arm and led Tib with the other. He caught his breath only in the elevator.

"And now what?" asked Piecky.

Tib nestled her face against Snorg the whole time.

"I know all the passwords," said Snorg. "We'll have surprise on our side . . ."

In a room they passed, he found coveralls for Tib.

At the main door the guard gave them an indifferent look. The thought did not occur to him that two of the three leaving were only material. He entered the password Snorg gave him, looked at the screen, and nodded for them to go.

Outside the warehouse, they practically ran. Snorg stopped a small automatic car, and they all climbed in. Even by vehicle, it was a considerable distance to Dringenboom's room. In all the corridors, the silence was unbroken and ominous.

They found Dringenboom in his room; he was still sleeping.

A blow, and the camera hung sadly from its cable. A sharp pull completely broke the connection.

"Abe! Get up!" Snorg shook his shoulder. "Tib's with me. Are you coming with us?"

Dringenboom rubbed his eyes. He looked at them.

"Don't call me Abe. I'm Abraham," he said. "She's lovely," he added, looking at Tib. "No, I'm not going with

38

you. Take the keycard for my truck and hit me on the head. Do it with that book, so there will be some blood . . . and get as far as you can from the city. That's your only chance."

"All right," said Snorg. "I'll tie you up too. It'll look better."

It took a while, because Snorg didn't want to hurt him too much. Finally Abraham Dringenboom lay senseless and tied up on his sofa, and there was even blood from the broken skin on his forehead.

They were driving to the hangar of the transporter machines when the corridor filled with the howl of sirens. It was beginning. Every few meters, a red light flashed. The cameras in the corridor all turned slowly. The fugitives made it to the hangar before the doors locked. Snorg found Dringenboom's truck. He slid the keycard in its entry slot, and the machine responded. All three of them got on the rising platform and in a few moments were inside the control cabin. Snorg drove the truck from the hangar. It was a dark day, the clouds heavier than usual. He activated the viewscreen. An information broadcast was being given.

". . . shocking theft of biological material at a value of more than 4500 money! Nothing like this has happened in our memory! An intensive search is being conducted for the perpetrator, who is a DG-rank officer of the Archive of Biological Material. His name is Tibsnorg Pieckymoosy. The defense forces are joining the search. They will guarantee that the stolen property is reclaimed without damage and that the perpetrator is captured quickly."

The screen showed a number of taped images, from various cameras, of Snorg carrying Piecky and with Tib walking beside him.

Snorg whistled through his teeth. "Those defense forces are several hundred he-men with perfectly functioning bodies full of muscles," he said.

"I would say we haven't a prayer." Piecky took his eyes from the screen. "But I'm grateful to you for allowing me to see this . . ." He gazed out the window. "I lost track of time, hooked up to those wires. There was an injection for sleeping, an injection for waking . . . and so on, in a circle."

Tib also had been staring out the window, silently, from the moment they left the hangar.

"Fortunately there was a guy my height opposite me, and we could talk," Piecky went on. "The guy also talked with Tib, so she wouldn't become totally stupid. I couldn't talk to her, because she couldn't see my mouth and she can't hear. She's getting smarter. At least that's what the guy said."

Snorg drove the truck to the mine.

Piecky watched with great attention as a powerful claw gathered pieces from a ruin that had once been a cathedral.

"And people lived in that . . . ?" he asked.

Snorg nodded.

Pieces were loaded into the truck.

40

"So that was how they lived before the war," Piecky said to himself. "They must have felt very lonely in such spread-out buildings."

When the truck was filled, Snorg turned it around.

"We're going back?" asked Piecky, uneasy.

"I have a plan," Snorg said.

The truck went at maximum speed.

"Tib, put a mask on yourself and one on Piecky," he said, nodding in the direction of the compartment that held the masks. But Tib didn't respond, because Snorg was facing the viewscreen as he spoke and she didn't see his lips. When he repeated it toward her, she took out the masks and suits, and then quickly and with surprising skill put them on herself and on Piecky. Snorg put on his own mask and suit. They came to the hill where the solitary, intact building stood.

Snorg stopped the truck, and the moving platform took them to the ground. The sound indicator he carried chattered. Tib carried Piecky in her arms like a baby. The protective suits they all wore were made of transparent material. Piecky was too short, so Tib wrapped the excess several times around him. They saw that they would have to walk a distance much greater than any they had ever crossed on foot. In addition, the dust came to mid-calf. For a while they stood and watched the truck leaving, on automatic, the huge machine growing smaller and smaller until it disappeared at the horizon. They turned and started walking. It was slow and difficult making their way through the dust and loose sand.

41

By the time they reached the building, they were covered with sweat. Tib was a little less tired, because her muscles had been kept in such good condition in the warehouse.

Inside, they found that the roof was in one piece, and the thick wood door as well, and there was even a fence and gate in the back. Snorg continued to hope that their escape would be successful, but Piecky thought it was a mistake for them to have left the truck. He said they should have driven as far as possible from the city and its defense forces. The city might then have given up its pursuit of them. Snorg privately agreed with Piecky, but he wasn't able to break altogether with the city. Having left it, the three were so extremely alone.

None of them removed the protective suit, because the dust was everywhere.

Tib sat and looked at Snorg.

"Ay w'shoor yood retoon f'mee . . . ," she said.

He smiled.

"Ay'd a dreem . . . that ay leff th'Room. Layt was all round . . . and thees straynge peepul, s'many peepul . . . Then thay put mee ther next t'Piecky . . . It's s'good that yoor heer 'gain," she said, watching his lips the whole time.

"Listen to her yap," said Piecky. "Next she'll tell about the injections . . . how a needle jabs you in the side, and bam, you sleep . . . and bam, you're awake . . . Like turning a switch on and off. And the gurneys every day going down the row, the three-level gurneys . . . always pulled by the same people in gray. And they'd always take someone away in them. And few returned, and if they did return, they were all bandaged up . . . I couldn't see much down where I was. Always one of us. And it was hard to talk, because every other guy in the row was out, and if you shouted, bam, you got a needle. But even so we exchanged information, like a chain, using just the right voice that could be heard but that wouldn't cause the needle. The worst was . . . how silent someone would be when they wheeled him by. Then the ones in gray would remove the bandages, and . . . he wouldn't have arms, or legs. It varied. The worst was when a gurney slowed down by you, and you'd think, will it stop? The ones in gray weren't sadists, but the gurneys had bad wheels . . . They tried to make them go as smoothly as possible, because they knew what we were feeling . . . But sometimes a wheel would catch and the gurney would slow down. But I decided that if they took me, I didn't want to come back. I don't have much body as it is . . ."

"On thoos gurnees thay took always three peepul," said Tib, whose eyes now were on Piecky's face. "Too came back, yoozhly, sometaymes one . . . I r'member Moosy, how she came back. Only one eye showt from the banjes, but it was Moosy . . . Colfi said she was coming back . . . and tole us how thay took off the banjes . . ."

"Enough!" said Piecky. "I don't want to hear that again. I know what she looked like . . . and then they took her a second time, and she didn't come back."

43

"Moosy," said Snorg with a groan. "That didn't happen on my shift. But they could have taken Tib too," he said to himself. "I was lucky, lucky that with her it happened on my shift."

"How, lucky?" Tib asked.

"That you're here with me now. There were so many things I didn't take into account."

"Ay coodn't anymor. Th'mussils jumpin, makin me s'tired . . . and talkin w'Colfi, b'cause ay coodn't see Piecky's mouth . . . and the rest. Ay wood of gone crazy. Ay din go crazy, but if it was longer, Ay wood f'shoor . . ."

They both talked, she and Piecky, interrupting each other. Piecky spoke while she spoke, but when she saw he was speaking, she stopped. Then she would break in again, to tell her story in her hoarse, halting voice. It was hard to express so many days in just a few hours. Then Piecky turned away to look at the thick brown cloud of dust swirling across the sky. He watched, rapt, and something shone in his face, something like bliss, which surely would have amazed Snorg had he seen it.

"Stop rustling that plastic," Piecky finally said.

They both looked at him.

"Listen, Snorg, I'm talking to you, because Skinny's eyes are fixed once more on your smug face . . ." He went on, and the way he spoke was so much like the old times that Snorg grinned with pleasure. "What I feel . . . that someday I'll fly among those clouds, high above

44

the earth, on wings, and it will be the best part of my life."

"Maybe they'll make you the controls of a machine, because your body is useless, but your brain, that's really . . . But first they have to catch us, and that won't be so easy for them. No camera saw where we went."

"What will happen when they catch us?" said Piecky. "Because I am certain they will." He wasn't impressed by Snorg's arguments.

"Shut, Piecky!" It was Tib. Snorg had never heard her talk in that tone. "Less yoo pr'fer thoos jekshins, ther."

"I say what I think."

"We should consider," said Snorg after a moment of thought. "It seems to me that two of us are not in any real danger, since this situation has no precedent. Two of us should be all right, though each for a different reason. Nothing will be done to me, because the preservation of life is a fundamental law for human beings. Once someone is named a person, then he can't stop being a person, so they would never turn an officer of the Archive of Biological Materials into just another specimen for the warehouse. And Piecky, you too will be all right. Your dream will come true: you'll look down on us from the height of a mine shoveler. They'll have to make use of us, you see, to justify all the effort and energy it takes them to catch us."

"Was that why we left the truck?" Piecky asked.

"No," answered Snorg after a silence. "There is no place to go ... Other than the city, there is nothing ... But here, Abe knows where we are, he remembers this little house, he'll bring us food. Abe is our hope."

This time the silence was broken by Tib.

"An mee, Sneogg? ... Wha 'bout mee?" She bent and fixed her eyes on his mouth.

"You. You're the only one," he said, turning fully to her, "a tragic fate awaits ... One woman wants your body, another your head and face. They're rich and no doubt deserving women, but I would die rather than let that happen."

"So it was thanks to Baldy that I got to see the sky," Piecky said softly, and said nothing after that. He gazed at the sky, at the swiftly moving clouds.

When the twilight turned from gray to the darkness of night, they fell asleep, huddled together, hungry and cold.

12

They woke to a gray, cold dawn. Tib was more talkative and animated than ever. She amazed him. In his memory she had been beautiful but not that aware of things. He saw that they were all developing mentally, not just he, who had been named a person, Tibsnorg Pieckymoosy.

He thought, "Maybe everyone, if given enough time ..."

They waited for Dringenboom to come. Snorg was counting on Abe's driving up in his giant truck and giving them food, and then all together they would figure out what to do next. Dringenboom was their only chance. They waited and waited, watching the string of vehicles in the distance carrying rocks from the city. Hunger gnawed at them. Around noon, a yellow sun showed through the clouds. It grew dazzlingly bright. Tib and Snorg stood side by side in a ray of sun and beheld the shadows they cast. Such a clean, clear sun. They saw it for the first time in their lives.

"If they made me the control unit of a machine, could I see this often?" Piecky wondered, peering out the window.

"I don't know. Maybe they would let you keep your eyes," said Snorg, but doubtfully. "You haven't been named a person, so they might treat your brain as just material. Only those people have a right to keep their eyes who lost their bodies to an incurable illness. But it's not impossible that you'd be installed in one of those great shovels . . . and you'd need your eyes for that. And with your intelligence, who knows? . . ."

He was interrupted by the roar of engines, a roar that definitely didn't come from a truck. Snorg paled, understanding that Dringenboom would never bring them food. The roar grew and made the ground vibrate. Multicopters began to land around the building, heavy flying machines of the defense forces.

"One ... two ... three," Snorg counted, feeling his face turn numb. Tib pressed to him with all her strength.

"Them ... Wha we did mayd n'senss," she whispered, watching the armored copters land.

Around the machines appeared small figures in gray uniforms, helmets, and bullet-proof vests. They jumped nimbly to the ground and waded through the dust to the building. Snorg saw that they were armed with rifles, and a few carried laser guns.

"All those cannons for us?" he thought wryly. "Do they intend to level the house?"

He didn't even try to count the commandos. There were at least fifty. They quickly took up positions around the house.

"Tibsnorg Pieckymoosy!" boomed a sudden, shrill voice. "You have no hope. Surrender. Surrendering the stolen biological material now will mitigate your sentence. Your accomplice, Abraham Dringenboom, has been placed under arrest."

Tib was looking hard at him. She seemed to understand. He repeated to her what the loudspeaker had said, making sure she could see his mouth.

"Tibsnorg Pieckymoosy!" the speaker repeated. Piecky said nothing, terror in his eyes.

"Shit ... shit ... ," said Snorg, standing in the middle of the room and holding Tib.

"Buh wee only wan t'live," she whispered, looking at him.

". . . will mitigate," the voice was booming, when a noise began at the door. Suddenly a powerful explosion blew the door apart. Two commandos jumped inside, like lightning, and fell to the floor, aiming at Snorg.

"Good maneuvers," he thought.

They were extremely capable. A third commando appeared in the smoking hole. He had a colorful winged dragon painted on his bulletproof vest, which reached below his hips. The man stood motionless on spread, muscular legs, aiming at Snorg with a revolver that had a long barrel. He held the gun with both hands, arms extended. In place of a nose he had a single black nostril, and he bared his teeth. The teeth, with the lack of eyelids, gave his face the look of a skull.

"You wanted to be first," Snorg thought. "For this you'll be able to buy yourself a new face. Unless they consider that the ones on the floor were first . . ." Snorg looked at the prone commandos. The one standing followed Snorg's eyes. More commandos rushed into the room through the broken door and immediately fell to the floor. The one standing, as if reading Snorg's mind, again swept his eyes over the prone soldiers. He stiffened, reaching a decision. For another brief moment he regarded Snorg through the plastic helmet, regarded him with those lidless bug-eyes.

And although none of the three fugitives had moved an inch, a shot rang out, and Tib, who had been shielding Snorg with her body, went limp in his arms. Snorg felt something constricting his throat. He didn't hear the second shot. The yellow flash before him became a row of bright spots and then went out.

Spellmaker

Andrzej Sapkowski

I

Later, people said that the stranger came from the north, through the Ropers' Gate. He came on foot, leading a heavily laden horse by the bridle. It was late in the day; the stalls of the ropers and saddlers were closed, and the street was empty. Although it was hot, the man had a black coat thrown over his shoulders. He drew attention.

He stopped in front of the Old Narakort, stood awhile, listened to the hum of voices within. The tavern, as usual at that hour, was packed.

The stranger didn't enter the Old Narakort. He pulled his horse onward, to the bottom of the street. There was another tavern there, smaller, called the Fox. It was nearly empty. It did not have the best reputation.

The tavern keeper looked up from a barrel of pickles and took the measure of the customer: not of these parts, wearing a coat. The man stood at the bar stiffly, not moving, saying nothing.

"What do you want?"

"Beer," said the stranger. He had an unpleasant voice.

The tavern keeper wiped his hands on his apron and filled a cracked earthen mug.

The stranger wasn't old, yet his hair was almost completely white. Under his coat he had a worn leather jerkin with ties at the neck and shoulders. When he removed his coat, everyone saw the sword belted behind his back. There was nothing remarkable in that; in Klothstur almost everyone went armed; but no one carried his sword behind him like a bow or quiver.

The stranger didn't sit at a table among the few who were there; he stood at the bar watching the tavern keeper. He took a pull from the mug.

"I need a room for the night."

"Nothing here," the tavern keeper grumbled, looking at the stranger's boots, which were covered with dust and full of mud. "Try the Old Narakort."

"I prefer this place."

"There's nothing." The tavern keeper had figured out the stranger's accent: a Rivian.

"I'll pay," the stranger said softly, as if unsure.

That was when the ugliness started. A pockmarked lout, who from the stranger's entrance hadn't taken his heavy eyes off the man, got up and approached the bar. His two comrades came and stood behind him.

"There's no room here, Rivian dirt," barked the pockmarked one, close, into the stranger's face. "We don't need your kind here in Klothstur. This is an honest town!"

The stranger took his mug and stepped back. He looked at the tavern keeper, but the tavern keeper averted his eyes. No chance that *he* would defend the Rivian. Who liked Rivians?

"Rivians are thieves, all of them," Pockmarked went on, exuding beer, garlic, and contempt. "You hear me, piece of garbage?"

"He doesn't hear you. He must have dung in his ears," said one of the men behind, and the other guffawed.

"Pay and get out!" shouted the beak-nosed lout.

Only now did the stranger turn to look at him.

"I'll finish my beer."

"We'll help you," said the lout through his teeth. He slapped the mug from the Rivian's hand and at the same time grabbed the belt that went across the Rivian's chest. One of the men behind raised a fist to deal a blow.

The stranger twisted in place, knocking Pock-marked off balance. The sword hissed from its scabbard and gleamed briefly in the light of the torches. There was a struggle, a scream. One of the customers bolted for the door. A chair overturned with a crash; crockery hit the floor, contents splashing. The tavern keeper, his lips atremble, saw the hideously sliced face of Pockmarked, who, clutching the edge of the counter, sank and disappeared from view, like a man drowning. The other two lay on the floor. One didn't move; one writhed and twitched in a quickly spreading pool of dark blood. In the air hung the

53

thin, hysterical shriek of a woman, hurting the ears. The tavern keeper shuddered, took a deep breath, began to retch.

The stranger moved back to the wall. In a crouch, poised, alert. He held his sword with both hands, drawing its point through the air. No one moved. Fear, like cold mud, numbed faces, constrained limbs, closed throats.

Guards came rushing into the tavern with much clanking. Three of them. They must have been nearby. They held strapped clubs at the ready, but seeing the bodies, they immediately drew their swords. The Rivian had his shoulders pressed to the wall and with his left hand pulled a dagger from his boot.

"Drop it!" shouted one of the guards in a voice that shook. "Drop it, villain! You're coming with us!"

The second guard kicked away a chair that kept him from getting to the other side of the Rivian.

"Bring help, Chax!" he shouted to the third, who had stayed closer to the door.

"No need," said the stranger, lowering his sword. "I'll go with you."

"Go you will, dog, but at the end of a rope!" The guard quivered with fury. "Drop that sword, or I open your skull!"

The Rivian straightened. He tucked the blade under his left arm, took the dagger in hand, raised it to the guards, and drew a quick but complex sign in the air. The many studs on the cuffs of his leather coat glittered.

The guards stepped back, shielding their faces. A customer jumped up; another scrambled for the door. The woman screamed again, wildly.

"I'll go with you," the stranger repeated in a voice like metal. "You three walk in front. Lead me to the mayor. I do not know the way."

"Yes, lord," stammered the guard, his head lowered. He made for the door, looking around uncertainly. The other two backed out after him. The stranger followed, sheathing his sword and dagger. As he passed the tables, the people covered their faces with the flaps of their jackets.

2

Ethmond, right high mayor of Klothstur, scratched his chin as he considered. He was not a superstitious man or faint of heart, but he wasn't thrilled at the prospect of being alone in the room with the white-haired one. Finally he decided.

"Leave," he told the guards. "And you, sit. No, not there. A little farther off, if you don't mind."

The stranger sat. He had neither his sword nor his black coat now.

"I am, ahem," said Ethmond, fiddling with the baton of office that lay on the table, "Ethmond, right high mayor of Klothstur. What have you to say to me, Sir Bandit, before you are thrown into our dungeon? Three men slain, an attempt at casting a spell—not a bad day's work, that. For such things people are impaled here in Klothstur. But I'm a reasonable man, I'll hear you first. Speak."

The Rivian unbuttoned a pocket of his jerkin and produced a scroll of bleached goatskin.

"At crossroads and in taverns, this is nailed up," he said quietly. "Is it true, what is written?"

"Ah," said Ethmond, seeing the script on the unrolled parchment. "So that's what this is. I should have guessed. Very well, then, the truth, the blessed truth. The signature reads Hrobost, king of Kra, Fonzor, and Apiph. That is so. But decrees are one thing, the law is another. In Klothstur here I maintain the law, and the order! I don't permit people to be murdered! You understand?"

The Rivian nodded that he understood. Ethmond huffed in his indignation.

"You have the spellmaker token?"

The stranger again dug into his pocket. He pulled out a medallion on a silver chain. On the disk: the head of a wolf with bared fangs.

"You have a name? It can be any name. I'm not curious—it just helps in a conversation."

"I am called Geralt."

"Geralt will do. From Rivia, I suppose, from your manner of speech."

"From Rivia."

"Yes. You know what, Geralt? This"—Ethmond patted the decree with an open hand—"forget about this. It's too deep. Many have tried. It's not the same thing, brother, as dealing with a couple of local thugs."

"I know. This is what I do, Right High Mayor. It is written in the announcement: a reward of three thousand rials."

"Three thousand." Ethmond puffed his cheeks. "And the princess for your wife, people say, though our most gracious Hrobost didn't put that in writing."

"I am not interested in the princess," Geralt said. He sat calmly, his hands on his knees. "It is written: three thousand."

"What times we live in," sighed the right high mayor. "Twenty years ago, who would have thought, even in one's cups, that there would be such a profession? Spellmakers! Traveling exterminators of basilisks and banshees! Itinerant slayers of dragons and lamias! Geralt? In your job, is it allowed to partake of alcohol?"

"Certainly."

Ethmond clapped his hands.

"Beer," he called. "And you, Geralt, sit a little closer. Ah, what can I do?"

The beer was cold and capped with foam.

"The times are rotten to the core," Ethmond continued with his monologue, taking a swallow from his mug. "All sorts of filth have multiplied. In Apiph, in the hills, an infestation of werecats. In the forests of yore a wolf might have howled: now it's vampires, trolls, ghouls, you can't spit without hitting a goblin or some other abomination. Undines in the shires, hags making off with offspring, hundreds of cases of that now. Diseases no one ever heard of. A person's hair stands on end. And now this!" He pushed the parchment scroll across the table. "Small wonder, Geralt, that there's a call for your services."

"This royal decree, Right High Mayor," Geralt asked, lifting his head. "Do you know the details?"

Ethmond pushed back his chair, folded his hands over his stomach.

"The details, you say? Yes, I know them. It's not at first hand, you understand, but the source is reliable."

"I'd like to hear them."

"You insist. Very well. Then listen." Ethmond emptied his mug, lowered his voice. "Our most gracious Hrobost, when he was still prince, in the reign of Demell the Decrepit, his father, showed us what he was capable of, and it was plenty. We thought that his escapades would cease with time. But shortly after his coronation, after the death of the old king, Hrobost outdid himself. Our mouths fell open. In a word: he got his sister, Adda, with child. Adda was younger than he; they were much together, but no one suspected; well, maybe the queen . . . In a word: we look, and lo, there's Adda with this belly, and Hrobost is starting to talk marriage. To his own sister, you understand, Geralt.

SPELLMAKER

A hellishly ticklish situation, because right then Cuthbond
of Globbur got it into his head to give his Dalka to Hrobost, sent a whole legation, and the king had to be sat on
so he wouldn't go and curse the emissaries up and down.
We managed that, and it was a good thing too, because an
insulted Cuthbond would have ground us fine. Then, with
Adda's help, because she had some influence over her
brother, we were able to talk the whelp into a quick wed-
ding. So, Adda gave birth when her time came. And now listen, because here is where it begins. What was born, few
saw it, but one midwife leaped from a tower window to her
death and another lost her reason and to this day only
mumbles. From which I conclude that the baby was not
pleasant to behold. It was a girl. She died immediately in
any case; I imagine no one was in a hurry to tie the cord.
Adda, mercifully, did not survive the birthing. And then,
brother, Hrobost did yet another really witless thing. The
changeling child ought to have been burned or, I don't
know, buried somewhere in the wild, not placed in a sarcophagus in the castle catacombs."

"It's too late now to exorcise," said Geralt. "They
ought to have summoned one of the Wise Ones."

"You mean those charlatans with stars and comets
on their pointy caps? Oh, there were dozens of them called
in, but that was later, when people realized what lay in the sarcophagus. And what emerged from it at night. Not that the
emerging started right away. We had seven years of peace after

59

the funeral. Then one night, there was a full moon, commotion in the castle, a scream, running about! But you know about these things, and you've read the decree. The baby grew in the tomb, grew plenty, grew teeth like you wouldn't believe. In a word, a gomb. You should have seen the bodies. As I did. Then you would have given our Klothstur a wide berth."

Geralt said nothing.

"So," Ethmond went on, "as I said, Hrobost brought in a whole troop of magicians. They jabbered one after the other and nearly came to blows with their gnarled staffs, which they must use to drive away the dogs that are sicced on them, which I bet happens daily. Pardon me, Geralt, if you have a different opinion of magicians; in your line of work you no doubt do, but to me they're all idiots and parasites. You spellmakers, on the other hand, inspire respect among the people. You are, how should I say, a more substantial lot."

Geralt smiled.

"But to return to our story." The right high mayor, peering into his mug, poured more beer for himself and the Rivian. "Some of what the magicians proposed was not bad. One said we should burn the gomb together with the sarcophagus and the castle, another advised that we sever her head with a spade, another advocated impalement with stakes of aspen in various parts of the body—during the day, obviously, when the demonness slumbered in her coffin, exhausted by her excesses of the night before. But unfortunately there was one clown of a sorceror, a floppy cap on his bald head, the humpbacked hermit variety, who came up with the notion that this was all magic, that therefore it could be undone, and that the gomb could be turned back into Hrobost's daughter, as pretty as a picture on the wall. One needed only sit in the crypt all night, wave a wand, and that would be that. Whereupon—you can see what a cretin this was, Geralt—he goes and spends the night at the castle. Not much was left of him, maybe only the cap and the staff. But Hrobost clung to the idea like a burr to a dog's rump. He forbade all attempts to kill the gomb and had frauds come to Klothstur from every corner of the land to change it back into a princess. What a motley bunch that was! Bent-over crones, gimpy monks, fleabitten bags of misery, you felt sorry for them. So, we let them work their charms, though most of their work was over a dinner plate or bowl. Yes, some were seen for what they were by Hrobost or the council, and a few were even drawn and quartered, but too few, too few. I would have hanged the lot. That the gomb meanwhile dined on whoever showed up, humbug or not, ignoring every incantation, well, I don't have to tell you. Hrobost no longer lived in the castle. No one did."

Ethmond paused to drink some beer. The spellmaker said nothing.

"This has been going on for six years, Geralt. The thing was born some fourteen years ago. We had a few other troubles in that time, we fought with Glothur of Kloffok, but that was for a respectable reason, to move back a border, not for daughters or social climbing. Hrobost got wedlock into his head, you see, and was examining portraits sent from neighboring courts that in former days he would have chucked into the privy hole. Meanwhile his old mania has returned, and now and then he sends out horsemen to find new magicians. And he promised that reward, the three thousand, which drew a few hotspurs, errant knights, even one shepherd, a known imbecile, may he rest in peace. And the gomb is fine. Except that sometimes she takes a bite out of someone. You can get used to it. One good thing about the heroes who come to break the enchantment on her is that now the monster can stay at home in the castle instead of having to eat out. And Hrobost's new palace is quite nice."

"Six years," said Geralt, "and no one could do anything?"

"Not a thing!" Ethmond shot the spellmaker a look. "Because there is not a thing, after all, that can be done. Some problems a person has to live with—although Hrobost, our gracious and beloved ruler, continues to put up those decrees at crossroads. At least there's been a drop in volunteers. The latest one wanted the three thousand up front. We put him in a sack and tossed him in the lake."

"There's no shortage of swindlers."

"A surplus, I'd say," agreed the right high mayor, his eyes on the spellmaker. "So if you go to the king, don't ask for the gold in advance. Assuming you go."

"I'm going."

"Well, that's your affair. But remember my advice. As for the reward, there's been talk lately about the other part of it, the princess as one's wife, I mean. I don't know who came up with that, but if the gomb looks as bad as some say, it's a nasty, nasty joke. Yet there have been fools who came on gallop to the court the moment they learned there was a chance here to enter a royal family. Two shoemaker's apprentices among them. Why are shoemakers so stupid, Geralt?"

"I have no idea. And spellmakers, Right High Mayor? Did they try?"

"There were a few. Usually, when they heard that the gomb had to be unsorceled instead of killed, they shrugged and left. That's why spellmakers went up in my estimation. But yes, one came later, younger than you, I don't recall his name, but possibly he didn't give a name. He actually did try."

"And?"

"Our long-fanged princess strewed his innards over a considerable area. Half a bow shot."

Geralt nodded. "That was all of them?"

"There was one more."

Ethmond was silent for a moment. The spellmaker didn't hurry him.

"Yes," the right high mayor finally said. "One more. At first, when Hrobost threatened him with the gallows if he killed or so much as maimed the gomb, the spellmaker laughed and started packing. But then . . ."

Ethmond lowered his voice to a whisper almost and leaned across the table.

"But then he set about it. You see, Geralt, here in Klothstur there are a few reasonable people, even in high places, who have grown sick of this business. Rumor has it that some of them quietly took the spellmaker aside and asked him to forget about the magic, just kill the blasted thing, and tell the king the abracadabra didn't work, his daughter tripped on the stairs, met with an accident. The king, of course, would be angry, wouldn't fork over one rial of the reward. To which the spellmaker said, `For free, gentlemen, you can deal with the gomb yourselves.' Well, there was no help for it, they bargained, a deal was struck . . . Except that nothing came of it."

Geralt raised his eyebrows.

"Nothing, I said," said Ethmond. "The spellmaker didn't want to jump in with both feet the first night. He skirted, he lurked, he reconnoitered. At last, they say, he saw the gomb—in action, no doubt, because that thing doesn't creep from her crypt to stretch her legs. After what he saw, he cleared out. Without saying farewell."

Geralt made a grimace that may have been a smile. "The reasonable people," he began, "no doubt still have that money. Spellmakers don't accept payment before services are rendered."

"I imagine the money is still there," replied Ethmond.

"Rumor doesn't say what it comes to?"

Ethmond bared his teeth in a grin. "In the opinion of some, eight hundred . . ."

Geralt shook his head.

"Others," grunted the right high mayor, "say a thousand."

"That's not a lot, if you take into account that rumor exaggerates everything. The king, after all, promises three thousand."

"And don't forget the hand of the princess," joked Ethmond. "Come, what are we talking about? We know you're not getting that three thousand."

"How do we know?"

Ethmond smacked the table with the flat of his hand.

"Geralt, please, don't lower my opinion of spellmakers! This has been going on for more than six years! The gomb finishes off about fifty souls a year—less now that folks keep their distance from the castle. I believe in magic, brother, I've seen things in my time, I know what mages, warlocks, and spellmakers can do, to some degree. But this lifting of the curse is complete rot, thought up by a humpbacked, snot-nosed beggar who got soft in the head from all the fasting he did in the desert. It's rot, and no one believes it—except Hrobost. No, Geralt! Adda gave birth to a gomb because she slept with her brother, and no magic in the world will help here. Gombs eat people and need to be killed, it's as simple as that. Listen, two years ago the churls of some hick shrop beyond Fonzor, where a dragon was chewing up the sheep, went in a group and beat it to death with stanchions and didn't even see the point of boasting about it. While we here in Klothstur wait for a miracle and bolt our doors at every full moon or tie our criminals to stakes by the castle so the monster can dine and return to her tomb."

"Not a bad punishment," remarked the spellmaker wryly. "Has crime dropped?"

"Not a bit."

"How do I get to the palace, the new one?"

"I'll take you there myself. What about the proposal of reasonable people?"

"Right High Mayor," said Geralt. "What's your hurry? The creature really could meet with an accident, quite apart from my intentions. Then the reasonable people should give thought to saving me from the wrath of the king and collecting that fifteen hundred rials rumor has spoken of."

"It was to be a thousand."

"No, Mr. Ethmond," said the spellmaker firmly. "The one you gave the thousand to, he fled at the mere sight of the gomb, he didn't even bargain. That means the danger exceeds a thousand. We'll see if it exceeds fifteen hundred. Of course, in that case, I'm gone."

Ethmond scratched his head.

"Geralt? Twelve hundred?"

"No, Right High Mayor. This is not child's play. The king offers three thousand, and I must tell you that sometimes breaking a spell is easier than making a kill. One of my predecessors would have slain the gomb if it were that easy, right? Do you really think they all let themselves be eaten because they feared the king?"

"Very well, brother." Ethmond gave a gloomy nod. "We have a deal. But say nothing, not a word, to the king about the possibility of the monster's meeting with an accident. My advice to you."

3

Hrobost was trim and had a handsome face—too handsome. He wasn't more than forty, the spellmaker judged. The king sat in an armchair of carved black wood, his legs stretched toward the coals of a fireplace where two dogs slumbered. Beside him, sitting on a chest, was an older man, powerfully built and with a beard. Behind the king stood another man, richly dressed, pride in his face: a dignitary.

"A spellmaker from Rivia," said the king after the short silence that followed Ethmond's introduction.

"Yes, sire." Geralt bent his head.

"What turned your hair white? A charm that backfired? I can see you're not old. But fine, fine. A joke, you needn't answer. You have, dare I assume, some experience?"

"Yes, sire."

"I'd like to hear it."

Geralt bowed lower.

"Surely you know, sire, that our code forbids us to speak of what we do."

"A convenient code, master spellmaker, most convenient. But you—without going into the particulars—have dealt with trolls?"

"I have."

"Ogres?"

"Also."

Hrobost hesitated.

"And gombs?"

Geralt raised his head and looked the king in the eye.

"Also."

Hrobost returned the look.

"Ethmond!"

"At your service, my lord."

"You gave him a full account?"

"I did, my lord. He maintains that it is possible to remove the curse from the princess."

"That I've known for some time. What method, master spellmaker, do you—ah, yes, I forget, your code. But one small comment: there have been several spellmakers here already. Ethmond, you told him? Good. From which I know that your specialty lies more with extermination than with the removal of spells. Extermination doesn't enter the picture here. If my daughter loses one hair of her head, your head goes on the block. That's it. Osrugh, and you, Sir Segelin, stay here and impart to our guest whatever information he requires. Spellmakers ask a lot of questions. Feed him and put him up in the palace. He shouldn't have to knock about in inns."

The king rose, whistled to his dogs, and departed, disturbing the straw that lay on the floor of the room. At the door he turned.

"You succeed, spellmaker, and the reward is yours. I may throw in a little extra if you succeed with style. Of course the jabber of the common folk about marrying the princess contains not a word of truth. You don't think that I would give my daughter to any vagrant passing through?"

"No, sire, I do not."

"Good. That shows you have sense."

Hrobost left, closing the door behind him. Ethmond and the dignitary, who had been standing, immediately sat down at the table and made themselves comfortable. The right high mayor tossed back what remained in the king's goblet, which was half full; he looked into the empty jug and swore. Osrugh, who now occupied the king's chair, watched the spellmaker from under his brows as he ran his hand along the carved armrests. The bearded Segelin gestured to Geralt.

"Sit, Master Spellmaker, sit. They'll be serving dinner soon. What would you like us to talk about? Our right high mayor must have told you everything. I know him, and he tends to say too much rather than too little."

"I have only a few questions."

"Come, out with them."

"The right high mayor said that after the appearance of the gomb, the king summoned many Wise Ones."

"True. But don't say 'gomb,' say 'princess.' That way you avoid making the mistake in the presence of the king. . . and avoid the consequences of it."

"Among the Wise Ones, was there someone known? Famed?"

"There were such then, and later. I don't recall their names . . . Do you, Sir Osrugh?"

"No," replied the nobleman. "But yes, there were those who enjoyed renown. Much was made of that."

"Did they agree that the curse could be removed?" Geralt asked.

"Agree?" laughed Segelin. "They agreed on not one thing. But such a statement was made, among others. It would be simple, not even requiring magical ability. All one need do, as I understand it, is spend the night, from sundown to the third cockcrow, in the catacombs, beside the sarcophagus."

"Nothing to it," snorted Ethmond.

"I would like to hear a description of . . . the princess," said Geralt.

Ethmond jumped from his seat.

"The princess is a gomb!" he roared. "The most gombish of the breed I ever heard of! Her royal highness the cursed changeling bastard is four cubits high, is shaped like a keg of beer, has a mouth that goes from ear to ear and is full of dagger teeth, and her eyes are red and her pelt tawny. Her arms, with claws like a lynx's, hang to the ground. I don't know why we haven't begun sending miniature portraits of her to the courts of friendly kingdoms! The princess, may the pox take her, is fourteen now: time to think of marrying her off to a prince!"

"Contain yourself, Right High Mayor," said Osrugh with a scowl, glancing at the door. Segelin chuckled.

"The description, if somewhat metaphoric, is precise enough, and that is what our master spellmaker wants, yes? Ethmond forgot to add that the princess moves with unbelievable speed and is much stronger than her size and build suggest. That she is fourteen is a fact, though it may not be significant."

"It is significant," said the spellmaker. "Do the attacks on people occur only during the full moon?"

"Yes," said Segelin. "If the attack is outside the old castle. Inside, no matter what the phase of the moon, people die. But it's only at the full moon, and not every, that she goes abroad."

"Was there ever an attack in daylight?"

"No, never during the day."

"Does she always eat her victims?"

Ethmond spat into the straw.

"Enough, Geralt, we dine soon. Phoo! She eats, she gnaws, she doesn't finish—it varies, depending on her mood. She might only chew off the head, or gut her victim,

71

but occasionally she'll lick her plate clean, in a manner of speaking. Like her mother!"

"Watch it, Ethmond," hissed Osrugh. "Say what you like about the gomb, but don't insult Adda in my presence—for you would not dare in the king's!"

"Was there anyone she attacked . . . who lived?" asked the spellmaker, pretending not to notice this outburst.

Segelin and Osrugh exchanged a look.

"Yes," said the bearded retainer. "At the beginning, six years ago, she went for the two soldiers standing watch at the crypt. One managed to escape."

"And later too," Ethmond put in. "The miller she attacked outside the town. Remember that?"

4

The miller was brought in—on the second day, late in the evening—and ushered into the little room above the guards' hall, where the spellmaker had been quartered. The man was escorted by a soldier in a hooded coat.

Conversation with the miller yielded little. He was frightened, he made no sense, he stammered. His scars told the spellmaker more: the creature had an impressively wide bite and truly sharp teeth, among them four very long upper fangs—two on either side. The claws were sharper than a lynx's though less curved. It was for that reason only that the miller was able to pull free.

Finishing his examination, Geralt nodded and led the miller and soldier to the door. The soldier pushed the peasant out, shut the door, and removed his hood. It was none other than Hrobost.

"Sit, don't rise," said the king. "My visit is unofficial. You were satisfied with the interview? I heard you were at the old castle this morning."

"Yes, sire."

"When do you set to work?"

"It's four days to the full moon. After the full moon."

"You want to see her first?"

"It's not necessary. But after feeding, the . . . the princess will be a little slower."

"Gomb, master spellmaker, it's a gomb. Let's not play diplomat. A princess she has yet to be. That is what I came to talk to you about. Tell me, off the record, plain and to the point: will that happen or not? And please, no hiding behind a code."

Geralt wiped his brow.

"The spell may be broken, Your Majesty. And if I'm not mistaken, the breaking of it is in fact done by spending the night in the castle. The third crow of the cock, if it catches the gomb outside her sarcophagus, lifts the curse. That is the traditional way of dealing with gombs."

"So simple?"

"It is not simple. One must survive the night, for one thing. And there may be deviations from the norm. Not one night, for example, but three. Consecutively. There are also cases that are . . . well, beyond hope."

"Yes." Hrobost grunted. "I hear that constantly from certain parties here. Kill the monster, because this is hopeless, incurable. I am sure they have already spoken with you, spellmaker, yes? To slay the man-eater without compunction, at the very beginning, and tell the king it couldn't be avoided. The king won't pay, but we will. Very convenient. And cheap. Because the king will have the spellmaker beheaded or hanged, and the money remains in their pockets."

"The king will have the spellmaker beheaded regardless?" Geralt made a face.

Hrobost looked the Rivian in the eye.

"The king doesn't know," he said finally. "But the spellmaker should consider that a possibility."

It was Geralt's turn to be silent.

"I intend to do what lies within my power," he said after a while. "But if things go badly, I will defend myself. You, sire, should consider that a possibility."

Hrobost rose.

"You mistake me. That is not what I meant. Obviously you will kill her if the battle waxes hot, whether I like it or not. For otherwise she will kill you, for sure. I do not say this publicly, but I would punish no man who killed her in self-defense. But I will not permit that she be killed without an attempt made to save her. People have already tried to burn down the old castle, have shot at her with arrows, have dug ditches, set snares. They stopped only after I hanged a few. But that's not the point. Listen to me, Master Spellmaker!"

"I am listening."

"After the third cockcrow she will not be a gomb, if I understand you right. What will she be?"

"If all goes well, a fourteen-year-old girl."

"With red eyes? With the teeth of a crocodile?"

"A regular fourteen-year-old girl. Except . . ."

"Except what?"

"Regular physically."

"Don't play games with me. And mentally? Requiring a bucket of blood every day for lunch? Loin of bumpkin?"

"No. Mentally . . . There is no way to tell . . . She may be at the level, say, of a child of three or four. She will need much care for a long time."

"That's clear. Master Spellmaker?"

"Yes?"

"Might she return to that? Later?"

The spellmaker did not answer.

"Ha," said the king. "She might. And what then?"

"If she dies after a long swoon, a swoon of several days, the body must be burned. And quickly."

Hrobost hung his head.

"But I don't believe that will happen," Geralt

added. "Let me tell you some things to do, sire, to lessen that danger."

"Tell me now? Isn't it a bit early in the game? Because if—"

"Now, Your Majesty," said the Rivian. "Outcomes vary. It may happen that in the morning you will find, in the crypt, the princess restored and my corpse."

"Really? Despite my permission for you to defend yourself? A permission, I have the impression, however, that you can manage without."

"This is a serious business, Your Majesty. The risk is great. Therefore hear me: the princess must wear around her neck, constantly, a sapphire, best a sapphire with an inclusion, on a silver chain. Constantly. Day and night."

"What does an inclusion mean?"

"That the stone contains a bubble of air. In addition, in the room in which she sleeps, one must every now and then burn in the fireplace boughs of juniper, yew, and hazel."

Hrobost grew pensive.

"For this, Master Spellmaker, I thank you. I will see to all these things, assuming that . . . But now listen carefully. If you determine that the case is hopeless, you will kill her. If you undo the spell, and the girl is . . . not normal, if you have the least doubt that you have not succeeded, you will also kill her. Do not fear; you will be in no danger from me. I will storm at you in the presence of people, I will drive you from the palace and from the town, nothing more. There will be no reward, of course. You might negotiate something for yourself, you know from whom."

Neither spoke for a while.

"Geralt," Hrobost said, using the spellmaker's name for the first time.

"Sire?"

"How much truth is there to what people say, that the child was the way it was because Adda was my sister?"

"Not much. A spell must be cast; no spell casts itself. But your union with your sister, I suspect, was the reason for the casting, so in that sense it was the cause."

"That is as I thought. Some of the Wise Ones said this, though not all of them. Geralt? Where do such things come from? Spells, magic, monsters."

"I know not, Your Majesty. The Wise Ones concern themselves with the sources of such phenomena. For us spellmakers it is enough to know that the concentrated will can bring them into play. And enough to know how to combat them."

"By killing?"

"Most often. That is what we are paid for most often. Few ask that a curse be lifted. As a rule, people simply want the danger to them removed. If the monster has taken lives, of course, there may be the added motive of revenge."

The king paced the floor, then stopped before the spellmaker's sword, which was hanging on the wall.

"With that?" he asked, not looking at Geralt.

"No. That is for people."

"I heard. You know what, Geralt? I will go with you to the crypt."

"Out of the question."

Hrobost turned, his eyes flashing.

"Do you realize, magician, that I have never seen her? Not after the birth and not . . . afterward. I was afraid. It is possible that I will never see her now, yes? I have the right at least to see her as you murder her."

"I repeat, Your Majesty, it is out of the question. It is certain death. For me as well as for you. If my attention wavers, my will . . . No."

Hrobost went to the door. For a moment Geralt thought he would leave without a word or parting gesture, but the king stopped and faced him.

"You inspire confidence," he said. "Though I have seen through some of your tricks. I was told what took place in that tavern. I know you slew those churls only for effect: to impress people, me. Obviously you could have overcome them without the sword. I fear I may never know whether you go to save my daughter or to slay her. But I agree to this. I must. Do you know why?"

Geralt did not answer.

"Because," said the king, "I believe that she is suffering. Is she?"

The spellmaker's eyes were penetrating as he faced the king. He did not say yes, did not nod, did not make the least movement, but Hrobost saw what the answer was.

5

For the last time, Geralt looked out the old castle window. Dusk was falling quickly. Across the lake glimmered the blurry lights of Klothstur. Around the old castle was a waste, a no-man's-land that the town in the course of six years had put between itself and the place of peril, leaving nothing but a few ruins, rotting timbers, and the gapped remnant of a stockade fence—apparently it didn't pay to take the thing down and cart it. Farther on, at the opposite end of the settlement, was where the king had moved his residence: the squat tower of his new palace rose black against the darkening blue sky.

The spellmaker returned to the dusty table at which, in one of the empty, plundered rooms, he had been preparing himself unhurriedly, quietly, carefully. He had time, he knew: the gomb would not leave her crypt before midnight.

On the table before him was a box, not large, brass-trimmed. He opened it. Inside sat dark vials, each in a narrow compartment padded with dry grass. He took out three.

From the floor he lifted a long package thickly wrapped in sheepskin and secured with a strap. Untying this package, he removed a sword with an ornamented hilt, its black gleaming scabbard covered with rows of runic signs and symbols. He bared the blade, which gleamed with the pure light of a mirror. It was all silver.

Geralt whispered a formula, drank the contents of two of the vials, first one, then the other, after each swallow placing his left hand on the pommel of his sword. Whereupon, wrapping himself tightly in his black cloak, he sat. On the floor. There were no chairs in the room, in any of the rooms of the castle.

He sat motionless, his eyes closed. His breathing, at first even, suddenly grew fast, hoarse, ragged. Then it stopped completely. The mixture that the spellmaker had used to assume full control of all the organs of his body was composed mainly of hellebore, jimsonweed, hawthorn, spurge, and wolf-wort. Some of the other ingredients had no name in any human tongue. For a man unaccustomed to this potion from childhood, it would have been a fatal drink.

The spellmaker immediately turned his head. His hearing, now sharpened beyond measure, easily caught from the surrounding stillness the rustle of steps across the courtyard overgrown with nettles. It couldn't be the gomb. It was too early. Geralt flung the sword on his back, hid his pack in the fireplace beneath the broken chimney, and as silent as a bat ran down the stairs.

In the courtyard, enough of the day was left for the approaching man to see the spellmaker's face. The man—it was Osrugh—recoiled with an involuntary grimace of fright and revulsion. The spellmaker smiled a crooked smile: he knew how he looked. The baneberry, monkshood, and glow-worm in the potion had turned his skin the color of chalk, and the irises of his eyes were now all pupil. But that enabled Geralt to see into the deepest darkness, which was what he wanted.

Osrugh regained his composure.

"You resemble a corpse already, sorceror," he said. "No doubt from terror. Fear not. I bring you a pardon."

The spellmaker said nothing.

"You did not hear what I just said, Rivian medicine man? You are saved. And rich—" Osrugh hefted in his hand a sizable purse and tossed it at Geralt's feet. "A thousand rials. Take it, mount your horse, and begone!"

The Rivian kept his silence.

"Don't stare at me that way!" Osrugh raised his voice. "And don't waste my time. I do not intend to stand here till midnight. Don't you comprehend? It is my wish that you leave the curse in place. No, don't think you have guessed the reason. I am not in this with Ethmond and Segelin: I don't want you to kill her. Simply go. Let every-thing remain as it was."

The spellmaker didn't move, not wanting the noble-man to realize how accelerated his motions and reflexes now were. It was growing darker rapidly, and in time, for even the dusk was too bright for his dilated eyes.

"And why, my lord, must everything remain as it was?" he asked, making an effort to pronounce each syllable slowly.

"That," said Osrugh, haughtily lifting his head, "is no concern of yours."

"And if I know already?"

"I am curious to hear."

"It will be easier to remove Hrobost from the throne if the gomb torments the people more and more. If the king's stubbornness utterly disgusts both nobles and commoners. Am I right? I rode here through Redania, through Gribbage. There is much talk there of how some in Klothstur see King Vizimir as savior and true monarch. But I am not concerned with politics, Sir Osrugh, with who succeeds whom to the throne, with palace coups. I am here to do a job. Have you never heard of professional ethics, a personal code of honor?"

"Consider to whom you speak, vagabond!" cried Osrugh in a fury, gripping the hilt of his sword. "Enough of this! It is not my wont to enter into discussions with such as you. Who talks of ethics, honor, a code? A ruffian who no sooner arrives than he murders honest folk. Who bends his knee to Hrobost, then behind his back bargains with Ethmond like a hired thug. And you dare to put on airs, flunky? Pretend to be a Wise One? A mage? A thaumaturge? Off with you, odious spellmaker scum, before I take the flat of my blade to your ugly face!"

The spellmaker didn't budge, stood calmly.

"Rather, off with you, Sir Osrugh," he said. "For night falls."

Osrugh stepped back a pace and drew his sword.

"You asked for it, weaver of charms. I will kill you. Your little tricks will not avail you, for I wear a turtle-stone."

Geralt smiled. The belief in the efficacy of turtle-stones was as widespread as it was mistaken. But the spell-maker had no intention of expending energy on a charm, nor more of endangering his silver blade by crossing it with Osrugh's weapon. He ducked under the swinging sword and with the base of his fist, with the silver studs of his cuff, made contact with the nobleman's skull.

6

Osrugh came to his senses, looked around, and found himself in total darkness. He was bound. Though Geralt stood near, Osrugh couldn't see him. But he knew where this was and screamed, long and in horror.

"Hush," said the spellmaker. "You'll draw her out before the time."

"Accursed murderer! Where are you? Untie me immediately, knave! You'll hang for this!"

"Hush."

Osrugh breathed heavily.

"You're leaving me to be eaten by her! Tied up?"

he asked, more quietly now, adding an obscenity at practically a whisper.

"No," said the spellmaker. "I will release you. But not now."

"Bastard," hissed Osrugh. "To divert the gomb's attention from yourself?"

"Yes."

Osrugh fell silent, stopped heaving, lay still.

"Spellmaker?"

"What?"

"It's true that I wanted to topple Hrobost. There were others, but I alone wished his death—an agonizing, maddening, decaying death. Do you know why?"

Geralt was silent.

"I loved Adda. The king's sister. The king's mistress. The king's whore. I loved her . . . Spellmaker, are you there?"

"I am."

"I know what you're thinking. That's not how it was. Believe me, I cast no curse. I know no magic. Only once, in my anger, did I utter . . . Only once. Spellmaker, are you listening?"

"I am."

"It was his mother, the old queen. It was certainly she. She couldn't bear to see how he and Adda . . . It wasn't I. Only one time, you understand, I tried to persuade her, but Adda . . . I lost my head and said it . . . Spellmaker, was it I? I?"

"It doesn't matter now."

"Spellmaker? Is it near midnight?"

"It is."

"Release me sooner. Give me more time."

"No."

Osrugh didn't hear the scrape of the slab as it was pushed from the tomb, but the spellmaker did. He bent over and with his dagger cut the nobleman's bonds. Osrugh didn't wait for words; he jumped up, clumsily limped on his numb legs, then ran. His eyes had grown accustomed enough to the darkness that he could make out the way that led from the main hall of the catacombs.

With a crash the slab covering the crypt hit the floor. Geralt, concealing himself behind the balustrade of the stairs, saw the hideous shape of the gomb running nimbly, swiftly, and unerringly after the departing clop-clop of Osrugh's boots. The gomb made not the least sound.

A horrid, frenzied, ringing din tore the night, shook the old walls, and went on, rising, falling, reverberating. The spellmaker could not tell the exact distance—his sharpened hearing deceived—but he knew that the gomb had caught Osrugh quickly. Too quickly.

He went to the center of the hall and stood right at the entrance of the crypt. He shrugged off his coat. He moved his shoulders to adjust the position of the sword. He pulled on his gloves. He had a moment or two yet. He knew that the gomb, even if completely sated, would be in no hurry to leave Osrugh's body. The heart and liver were a valuable store of nourishment for her long sleep.

The spellmaker waited. There were about five hours to morning, he estimated. The crowing of a cock could only mislead him. In any event there were most likely no cocks in the vicinity.

He listened. She walked slowly, shuffling across the parquet floor. Then he saw her.

The description was accurate. A disproportionately large head set on a short neck. Around the head, in a circle, a tangled writhe of reddish hair. The eyes glowed in the dark like two carbuncles. The gomb stood still, eyes on Geralt. Suddenly she opened her jaws—as if to show off her rows of white pointed teeth—then clamped them shut, as one closes a chest. And she leaped from her place, with no preliminary movement, and made for the spellmaker, her bloody claws outstretched.

Geralt jumped to one side, turned in a lightning pirouette; the gomb lunged at him, also spun, lashing the air with her talons. She kept her balance, attacked again, instantly, in half turn, snapping her teeth an inch from Geralt's breast. The Rivian jumped to the other side, three times changing the direction of his spin, in a flapping twirl that confused the monster. As he jumped back, he hit her, hard, without swinging, in the side of the head with the silver barbs set along the top of his glove.

The gomb roared, filling the catacombs with thunder, and dropped to the ground and began to howl, a guttural, evil, enraged baying.

The spellmaker smiled grimly. The first test, as he had hoped, succeeded: silver was poison to the gomb, as it was to most creatures brought to life by magic. So there was a fair chance that this beast was like others, that therefore the curse could be lifted from her. Also, his silver sword, as a last resort, could save his life.

The gomb didn't hurry with her next attack. This time she approached slowly, baring her fangs, drooling repulsively. Geralt retreated, went in a half circle, planting his feet with great care. He moved now slower, now faster, putting the gomb off stride whenever she crouched to pounce. As he went, the spellmaker unloosed a long, thin, strong chain weighted at the end. The chain was silver.

In the moment the gomb sprang, the chain whistled in the air and, snaking, in a blink was wrapped around the monster's shoulders, neck, and head. The gomb fell in midleap, emitting a scream that pierced the ears. She thrashed on the parquet floor, roaring, either from fury or from the burning pain caused by the hated metal. Geralt was satisfied: killing this gomb, should he need to, would present no problem.

But the spellmaker did not draw his sword. So far nothing in the creature's behavior gave reason to think that her condition was incurable. He withdrew to an appropriate distance and, not taking his eyes off the shape that heaved on the floor, breathed deeply and concentrated.

The chain broke, its silver links sprayed in every direction like rain, ringing on the stone. Blind with rage, the gomb hurled herself at Geralt. He waited calmly and with his raised right hand before him made the Sign of Aad.

The gomb was thrown back several paces as if hit with a hammer, but she kept on her feet, extended her claws, opened her jaws. Her hair was blown back and fluttered as if she pressed against a furious wind. With difficulty, rasping, step by step, she came at him slowly. But came.

Geralt frowned. He hadn't expected that such a simple sign would completely paralyze the gomb, but it was a surprise that the beast was overcoming its resistance so easily. He couldn't maintain the sign long, it was too draining, and the gomb now had no more than ten steps to take to reach him. He released the sign suddenly and jumped aside. As he expected, the gomb, unprepared, flew forward, lost her balance, fell, slid across the floor, bounced down steps and into the pit that was the entrance to the crypt. From below came a resounding bellow of the damned.

To gain time, he ran up the stairs to the gallery. He hadn't gone halfway before the gomb emerged from the crypt, rushing like an enormous black spider. The spellmaker waited for her to mount the stairs after him, then vaulted the balustrade and jumped down. The gomb turned on the stairs and came bounding toward him in an incredible jump. She was not so fooled this time by his pirouette—twice her talons scored the Rivian's leather jerkin. But another powerful blow with the silver barbs of his glove repelled her, staggered her. Geralt, feeling a great anger grow in him, rocked, bent backward, and with a strong sideways kick swept the beast off her feet.

The roar she gave was louder than any before. Plaster dribbled from the ceiling.

The gomb was up again, quivering with insane fury and thirsting for blood. Geralt waited. He had drawn his sword; he made a circle in the air with it, went around the gomb, taking care that the sword did not move in the rhythm of his steps. The gomb did not lunge; she approached slowly, following the bright trail of the blade with her eyes.

Geralt came to a sudden stop, froze with the sword raised. The gomb, perplexed, stopped as well. The spellmaker drew a slow half circle with the edge, took a step toward the gomb. Then another, then he leaped, twirling it above his head.

In a crouch, the gomb zigzagged back. Again Geralt was near, the blade flashing in his hand. The eyes of the spellmaker smoldered with menace; from his clenched teeth came a rumbling growl. The gomb again retreated, pushed by the force of the concentrated hatred and violence that emanated from the advancing man, in a wave that entered her brain, her core. Frightened to the point of pain by this emotion unknown to her, she uttered a shuddery, strangled shriek, turned, and bolted madly into the dark maze of the castle's corridors.

Geralt, shivering, stood in the center of the hall. Alone. It had taken a long time, he thought, for that dance at the edge of the precipice, for that berserk, macabre ballet-duel to lead to the end desired: his attaining psychic unity with the adversary, his reaching the level of focused will that filled the gomb. The vile, sick will from which she arose and on whose power she fed. The spellmaker shivered at the memory of the moment when he took into himself the charge of evil, to level it like a mirror back on the monster. He had never before encountered such unalloyed bile, such a murderous frenzy, even among the basilisks, who were known for that.

All the better, he thought as he walked to the entrance of the crypt, a huge puddle of black on the floor. All the better, for all the stronger was the blow that the gomb had received. It would give him a little more time to do what he needed to do, before the beast shook off her shock. The spellmaker doubted that he would be able to make another effort like that. The effect of the elixirs was weakening, and dawn was still far off. The gomb must not return to the crypt before morning, or all his work was for naught.

He descended the steps. The crypt was not big; it held three stone sarcophagi. On the one nearest the entrance the lid had been half pushed aside. Geralt took from his pocket the third vial, quickly drank its contents, climbed into the tomb, and sank down. As he had thought, the tomb was for two—for a mother and daughter.

He closed the lid only when he heard, above, the howl of the monster. He lay down beside the mummified remains of Adda, and on the slab above him he drew the Sign of Yrd. He laid the sword across his chest and on it set a small hourglass filled with phosphorescent sand. He crossed his arms. He no longer heard the cries of the gomb at loose in the castle. He no longer heard anything, for the marguerite and the celandine had begun their work.

7

When Geralt opened his eyes, the sand in the hourglass had all sifted to the bottom, which meant that his sleep had lasted longer than needed. He strained his ears but heard nothing. His senses were normal again.

He took the sword, brushed a hand along the lid of the sarcophagus, muttering a formula, then easily—by a few inches—moved the slab ajar.

Silence.

He moved the lid farther, sat up, and holding his sword in readiness lifted his head from the tomb. It was black in the crypt, but the spellmaker knew that it was morning outside. He started a flame, lit a miniature torch, raised it, throwing eerie shadows on the walls of the crypt.

The crypt was empty.

He crawled out of the sarcophagus, sore, numb, cold. Then he saw her. She lay across the tomb, naked, unconscious.

She was homely. Scrawny, with small pointy breasts, dirty. Her hair—a pale red—almost reached her waist. Setting the torch on the slab, he knelt beside her, bent to her. Her lips were white; her cheekbone had a large red scratch where he had struck her. Geralt removed his glove, put aside the sword, and unceremoniously lifted her upper lip with a finger. Her teeth were normal. He reached for her hand, which was entangled in her hair. Before he touched the hand, he saw her eyes were open. Too late.

She clawed at his neck, clawed deep; his blood spattered her face. She wailed, going for his eyes with her other hand. He fell on her, seizing the wrists of both hands, pressing her to the floor. She snapped with her teeth—now too short—at his face. He pounded his forehead into her face, pressed harder. She did not have her former strength, she could only twist beneath him, wailing, spitting the blood—his blood—that had filled her mouth. The bleeding was fast. There was no time. The spellmaker cursed and bit her hard in the neck, just below the ear, sank his teeth deep and shook until the inhuman wail became a thin, desperate scream and then choking sobs—the weeping of a fourteen-year-old girl who had been hurt.

He released her when she stopped moving; he got to his knees, tore a scrap of cloth from the pocket on his sleeve, pressed it to his neck. He groped for the sword that lay nearby, pressed its point to the throat of the senseless girl, leaned over to examine her hand. The nails were filthy, broken, bloody . . . but human. Completely human.

The spellmaker got up with difficulty. Through the entrance to the crypt one could now make out the moist gray of morning. He walked toward the stairs, but wavered, sat heavily on the parquet floor. Through the soaked cloth the blood flowed down his arm, dripped from his sleeve. He unbuttoned his jacket, tore his shirt, ripped, made strips, tied them around his neck, knowing there was little time before he passed out . . .

He tied the strips in time. And passed out.

In Klothstur, beyond the lake, a rooster, shaking the chilly dew from his feathers, gave a raspy cry for the third time.

8

He saw the whitewashed walls and beamed ceiling of the little room above the guards' hall. He moved his head, winced with the pain, groaned. His neck was all bandaged—thickly, professionally.

"Lie there, magician," Ethmond said. "Don't try to move."

"My . . . sword . . ."

"Yes, of course. The most important thing, clearly,

is your silver spellmaker sword. It's here, don't worry. The sword, the little box. And the three thousand rials. Yes, yes, don't try to speak. I'm an old fool, and you're a wise spellmaker. Hrobost has been repeating that for the past two days."

"Two . . ."

"Two, of course. She opened your neck quite a bit, we could see everything inside. You lost much blood. Lucky for you we rushed to the old castle right after the third crow. No one in Klothstur slept that night. They couldn't. The noise you made was awful. I'm not tiring you with my chatter?"

"The . . . princess?"

"The princess, well, she's a princess. Skin and bones. And with not a whole lot upstairs. She cries all the time. Wets the bed. But Hrobost says that'll change. Change for the better, I'm thinking, right, Geralt?"

The spellmaker closed his eyes.

"Very well, I'm leaving now." Ethmond got up. "You rest. Geralt? Before I go, could you tell me one thing? Why did you want to bite her like that? Geralt?"

The spellmaker slept.

Key of Passage

Tomasz Kołodziejczak

I

The jaegers came to the village at dawn, as they always did. You might have thought that the previous night had coughed them from its dark belly, or that they were the night itself, condensed and clotted into physical form. The black horses cantered on four-jointed legs spread like spider limbs. The heads of the horses were barely visible in their quivering collars of skin; only now and then did you catch the flash of white teeth or the gleam of a yellow eye with a vertical iris. Their muscular sides were covered with ornate caparisons—purple, bearing the swastikas of the Margravate.

The four riders sat stiff in their saddles, looking high above their steeds of jet and above the heads of the people gathered along the roadside. The jaegers were armed with long swords and had axes fastened to their saddles. Across the black chain mail they wore, silver threads were woven in warding patterns. From their shoulders flowed dark-violet capes trimmed with black fur. Their spiked helmets hid half their faces, yet you could see, through the visor, the glittering eye of the symbiotic worm that lived inside each jaeger; the other eye, slightly more human, was snow white with a black dot in the center.

The riders halted at the church square of the village and waited impassively for the men to assemble.

The men didn't delay. Calls came from all directions. Bare feet slapped on broken asphalt. Raised voices warned curious children to leave, and you could also hear the frightened cries of women and the barking of dogs. No one knew how patient the jaegers would be today, or how they might punish those who were late.

The horsemen stood in a row, the haunches of their steeds practically resting on the ruins of the burnt church. The heads of these creatures swung from side to side, as if they were hearkening to a voice or trying to catch a scent. Sometimes they extended a neck, so that the collar of skin retreated to reveal an almost hairless head, and then the yellow eyes would fix on a person, as if to say, "Today is your turn."

At last the jaegers saw that they need wait no longer.

"Where is the mayor?" asked one.

"Here I am, lord." An older man pushed through the crowd. Tall, spare, his hair cut close, he wore faded jeans and heavy wooden clogs. His linen shirt had long outlived its color. A closer observer would have noticed brown strips along the shoulders—cuts made by a sharp instrument, then meticulously darned—and the fact that every button, though well sewn on, was different.

"You have summoned all your people?" The jaeger spoke slowly and heavily. The voice grated, as if all feeling had been chiseled from the words.

"Yes, lord. Every man not working in the gardens is here." The mayor lowered his head. It might have been a gesture of respect. It might also have been to avoid making contact with the eyes of the jaegers. And with the eyes of their worms.

"I charge you to repeat to those not present everything that is said here, so that they obey the law."

"I understand, lord. Your words will be repeated to them."

That's how it was always done. The jaegers, in the name of their masters, could kill, torture, ensorcel. They could wipe away an entire village. But the slaughtering had to be done in accordance with the code. Their code was full of paragraphs no human could understand. It did not matter whether it concerned the hunt for fugitives, work in the gardens of the rulers, the meting out of punishment, or conscription. Order. *Ordnung muss sein.*

"We seek an outlaw. He may be in this area. We want him alive. There is a reward. If anyone gives aid to him, we kill you all."

"What does this man look like, lord?" the mayor asked, unperturbed, as if he had not heard the threat. "How will we know it is he?"

The rider did not reply at once. He turned to look at his companions. His thin lips twisted into something like a smile.

"A man, you say? Let it be a man . . . You will know, beyond a doubt."

"I understand, lord. We will know." The mayor bowed again. "To be safe, we will stop all strangers, even if they are licensed merchants."

"Good. Your cooperation will be remembered. Praise to the Masters."

"Praise," answered all the gathered, kneeling.

"Their power gives life and death." The voice of the jaeger grew in strength, finally holding emotion: adoration. "It gives wisdom and dominion. It gives time and space. Praise to the Masters."

"And to their servants," finished the villagers. The audience was concluded.

When the jaegers had disappeared around the bend in the road, the people began dispersing to their occupations and so did not see that when the black riders left the village, their forms began to fade. After a while only a thick shadow hung above the roadway, poised like a motionless predator.

The mayor remained in the square by the burnt church, consulting with several important villagers. They stood in a semicircle, their backs to the ruins; in that way they did not need to look at the cage dangling from what was left of the old belfry and at the skeleton in the cage, its bones trailing the tatters of a priest's vestments. The men smoked their grass cigarettes as they planned the hunt for the outlaw, discussing how many could be taken from their work in the fields. They drew straws to choose who would announce the will of the jaegers to the neighboring villages, which were smaller and situated farther from the main road.

No one paid attention to the barefoot boy with the torn clothes and scraggly hair; he was maybe twelve. Hidden among the fallen walls of the belfry, this boy listened carefully, first to the orders of the jaegers, then to what the mayor and the elders said in their council. Only when they too had left did he venture out. Not deliberating, he ran to the edge of the village, cut across a potato patch that happened to belong to the mayor, and hurried in the direction of the pine woods dark on the horizon.

2

The pyxel appeared at a most inconvenient moment for Robert. As usual on such appearances, the air flickered a little, an invisible violin began to play softly, and there was a whiff of vanilla. The pyxel materialized some thirty centimeters above the tabletop. He windmilled his little arms, piped, "Oh shit," and fell to the table with a crash surprisingly heavy for an insubstantial being.

He got up, brushed himself off, adjusted his official cap, and turned a serious face to Robert and Bess, who were sitting on either side of the little café table.

"Of you here present, which is the Robert Gralewski?" he asked, scrutinizing.

Bess gasped, amazement on her face.

Robert adored it when she was amazed. Actually, he adored her every word and gesture. He had become smitten with Bess about fifteen minutes ago. The moment he saw her at the café door, he popped an EZ philtrum, felt the familiar tremor in his cheeks—and was instantly head over heels. Having already arranged to meet her, he thought, What could be nicer than a rendezvous with the one you love?

She was perfect.

"They can't distinguish gender in humans," he explained quietly, patting her hand. "A construction flaw."

"I am repeat, of you here present, which is the Robert Gralewski? Which the?" asked the pyxel. Pyxels not only couldn't distinguish gender, they also had trouble with Polish verbs and word order. Well, but these comp sprites that had been programmed to remote-communicate with humans were of the telepathic variety and didn't need grammar.

"That's me," said Robert. "The password is six-three-seven black walnut cracks between teeth."

"Roger password received," said the pyxel with clear satisfaction. "You are summoned to Central Command, by Guard of the Shield Ogalfin."

"Please tell him I'll be there in an hour. Over."

"Over very welcome. Ding ding, end transmission," said the pyxel and vanished. Robert put a finger on the place on the tabletop where the messenger had stood. It was warm.

"What was that?" asked Bess, cocking her head. A shock of hair fell across her face, covering the delicate row of input sockets along her neck. Bess was not only lovely but smart too. She worked at a big information concern as a net jockey. Robert had once used the services of her company; they were introduced at a bank. Bess fell for him, alas without reciprocation, though objectively he had to admit that she was a knockout. He dated her on a few occasions, but today was the first time he had used an EZ philtrum. And look how it turned out: he's crazy about her now, she's crazy about him, and duty calls. He was appalled at his lack of foresight: buying the EZ philtrum but not also a kwik E neutralizer. So there was a bit of suffering ahead for him, of the parting-is-sweet-sorrow sort. (On the package it said: "The effect may last more than four hours. The manufacturer cannot be held responsible if public humiliation, legal action, or death occurs after the drug is taken.")

"Excuse me, darling, but that pyxel was from the Commandant. I have to go."

"Of course you don't have to," she said mildly, but he could hear the steel in her voice. "You'll simply call him and tell him you're busy."

"But . . ."

"Please." Again she smiled, and Robert realized that for love he was ready to, yes, even risk the displeasure of Ogalfin. Bess was now everything to him, everything . . .

"Very well," she said suddenly, getting up from the table. "This happens. I have some work to do myself: there's that Phoebus report for tomorrow. Ciao."

She gave him a peck on the cheek and walked out. Left. Life had lost all meaning.

Elves were strange. Robert liked them, liked working with them, but could never really figure them out. He didn't fret over that: there were plenty of people in the world no less strange than elves, yet the world kept turning. It would keep turning, even if some felt that with the advent of magic on Earth our planet should have come to a stop, with the sun going around it like a roulette wheel.

Taste, for example. Each to his own, maybe, but the elves' could have been better. When they took over Warsaw, they fell in love with the Palace of Culture, Stalin's dreadful gift to the city. "What wonderful architecture," they said. "How sublime! What class!" They removed the towers that had been put up around the palace in the 2020s; they leveled a considerable section of Midtown and with an enchantment placed three copies of the building there. Joined by bridges of light, these structures, according to the elves, would concentrate the life-affirming power of the sun.

Robert's grandfather, born in 1947, kept diligently shelved in his memory various facts from the past; he especially liked those that were completely useless and unconnected in any way to the present day. When he saw four

Palaces of Culture pointing at the sky with their golden spires, he concluded:

"I knew right away those elves were all Jews and Communists."

How wrong dear old gramps was. The majority of the elves embraced the Catholic faith and went to Mass more often than most humans. And Communism wasn't their favorite system, because a king ruled over them, and they all had titles, baron and up, and a minimum of fifteen honorary names. Their style.

Police headquarters was located in the Northern Palace of Culture. Getting there shouldn't take long.

Robert left the Architects' Café a little after Bess but saw only the cab of her departing rickshaw. The trusty pneum, wheezing and whistling, brought Arrow. The pneum handed Robert the reins; compressed air hissed from between his teeth and from his joints.

Robert climbed into the saddle and slowly set off down Koszykowa Avenue toward Chaubinski. New horseshoes clopped along the asphalt; the horse gave a little snort every now and then; the metal buckles of Robert's belt clinked against the barrel of his automatic.

There wasn't much traffic for 21:00—mostly folks on foot, a few carts. It was only at the viaduct that Robert passed the first automobile. The vehicle crawled uphill with great effort, puffs of vapor coming from its stack. On the roof was the sign of the Watch Cat clan, a powerful symbol that provided the drive. The air around the vehicle rippled slightly from the nanocadabras making sure that other signs didn't come too close, which could cause an accident.

Robert automatically moved to the right lane. His tattoo was strong enough to interfere with the car's defense system, and such warding tangles usually resulted in boils. How could a man deeply in love walk around with boils on his back? And not only there.

He turned at Holy Cross Boulevard. The gate of the Northern Palace zone was up ahead. No joking here—he was entering one of the most heavily protected areas in Poland. He jumped from his horse, uttered the regulation cipher spell, and when the guards approached with their armor and axes, he handed them his plastic ID.

"Cadet Robert Gralewski. I was summoned."

"We have confirmation. Proceed," said the guard—with a pleasant smile. The man must have been ill.

The door thrown open from Ogalfin's office nearly hit Robert's face. Robert stepped back. Two policemen erupted into the hallway. After them, escorted by two others, came a man in handcuffs: a young skinhead with a curly beard and Day-Glo orange T-shirt that showed the familiar triumvarite of Lenin, Hitler, and Che Guevara and over them the eye of Sauron. The prisoner fixed his attention on Robert and for some demented reason decided to share with him his worldview.

"Down with the monarchy! Elves go home! Long live the socialism of the people!"

The guards allowed the youth to vent his propaganda but then led him firmly to the elevator. Robert stepped into the elf's office.

When Ogalfin was agitated, he spoke in a way that befitted neither his rank—High Commandant of the Recon Corps—nor his age, which was about three hundred.

"Can't people kill each other anymore for simple gain?" he yelled, pacing. His uniform was perfectly tailored and pressed, his epaulettes gleamed, and the creases of his trousers looked as if they had had the help of a steamroller. The misericord dagger bounced against his thigh at every step. Its scabbard was gilded, beautifully ornamented, and no doubt worth a fortune.

The elf had a smooth face, crossed by lines exactly where lines were needed to convey reliability and experience. His thick black hair was cut close, and the various earrings on his pointy ears indicated his rank. Ogalfin came from one of the most illustrious lines inhabiting this part of Europe, and he was related by blood to rulers in almost every corner of the planet. Even when he got drunk or swore, he did it as a leader.

During the invasion Ogalfin had led the Podlaski Division. He initiated and won four battles. He took half of Poland, the Czech Republic, and a piece of Slovakia. Now he ruled here, and frothed at the mouth only when paperwork took up more of his time than going after miscreants.

"Body counts, I understand that, sometimes you can't avoid it. Though I don't boast, don't try for that. Now we have this sect, doing ritual murder. And the king, blessed be his name, says to me that our prime is troubled by the increased interest in sects, weird cults, magic! Magic, can you believe that? It's bizarre, humans taking up magic . . . Our prime, he's a good man, but sometimes, when he says . . . I'm telling you, lad, the ritual murder rate shot up over 20 percent this year. Can no one in this country, damn it, simply kill for gain? And so the king, blessed be his name, wants an explanation, trials. This is nothing we can wave a wand over, is it, lad?

Ogalfin plopped into the chair behind his desk, threw his head back, and stared at the ceiling, as if to find something there other than the usual animated fresco. His indignation was over. In a moment the hard work would begin. Robert stepped over the memo turtle dozing on the floor (elves adored turtles: further proof that their aesthetic sense was an embarrassment).

"You are reminded," the turtle announced, sticking out its head from its shell. "Upper delta, quadrant black, the code six-eighteen-pi."

"Thoughtful of you," Robert acknowledged and sat down beside Ogalfin. "What's going on, Commandant? Why did you call me in?"

"The assignment you wanted: a foray outside the city. Our instruments have picked up an emanation in the Zone."

"What is it?"

"An artifact. Our satellites place it near what used to be Green Mountain City. It's no more than a dozen kilometers outside the Zone but still in unmagical territory controlled by the Margravate. Some villager found an amulet in the woods, or maybe a pectoral from the time of the last war. Or, out hunting, he caught an animal that had fallen under the Zone's influence, and now he has at home a pile of fay bones filled with nanos. The emanation is not strong, but our techs say they can extract a ton of power from the object. We have to take it before the enemy knows it's there. And this is a perfect opportunity for you to get some practice in the Zone."

"Which division?"

"You'll go as assistant to Hardadian of the Strong Hand. I don't believe you know him. An excellent warrior. He came to Poland three years ago and ever since, practically the whole time, has been working in the Zone. Hasn't even given Warsaw a proper visit. You might teach him a little of the language, you'll have the chance. But enough of this chatter. You depart in an hour."

3

Women are like colds—one gets saddled with them at the worst time. Kajetan Kolbudz agreed with that adage as applied to younger sisters. It was told to him once in confidence by a man staying at the Old Pine Cone. The man must have meant his wife; he had only just escaped her, fleeing through a field of cabbage owned by the village elder, where he ran into Kajetan, who happened to be appropriating a few green heads. The two swore an oath of secrecy and eternal brotherhood, exchanged a few thoughts on life's trials, then continued with their business: decamping from a spouse and committing vegetable larceny, respectively.

That took place three years ago, but with each passing day Kajetan appreciated more the experienced man's wisdom. In that time, the boy's lot had not changed much. His father's face faded in memory, and his mother grew wearier and had greater difficulty working in the field. Fortunately the son grew and could help in the running of the family. The family was his mother, himself, his four-year-old brother Jack, and his eight-year-old sister Dorothy. The same Dorothy whose appearance now on the path brought to mind the adage about women and colds.

There was no time. Kajetan had run a distance, with more to go, and his destination was a great secret. But not so great a secret, apparently, if little nosy Dorothy had figured out where he was running. She must have followed him when he sneaked out last night. Unless her showing up here was a coincidence. This thought gave him hope.

He stopped, out of breath. His sister was short for her age. In a drab dress, with long blond hair tied in braids, her feet dirty, her calves and knees all scratched, she stood in the middle of the field alone, evidently expecting him.

Except there was no time. He couldn't look after her now, couldn't take her with him, but also couldn't leave her here. What had seemed a chance to be wealthy, to grab a better future for the family, was today a terrible danger. Not only those close to him could be destroyed but the entire village. Including this stupid sister.

The jaegers were looking for the outlaw.

"What are you doing here, Dotty?" he asked.

"Waiting for you, Kajtek. Let's go together."

She lisped a little, because of the gaps in her teeth. She didn't seem at all frightened.

"We're not going anywhere together! Go home!" he shouted, but even as he said this, he knew it was a mistake. Her lips pouted; her eyes brimmed with tears.

"Dotty, don't you start now!" He went and patted her quickly. "No bawling. Does Mama know where you are?"

"She went to the plantation this morning. She took Jack."

"She didn't tell you to stay in the house? She didn't give you any work to do?"

"Maybe she did, but when the black ones came"— Dorothy shuddered at the thought of the jaegers— "Granny sent me to the fields to tell the people. Then I knew you would be running to the woods again, like you do every night—"

"What are you talking about? At night I sleep!"

"Don't fib. Mama and Granny sleep after they work, but I wake up a lot, Kajtek. Don't you remember Daddy saying what a light sleeper I am? Three times I saw you leave, and the fourth time I followed. I lost you here, so I came back here. See how smart I am?" She grinned, showing all the gaps in her teeth, and Kajetan didn't know which to curse, her meddling or his carelessness.

"Listen, Dotty," he said after a moment. "You can't come with me. Go home."

"No," she said calmly. "Unless you want me to tell everybody you have a *se-cret!*"

Kajetan knew that his little sister meant it.

"Women are like an awful cold," the man in the cabbage patch had said, "the kind you can't shake for a week."

Kajetan took his sister by the hand, and together, quickly, they went into the woods. There was no time to waste. He had to tell Ha-hon about the jaegers.

"Sit here and don't move, you hear?" Kajetan pushed Dorothy into a clump of leafy burdock. "Even if an ant bites you, even if something itches, even if a little bunny goes by! Don't move!"

"Okay, Kajtek." The little girl seemed to under-stand. Her readiness to obey filled the boy with forebod-ing. He hunkered down, put his hands on her shoulders.

"Listen, Dotty, this is not a game. If you don't do what I say, something really, really bad could happen. To you and to me too. And Mama. Will you sit here?"

"I will." She looked steadily into his eyes.

"Good. I'll be back soon." He got up and carefully looked around.

"Kajtek?"

"What?"

"If a little fox goes by, can I move then?"

"No!" he nearly shouted. She wanted to discuss it further, but he wouldn't go into the question of little bunnies versus little foxes. He ran the last leg, passing the familiar trees, the glade of berries, the fallen trunk, and finally reached the fence that lay rotting on the ground, overgrown with weeds. He crossed it and made for the wooden columns among the bushes, what was left of a house that had stood here long ago.

It might have been a hunting lodge or the summer home of a rich man, or a military post. Whatever it was, the building had been leveled by nature, and a few fragments of wall were all that marked its former existence. The greenery twining around them was different in a subtle way from the other forest plants, showing a definite rectangle where the foundation had been: a little less lush, and a little lower. Enough for Kajetan to know at once that this place was a remnant of the old world. His surprise and delight increased when practically at the center of the rectangle he found a square hole leading to a small basement. Beneath the earth were treasures: empty, unbroken bottles, rusty nails, the skull of a horned animal, a metal mug. The mug could be used at home, but all the other objects Kajetan exchanged for food. And since this discovery was made right after the death of his father, when they often went hungry—he and his mother—Kajetan considered the forest ruin his good luck spot.

So it was natural for him to have brought here the creature he met in the woods. With this creature in his lucky spot, he believed, he would again be able to put food on the table. But things were turning out differently.

"Ha-hon!" Kajetan called. "It's me, Ha-hon. You can come out."

There was a rustling at the branch-covered entrance to the hole. The tangle of stalks that Kajetan had dragged together stirred, moved aside, and facing the boy stood a most peculiar man.

Ha-hon was only a meter high, solidly built, with arms disproportionately long and legs disproportionately short—except for the feet: possibly if you added the lengths of leg and foot, Ha-hon's lower extremities would have exceeded those of the tallest villager. The fingers of his powerful hands were remarkably long and supple, having an extra joint and nails on both sides. The misshapen body was topped by a round head. Ha-hon was almost completely bald. He had large blue eyes, almond-shaped; his nose was enormous and as bulbous as a potato that has been in the cellar too long; his large mouth had two rows of bright-yellow, gleaming teeth. In his case the expression "a sunny smile" was literal.

But Ha-hon was not in the best condition. A long scratch ran down his cheek, and it wasn't healing well. He had trouble moving his left arm; he grimaced whenever he had to lift it. He was weak, wounded, and very likely ill.

But seeing Kajetan, he broke into a lemony smile.

"You have it?!"

"Not yet, but I know where it is."

"Good." Ha-hon scrambled the rest of the way out of the hole and stepped toward Kajetan. When they shook hands, the boy's hand was completely covered by the troll's paw. "But if you do not have the substratum, why did you come?"

"The jaegers know you're here. They're setting up a hunt. You must hide better!"

The troll did not answer right away. He raised his left hand to his neck, touched a metal pendant there.

"I am almost ready. Get me what you promised, and I will flee from here."

"But you'll return, to help?"

"I gave my word. Do you not remember?"

Kajetan remembered, of course: how could he forget what had happened only a week before? When he met the troll in the woods, he was gathering mushrooms, as he usually did in the early hours at this time of year. He had left the house at dawn, when the ground was wet with dew and the last chill of the night still penetrated a torn shirt. He left with an empty sack on his back and a basket in his hand. The old wicker was cracked in many places, but Kajetan's mother had lovingly repaired the holes, and she made a new handle from a piece of a cane and withes of willow bent by being soaked in water. This old-friend basket had brought home more than one meal. Mama prepared the mushrooms in different ways; a portion of them she dried for the winter, and sometimes she bartered with them.

Many people in the village were afraid to go looking for mushrooms. An unskilled picker risked death, as the villagers had been harshly reminded a year earlier, when little Helen was fooled by a werechamel imitating a chanterelle. There was nothing to bury; they found only a few scraps of her dress beside the monster's swollen bulb. They did then what was usually done: dug up the earth, pried out the bole hidden there, put branches and pine needles around it, and burned it. But that didn't bring back to life the seven-year-old Helen, and Kajetan got new customers for his mushrooms.

A week ago he was returning with his basket full, when the underbrush behind him swayed more than it should have. He whirled, dropping the basket, and the mushrooms went tumbling across the moss.

A strange being stood there, human-shaped and yet not human, and his clothes, once fine, were now torn and muddy. He seemed no threat—seemed actually in need of help. His weary face was covered with dirt and dried blood. He breathed heavily, as if after a long run, and every breath made him wince. His left arm was oddly twisted; perhaps he was trying to protect his nerveless fingers. In his right hand he clutched a long black object. A gun, Kajetan thought.

"I should run" went through his head, but he didn't move, sensing that the creature had no connection with the jaegers and their masters—unless it was fleeing from them.

"Help me." Those were the creature's first words. "Please."

Then Kajetan learned things he had never dreamed of.

Ha-hon came from a race of trolls who inhabited a world separate from the world of men. The troll used words Kajetan didn't understand: the eidolon membrane, the osmosophoresis of imaginings, the gradients of magic fluxions. Ha-hon's people were at war with the lords of the jaegers. The barlogs had attacked the troll world, as they did the human world, but met with much more resistance from the trolls. The war was still waging, savage, merciless. Ha-hon belonged to a special group of scouts who had been sent to the world of men to spy on the barlogs. He was captured and imprisoned for two years by the jaegers. Several days ago he contrived his escape, and also managed to steal this unusual object—here Ha-hon showed his treasure—a key that allowed you to cross the walls between the worlds. The troll wished to return to his people and could do this, but it was difficult.

The key, belonging to the barlogs, was tuned to their magic. Ha-hon needed to harness it, and for that he needed more power, time, and the performance of a certain ritual. Also, the damping of the artifact's aura, so that it would not be picked up by the hunters, had taken much energy. He asked Kajetan to keep his secret and to assist him.

"When I return to my people, I will recover my strength," he said, "and then I will repay you. What do you wish? I will do what lies within my ability and the ability of my countrymen."

Kajetan did not answer right away. He took the measure of this being who was no higher than he though obviously much older and wiser. In only a few minutes the troll had revealed to him more about the mysteries of the world than the boy had learned in all his twelve years on earth. What should he ask for? Food? A weapon? Clothing?

"I wish you would take me from this place. Me and my whole family, Mama, Granny, my sister and brother. Can you do that?" Kajetan asked, looking into the troll's eerie eyes.

The troll held the look. "Yes, I can take you all to a better world," he said. "And I will do this thing, I swear, if you assist me."

So Kajetan obtained the herbs that hastened the healing of the wounds Ha-hon had received, most of them at the hands of his torturers. He brought the troll food to eat, often from his own plate. Finally, he provided the objects required for the ritual of passage—the bark of a birch tree, fur from a dog, water from a deep well, and other things that seemed to have nothing to do with high magic.

"Passage between worlds is not like walking through a gate," explained Ha-hon, though Kajetan couldn't always tell whether the troll was speaking to him or to himself. "It is like oozing through a barrier, like water that seeps through a fabric. First I must build a special frame, a weaving frame to hold the fibers of your world. Then I must have pieces of your world's power. Then the key allows me to part the threads of the weave, allows me to replace the tight fabric with a net that has holes, larger and larger holes. It is through such a hole that I escape. Do you grasp?"

Kajetan nodded eagerly, grasping nothing.

The key was a small, elongated object the color of iron, though at the touch it felt more like stone than metal. When Ha-hon held it, it barely jutted from his hand. Curiously, when the troll let Kajetan hold it once, the key was almost completely hidden in his hand, a much smaller hand than the troll's. The magic object resembled a knife somewhat, having a hilt that was half its length. The blade was a flat triangle, its edges dull, not sharp. The key was covered with drawings so very tiny that when Kajetan lifted it to his eyes, he could make out only squiggles, which seemed arranged in patterns. Ha-hon had tied a piece of string to the key and wore it around his neck, under his shirt.

"The problem," he explained, "is that the jaegers drained my power from me; I am now like a gutted fish. And I spent a week in the forest, running, circling to put them off the scent, and meeting with many dangers. I need a few days to regain my strength, so I can control the key."

Kajetan was proud. He once overheard his father talking with another villager about people who lived far away and fought the jaegers. They were strong enough to live in freedom, those people, and the barlogs could not cross the border of their land. The grownups spoke of this in whispers, in secret, themselves not fully believing what they said. And now here was a man—well, not exactly a man—who came from a place free of the barlogs, who fought them, and who asked for Kajetan's help.

In the next week Kajetan not only did his usual tasks but also cared for the troll. No one in the village, not even his mother, knew about this. Ha-hon said that he needed two or three more days to build up in himself the perfluctive force that would enable the opening of the hole in the net. Except that now he didn't have those two or three days: the jaegers were after him.

The troll didn't seem worried.

"They do not know I am here, otherwise they would have taken me already. Four jaegers is a common unit, so their coming to the village was usual reconnaissance. I covered my tracks well. They are no doubt looking for me in the mountains too and by the sea. Obviously there is no point taking risks. We have a little time to spare but must act quickly. Will you be able to bring me the final substratum tomorrow morning?"

"Yes, Ha-hon. I'll be back here at dawn, but don't leave the hideout."

The troll looked at him, his head at a slight angle.

"The child is concerned about me. Imagine. Boy, just make sure that no harm befalls you on your way home. It is time anyway for me to start the ritual. Go, go."

Kajetan turned on his heel and in a moment had put the forest ruins behind him, hidden by thick bushes. Dorothy should be waiting for him somewhere here, unless she got bored or saw a little fox or bunny, or was thirsty, or had to pee, or simply decided to leave.

Incredibly, she was waiting where he had left her.

4

The Apache hung twenty meters above the ground.

The elf spat the matchstick from his mouth and tied the automatic to the line. Once more he adjusted the bow on his back, the sword strapped to his side. He tucked one of his pointed ears inside his helmet. Elves did everything exactly, on principle.

"Geronimo!" he yelled then and jumped.

Robert waited a moment and went to the open cabin door. He peered out. Seeing that the elf was unhitched, he grabbed the line and stepped into the air.

He cushioned his fall, but felt a pinch in his left knee. He unhitched immediately.

"Clear out!"

"Good luck!" he heard above him. The chopper turned its nose east and started moving. Soon it was only a speck in the blue sky.

"I don't like it," said the elf. Robert wasn't sure whether his comrade meant traveling this way or the landscape that now lay before them.

They stood on a patch of sand surrounded by seedling firs. Some twenty paces lay between them and the edge of the forest. The trees were different colors, and Robert had the impression that some were moving their branches in a direction other than the direction of the wind. A few had eyes that blinked.

"To work," Robert said. He knelt and took a small black instrument from his thigh pocket. He smoothed the ground with his hand; the fine sand rippled through his fingers. A glance up at the elf. "Is this all right?"

Hardadian had set the little pendulum swinging. He watched its movement carefully and finally nodded. Satellite recon by the Americans was confirmed: this piece of ground— an ordinary variety of grass, an occasional shrub—was free of enemy cadabras. They could set up their equipment here.

Robert dug a shallow hole in the sand, placed the device in the hole, and covered it up. He lifted his left hand, pulled back the sleeve to reveal the band on his forearm, and punched in the activating code. The ground beneath his feet moved. Six thin rods emerged, bending upward and inward like the legs of an overturned beetle. Robert looked at the communicator.

"We have contact with the base. Three minutes remain."

"Let's go!"

They went. Before them was the Zone, a thirty-kilometer strip of land across which for half a century now armies and bands of looters had come and gone, fay caissons and columns of tanks, cohorts of armored horsemen and the gray shades of phantom spies. Scars of old battles were left in the form of eldritch force fields, wandering concentrations of nanos, weird beasts. An added danger was the military divisions still in operation here. Beyond this belt of damaged reality began an unmagical region, the Marches, the kingdom of the barlogs and their servants.

The man Robert and the elf Hardadian did not need to go that far. The American satellites had pinpointed the artifact on this side of the Oder. Had it been on the other side, the elf would have been accompanied not by Robert but by Georg Baum, an emissary of the Free German Government in Exile, a branch of which had taken up residence in Warsaw. Fortunately for Georg (Warsaw girls were pretty, Polish beer was good) and unfortunately for Robert (the same two reasons), the artifact had shown up east of the river, in the region where Kozuchow once stood. The satellites had determined its position to within fifteen kilometers—not bad, considering that the sputniks constructed on elfin specs were mainly of linden wood covered with runic carvings and then soaked in mithril. When it turned out that these in fact orbited and transmitted, at least three NASA employees became clinically depressed and one had to be institutionalized.

The whole industrial effort of the USA, which country had been devastated by its war with the Canadian barlogs, was now channeled into maintaining an orbiting network to monitor the enemy's colonies on Earth. With this network, the Allies were able to stem the barlog expansion. In Europe the status quo had been preserved for two decades. Over that time the jaegers had not enlarged their territory in Poland, Brittany, or Padua. Only in the north had they reached the ocean, joining with the Baltic barlogs where Denmark once was.

The Apache had carried Robert and Hardadian as far as it could without risking discovery. Because headquarters did not know the precise location of the artifact, they decided to send two scouts to investigate onsite. The two were to make their way through the Zone, avoiding both emanations and enemy patrols, and find the artifact, which lay in occupied territory. Finding it, they would call for help, and a helicopter from Fort Thorn would come in fifteen minutes. In fifteen minutes the jaegers would not have time to react and engage them—as they unavoidably

would if an expedition were sent in. The artifact wasn't
worth that.

In the magic forest, the elf led. They went at a stiff pace
but with a wary eye. The trees were close together, com-
peting for the sunlight. Firs predominated, but there were
also birches, rowans, willows. The grass underfoot grew
sparse. Clumps of ferns, an occasional thicket. The strong
June sun penetrated and fell in greenish gold on the
ground. Into such a forest one could take one's family berry
picking—if one didn't care for one's family.

Hardadian took his bow in hand; Robert held his
MP7 at the ready, setting it to 3. The elf walked with confidence, though now and then he stopped and froze a moment, to turn aside suddenly and go around a tree, mound,
or fallen trunk.

This was not his first time crossing the Zone, which
meant something—though not much, because the forces
shifted, changing the loci of peril and even the topography,
the distances between A and B. (And space-time problems
could arise: one scout claimed that in the middle of the forest
he came upon Lower Manhattan, and another reported sight-
ing a penguin.) But fragmentary information was better than
none, and an elf, besides, was far more adept than the most
spell-sensitive human at foreseeing and countering snares.

Robert's talent was 8.76 pratchetts on the ten-
point Smith-Smythe-Vujowic Scale, which placed him in

the top three permills of the human population. Sometimes he was smug about that, but usually not when he had to slog through wilderness lugging thirty kilograms of equipment. He swore under his breath, and for the forest the feeling was mutual.

From one of the trees a green, shaggy shadow detached itself and silently followed the intruders.

It was not a bona fide monster. One could even say that it was not a bona fide anything, merely a large and moving rift in the continuum, a wandering node of fairy woven by nanocadabras into an invisible skeleton, which then clothed itself in the flesh of its surroundings: a torn blanket of moss became the creature's skin, stones became its teeth, the sharp points of broken branches its claws, and perfectly innocent spiders were made to spin round webs where any self-respecting animal had eyes.

The creature jumped on Robert's back, spreading its four spectral arms and opening its maw, whose proportions suggested that the forest nanos had experience once, somehow, with fishes of the deep. The moment the wooden claws touched his neck, Robert leaped to one side, the barrel of his gun seeking a target. The elf was swifter. Where a second before Robert's head had been, an arrow whistled from Hardadian's bow. The elfin bolt with a flash of silver stuck in the monster's spidery eye. There was a huff, a crack, a snap, as of a tree falling.

The monster came apart, the constituents of its body hitting the earth, but the arrow, which by logic should have fallen with them or flown on to the trees, disappeared.

Robert, whispering defensive charms, swept the nearest trees with his automatic. The elf already had another arrow nocked and ready. The wood of his bow glowed red.

"Dendroids rarely hunt in pairs," said Hardadian, lowering his weapon after a while. "That one wasn't too bad."

"You were the threat. If I hadn't got out of the way in time, I would have a third eye now."

"A third might help."

"Anyway," said Robert, "thanks."

"Let's move on. We have seven more kilometers to cover before dark. And there are worse things here than dendroids."

Over the next few hours Robert learned that the elf was right. As elves tended to be.

The jaeger guardpost was unexpected, not in any of the plans that headquarters had provided. It loomed among the trees—a high wooden building that resembled a windmill in that each of the four walls had a six-bladed wing and turned, with such synchrony that the blades did not hit each other.

The elf sensed it first.

"May a hairy horse hoof!" he swore, using one of the many elfin profanities that never failed to amuse Robert. Rumor had it that at the royal court there was a special Keeper of the Curse, whose task it was to think up new choice expressions.

"May an infirm pachyderm with the runs," Hardadian added, in his disgust at the serious departure from the plan this jaeger guardpost represented. "When we get back, I'll make those astro bastards eat their charts! Just yesterday they told me they had coordinates, images. What the duck is going on?"

"The fuck," Robert corrected him. "What do we do now?"

"Look." Hardadian fingered an outline of the building. "Border guards. Those turbos are generating Köff space, thick as jelly with nanos and tetras. We won't pass without being discovered. Here we're OK, Köff waves are broken up by the trees, but on that meadow we'll be as visible as a fly on a windshield."

"Can we go around it?"

"Wait." Hardadian shrugged off his pack and from its side pocket took out a ring of yellow metal covered with inscriptions. He put in on an index finger, turned it three times to the left, two times to the right as he murmured words. Robert recognized only the first verses of the mantra used to begin a cohesion séance. Hardadian was attempting to break into the spatial matrix of the jaeger kibosh to assess its range. This was higher stuff: no human, even with Robert's proficiency, could finesse such hoodoo. Someone might spend his life in study of the formulas that the elves learned over their three to four hundred years—but that student would never wield their power. Unless perhaps it was in Warsaw, where the natural gradients of glamour were significantly elevated by the presence of thousands of elves and their devices, protective shields, and residual discharges. In the city, well-magicked humans worked side by side with elves, conducted experiments, assembled artifacts. But here, in this wild, all the might had to come from inside the caster of the spell. Robert would have been able to produce a few phenomena or manifestations on his own—but any attempt he made to confront the war weird of the barlogs would have ended badly.

Hardadian probed the guardpost environs a while longer, then quietly removed the ring and returned it to his pack.

"And?" asked Robert.

"Doesn't look good. A strong generator, throws up a fence some fifteen kilometers to the north and seventeen to the south. Which means we must reroute. At our pace that's a loss of six, seven hours."

"So much? What rotten luck, that we had to hit precisely the guardpost."

"Rotten luck?" Hardadian was surprised.

"Finding this blasted windmill right in our path. Unless maybe they're lying in wait for us?"

"I wouldn't worry about that," Hardadian said with a smile. "The guardpost isn't exactly there."

"What do you mean, not exactly there? What am I looking at, an ice cream cone?"

"Had we emerged from the forest five kilometers on, we would have encountered the same guardpost. It's everywhere on the meadow, and at the same time nowhere. Whenever an intruder approaches the barrier, the building appears."

"That makes no sense . . ."

"What makes no sense? Why no sense?" said the elf, annoyed. "It's the same way with those . . . what, electrons of yours. In an atomic shell they're everywhere, statistically. But when a photon hits, it turns out they're mostly at that one point. Your whole world is built of such absurd particles, and you tell me that a probabilistic meadow doesn't make sense!"

"All right, then, what do we do?" Robert didn't care for discussions on quantum physics or quantum magic, not understanding either, though both worked.

"Circling the fence will take too long. And the forest itself isn't safe. All kinds of obstacles in it could slow us down. How far are we from the destination?"

"The last usable satellite reading puts the artifact ten kilometers from here."

"In other words, two hours. Chopper?"

"One could be here in a quarter of an hour."

"What I'm thinking is, how far are the jaegers? And how quickly can we reach the artifact?"

"You're not suggesting . . ."

"We have no choice. We must cross the meadow, then run as fast as—how do you Poles put it?—with the poker up the rear."

Sheathed in charms, the elf and the human flitted from tree to tree, crouched behind bushes, crawled through tall grass. Robert felt that he couldn't have been more visible, that the sun at its zenith was making his figure leap from the forest's dark background to the eyes of every guard. His soldier's instinct told him to wait for dusk, to lie motionless under leaves, to darken his face with paint. A part of his mind watched analytically this scene in which he was a player.

Their spells worked far better than any cover of grass or branches. But what shielded them in one spectral band of the guardpost scanners must leave traces in another. Their blocking would sooner or later cause fluctuation in the tetra field and come to the attention of the guards. Meanwhile the windmill was within fifty paces, and still they were unobserved. For Robert, further evidence that his partner was a master.

The closer they came, the less like a windmill it appeared. The wings had six blades each—at least at first

129

glance. On closer inspection, it was not six but four, or maybe three, though sometimes eight. They turned so regularly that in a sense they were the opposite of a windmill: it was not the wind that moved them but they that set the air in motion. The tension of nanos at the wings was so high, strange shapes flickered. The farther from the hub, the fewer the shapes.

The structure itself was made of black wood, shiny like ebony, but with no grain, cracks, or insect holes. The horizontal planks, perfectly straight and even, made a rectangular solid that tapered a little at the roof. Three meters up, the building was surrounded by a gallery so narrow that a person standing on it would have had to press himself to the wall to keep the windmill blades from slicing off his nose.

Above the gallery—at least on the side they were approaching—was a square window framed by bas-relief figures representing a creature with a number of heads that exceeded the terrestrial average. Greater detail could not be seen at that distance. The window opening was darker even than the wall; its dense, dull black suggested depth and such mysteries of multidimensional space as would have been the professional delight of any topologist.

The two scouts separated. Robert crawled along a shallow, grassy ditch; Hardadian advanced to his right, hopping from clump to clump of underbrush. Finally he stopped, gave the sign that there was no more cover. He took the bow from his shoulder. Robert delicately parted the grass, moved forward a little to get in a better position.

Slow breathing. The battle mantras. Rhythm and concentration.

He recited the enchantments evenly, calmly, accenting those phrases that applied to what would soon commence. It was in a language he didn't know. He had learned these sentences by heart in the academy, as a cadet; years of drilling had stamped them on his mind, and many repetitions in military actions had refined them.

The mantras harnessed his thoughts to one goal; they ordered, prioritized, discarding all that was unnecessary. They fused the physical organism, upping muscle capacity, neural speed, acuity of vision. They wrapped his body in the best armor: transparent, light, supple, yet protecting him from the blows of ordinary weapons as well as from bolts of magic.

Robert could now go against any man or jaeger. For barlogs, there was the elf. But barlogs weren't expected here.

Hardadian stood up. The twang of his bow was like the scream of a hawk. The silver arrow cut the air with a high whistle, making for the black window. The elf sent other arrows after it.

The first was consumed before it reached its target, the second also, but the third broke through and flew into the pit. In an instant the windmill changed color, turned snow white, and the blades came to a halt. Mingled in the roar of the explosion, the cries of the defenders. Through the walls came their silhouettes. Human-shaped auxmorphs materialized at the base of the fort. Some, injured by the blast within, fell as they appeared.

The dozen or so who survived formed swords and axes and made for the elf. Hardadian stood calmly, plying his bow, and arrow quickly followed arrow.

The MP7 belched. Robert fired in short three-round bursts. The bullets pierced the chests of the aux-morphs but could damage only the ones who were almost completely materialized. The elf dispatched the ones still spectral.

None of these creatures reached their attackers. But that was not their purpose: the defense system had generated them to make contact with and test the enemy's battle aura. Behind the expiring soldiers appeared their leaders, the true defenders of the fort, warriors of the panzer race: four-armed, clad in plates of fay, wielding maces of iron. These bodies were based on the human pattern, but atop their heads were clusters of ruby eyes, spider eyes, the facets arrayed to indicate clan. The closest three panzers were Mittwochstamms, who for years had made up most of the army that fought elves and humans on the old Polish-German border. Possibly they remembered the blood, terror, and pain, the dark time when all Europe had been turned into a land of death.

Robert hated the Mittwochstamms.

Hardadian threw down his bow practically at the same moment that Robert cast aside his MP7, both useless against the panzers. Drawing their swords, elf and human charged with a cry. Hardadian danced gracefully as he closed with the enemy. He seemed to have been hurled among the crushing machines of a great factory. The maces and arms of the panzers threshed the air about him, but he eluded them, deftly sidestepping pulpy death each time by a hair. His own blows were dealt with swift precision, hewing, stabbing.

The fight was soon over. Robert chopped one of his opponents in the neck, nearly removing the head. The elf sank his blade into the skull of another, and paste sprayed in all directions from the severed eyestalks. The third creature fled, but fleeing evidently weakened its defensive field, because with one short curse Hardadian brought it to the ground, then slew it.

The windmill winked out, and with it vanished the corpses of all the auxmorphs.

"We've gained a path," said the elf. His voice was steady, but in his eyes still danced the light of battle madness. "The jaegers now know we're here. Let's move!"

5

This time Ha-hon waited for Kajetan.

The place where the old building once stood had been cleared of bushes by the troll. Through the moss now ran furrows, a hand's width and dug down into the black soil; these were arranged in spirals, or in the sweeping letters of a secret script, or in the shapes of animals. The lines all met at the center of the clearing, where Ha-hon had set stones in a circle, a circle so large that Kajetan would not have been able to jump across it even with a running start. Most of these stones Kajetan had brought himself, for it was easier to gather them in the fields than here in the woods. There were twenty-four—the largest the size of a child's head, the smallest like a child's clenched fist.

As the troll once explained to the boy, the channels carved in the moss were to fill the stones with the power of the earth. When focused on the objects collected inside the circle, that power would enable the key to open the gate to the troll's home world.

There were four objects inside. A blood-red crystal: the troll's amulet, which remembered the way back. A scroll of yellowed paper covered with black marks: the formulas that permitted you to part the successive curtains between one reality and the next. An oak branch to draw the force of all plants. An elk bone to provide the strength of all beasts.

Ha-hon sat beneath the arch that would span worlds. He had built it himself. In a forward squat, he was pressing his long hands to the ground. His eyes were shut. He gulped the air—as though by force of will alone he was holding back an earthquake, a tornado.

"You have it, boy?" he asked, not opening his eyes.

"Yes," said Kajetan, approaching the troll slowly, carefully, trying not to step on any of the lines cut into the moss. If something flowed there, even if invisible, it might hurt his bare feet. Coming up to the circle of stones, he saw that the troll held in his left hand the key of passage.

"Good." Ha-hon opened his bulbous eyes, which now were burning. "The moment nears."

"There are no jaegers in the village. Our people are still gathering. You have time."

"Give me the egg." The troll stretched out his hand.

"But . . ." Kajetan hesitated, reluctant to step into the circle. He stood at its edge, shifting from foot to foot.

"Afraid?" Ha-hon smiled.

"Me? Never!" Kajetan stuck out his chest yet still did not move.

"You should be afraid, boy. Many lines of magic converge here, and you possess none yourself. Worse, I do not have my own key, only this." He raised it on his open palm. "It is the key of the barlogs, as you curiously call them. I must adapt to it the aura of my world. It would be different if those scum had not taken mine. Believe me, much different . . . But no matter, give me the egg."

Kajetan reached into his pocket and took out a chicken egg, which had been wrapped in straw for protection. He didn't understand why an egg was needed: Ha-hon had said something about the circle of rebirth, the shell of appearance, the calibration of ectoplasm. To obtain the egg the boy had risked an expedition to a neighbor's henhouse. For stealing, one could be whipped.

Kajetan raised a leg above the circle of stones. He paused, as if to test the water. Nothing happened. His foot was not scalded. He boldly crossed the circle then, went to Ha-hon, and handed him the egg. The troll took it, weighed it for a moment in his closed hand, then with violent suddenness popped it into his mouth and chomped.

Kajetan was hit by a wave of heat. Spots danced before his eyes; the world changed color. Only now did the boy feel the pull of the currents that were merging on the troll. He swayed, would have fallen if Ha-hon's hands hadn't held him up.

"I do regret this . . . ," said the troll, and from the corners of his mouth trickled a sticky, iridescent fluid.

Hardadian came to a stop. Winded, panting, Robert stopped too and leaned against a tree trunk; he bent over and drew the air into his lungs.

"Oof, thanks . . ."

"For what?" The elf's tone was not pleasant.

"For the rest."

"I'm not resting." Hardadian straightened, stood almost on tiptoe, craning his neck as if to catch a scent. "I feel . . . it's strong. A ritual," he whispered. "But that's not possible . . ."

Far to the west, the tower tops of the jaeger stronghold gleamed red. A shadow hovering at the edge of a village began to thicken. The dragons of night opened their jaws, and black riders emerged on the road, on their spider-legged steeds.

Hardadian turned in his hand the brass medallion he had taken from his pack. He fingered the gems set in it, gazed at their sparkle, felt their temperature.

"We didn't foresee this," he muttered.

"What? Foresee what?"

"It's not an ordinary artifact, not some amulet one of our chieftains lost on a battlefield or the bone of an enchanted animal. It's not from here, from Earth. It's a key of passage, a key that opens portals to other planes and shows the way to the ruins of the sacred city Olmeh. And the one who holds it has begun the ritual of passage. All this time he hid from us and from the jaegers the fact of his possession. He must be a great mage. It is not a man we will find there, Robert."

"What then?"

"I don't know."

"I am sorry," the troll said, drawing to him the stunned Kajetan. His hands closed around the boy's neck. "This is not my magic. I have not the strength myself. The egg gave me life. You must provide now the final thing: death."

The jaegers galloped through the village. A wake of flame and screaming followed them. The disobedient must be punished. *Ordnung muss sein.*

The boy felt the long bony hands of the troll around his neck; the fingers with nails on both sides dug into his skin. He did not resist at first, in his shock and fear. Perhaps it was the digging nails that brought him to himself. He was being pressed to the ground, could hardly breathe, and a sharp stink filled his nostrils. He tried to push the troll away. He was unable to, yet the grip on his neck loosened a little. The troll was much older and wiser than he, the boy realized, but not that much stronger.

Kajetan struggled again, now putting everything he had into it. He kicked, he shoved at the troll's face with his shoulder, he punched the troll's arms. It helped for a moment, but again Ha-hon was pressing down. He got a better grip, and Kajetan couldn't breathe at all now. In despair he flailed, pulled at the troll's hair, pushed. But without air he was weakening, dying.

Seeing that his victim's resistance was over, the troll changed the grip again, to throttle the boy more quickly, but this allowed Kajetan a breath. Reanimated, he fought with all his might, and must have struck an eye, because Ha-hon yelped with pain and momentarily lost his advantage. Kajetan hit again, threw the troll off, got to his feet, and jumped out of the stone circle, still feeling the troll's hands around his neck. He stumbled but was able to regain his balance. He ran full tilt into the forest, making for the village, not looking behind him, though he heard furious panting, the crack of broken twigs, the thud of feet. The branches hit his face, the tree trunks threatened collision, every root, mound, and puddle was a mortal danger, because if he slipped even once or tripped . . .

He ran for a long time before he knew that he was not being pursued. Hardly daring to believe it, he didn't stop, he only slowed a little. Finally he looked back. Wiping his runny nose with a sleeve, he felt how badly his neck hurt, only now. He put a hand to it, but there wasn't that much blood. The forest appeared quiet, peaceful.

Kajetan couldn't trust in that. Again he ran. He stopped only when he reached the village. He made straight for his house. He would tell his mother what had happened, as soon as possible. Ha-hon might be an enemy of the jaegers, but he was also an enemy of humans. Fear and fatigue in the boy began to give way to anger. The troll had tricked him. Promising so much, the hope that they could leave this nightmare, that they would no longer go hungry—he, his mother, Dorothy. Let the jaegers catch the troll and drag him back to their fortress, let them take revenge on the ugly creature for what he had done to Kajetan!

"I've lost the signal," said Hardadian, throwing out his hands.

139

"How?"

"How? Just like that. He must have stopped the ritual."

But first he had to make up some story for his mother. He couldn't tell her that he had been helping Ha-hon. For that there might be a dreadful punishment—not just he, the whole village might be killed. How many times had the jaegers killed an entire family because one person did not even a big thing, a little thing, nonsense: possessing a forbidden object, not working hard enough, saying one rude word. And he, Kajetan, had hid their enemy, an outlaw, in defiance of the jaeger warning. This couldn't end well. Especially when the troll, under torture, was sure to tell all about Kajetan's role. So it wasn't a good idea to inform the jaegers about the outlaw. Maybe the villagers themselves should find and kill him. They could show their masters the corpse afterward.

He must tell his mother everything. Let her decide what to do.

Entering the yard of his home, Kajetan wiped his face again, straightened his shirt. You have to look your best when you do important business—though only twelve, he had learned that lesson by watching the grownups.

He quickly crossed the sandy yard and opened the door. Now he felt safe, greeted by the warm, familiar smell of his home. The fear left him: he was ready to tell the truth.

"Mommy," he began. "Something happened . . ."

"Ah, it's you." His mother hadn't heard his first words, hadn't yet noticed the marks on his neck and face. She sat half turned from the door, at the table black with age. A piece of material was spread out there, and on it lay a mound of something dark and crumbly. She was dividing the substance into smaller piles, using a knife blade, working with the utmost care so that each pile would contain exactly the same number of brown grains.

"See, I got some sugar for you children. Dotty will be so happy."

"Mommy . . ."

"And yes, did Dotty meet you?"

"Dotty? Meet me? Why . . ."

"She was sitting here with me but got bored and said she'd go find you. To the forest! She said she knew the way and where you were. You didn't see her? But what happened to you, Kajtek? What are those cuts on your neck? Kajtek?!"

They were almost in time. When they ran into the forest clearing, they saw the dissipating aura around the low, bent figure. The troll was on his knees, both hands raised to the sky. On his neck hung the key of passage. He was chanting the final words of the spell. His hands and face were red with blood.

He saw them too. For a brief moment the eyes of Ha-hon and Robert met. It even seemed to the human that the troll smiled slightly. Then the creature was gone.

"What was that?"

"What I didn't expect. One of the trackers. A mighty warrior. They are able to travel among worlds. Serving no one, only themselves."

"Worlds?"

"I don't know for what reason he came, but he was hiding from the jaegers."

Then—

"We must catch him, Hardadian!" Robert's voice surprised the elf. He had never before heard such iron in it. "I must go after him!"

"Dangerous. His power is great, perhaps greater than mine. But why . . ." The elf fell silent, because now he saw what Robert had seen. Blood on light hair. Torn clothes. On the cheek of the dead child, a beetle crawled.

"I must," the man repeated.

"Let's do it, then," said the elf with a nod.

The forest froze where the jaeger steeds passed. A burst of magic split space. The transfer was beginning.

6

"Manè karata, manè tevol, kadam kadam." The elf's eyes glittered.

A stream of light like a white worm burrowed through the darkness. It curled, looped, gathered, and swelled, etching structures of white across the void. It drove all blackness from the world, making room for day.

The elf stretched out his hands, and from them too light flowed, every color, furling at his fingertips, spilling and sparkling like water from a fountain. The circle of heat increased.

The forest had disappeared somewhere, Robert realized. They were in the Nonworld.

On a vast plain. To the horizon was yellow earth, and strips of sky-blue grass undulating in a warm yet acrid breeze. In the distance Robert saw the tangles of strange trees. Beyond them were towers, slender, high, rising directly from the ground, not surrounded at the bottom by walls or lesser buildings. These towers commanded the plain. Red, curved, twisted, they leaned on one another, then separated, leaving wells of space among them; they bulged and thinned; they sent arms to one another, creating bridges. Their windows were empty holes. Despite the distance Robert could see the rust of entropy on the towers. The stairways were broken; jagged openings gaped in the turret roofs; bridge arches, fragmented, led nowhere.

"Behold the ruins of the city Olmeh. Of the Kingdom of Passes. This is the verge of the world," said Hardadian, and his shadow fell on Robert. Robert looked up and shivered. His guide, who had been dressed in the army fatigues of the elves, was gone. In his place stood a powerfully built warrior in splendid armor. On the breastplate gleamed the colors of Hardadian's house. A red cape fluttered from his shoulders to his knees. The elf's bow was twice as thick as before, and the sword he unsheathed pulsed like a ruby.

The sky above them was pitch black.

"There he is," said the elf, pointing with the blade, and Robert saw a small silhouette. The troll was running toward the ruined towers.

"And there they are." The sword edge shifted to indicate the horizon. Robert strained but didn't see them at first: black specks against a black sky. Four jaeger steeds were galloping in their disjointed way, the riders bent low in their saddles. The pursuers were attempting to intercept the fugitive before he reached the towers.

"Begin!" ordered Hardadian. Robert closed his eyes and began reciting the Third Battle Mantra. He could feel his nanos throbbing in his veins, his heated brain activating routines that had lain dormant, his heart pounding above reasonable speed. The mantra charged both his body and his will.

The elf whispered a brief spell, a wind hit Robert's face, and when Robert opened his eyes, he found that they were facing the fugitive, and at their backs rose the giant towers of Olmeh. The jaegers were approaching from the side.

The troll did not realize at first that he had new adversaries. A moment before, he was confident that he would make it to the towers, where no jaeger shadow dared enter, and there he would be able to perform the second part of the ritual. Now in his path to asylum lay a complication.

He didn't falter. Not slowing, he shouted spells. His clothes fell from him as a snake sloughs its skin. All that remained the same were the piece of string around his neck and the gray object tied to it. The troll's body took on more and more a form for battle.

Hardadian stepped forward, his sword cutting the dense air of the Nonworld.

The jaegers arrived. Robert held his automatic at belly height, and its barrel spat flame. The bullets pushed through the air like borers through the stump of a tree. The closer the jaegers were, the more slowly the bullets went. Not one reached a horse or rider.

The chargers extended their necks, and their heads now shone with the slippery wet black of the abyss, writhing masses. From their throats came a steady rumble: the roar of a predator fused with the hum of a hornet swarm.

The jaegers clutched their weapons—axes on curved handles, the blades serrated. Their symbiotic eyes poured streams of shadow, like lanterns that ate rather than gave light. The jaegers screamed, and their mouths vomited auxmorphs, a horde of helpers, many-headed chimeras that were mainly fang, poison barb, and scalding eye.

Hardadian let his arrows fly at these, and several were felled by bullets; the rest crawled through the air, buoyed in the streams of black light emitted by their masters.

They drew near. The ground shook, its vibration filling the body with hurt and chill.

Robert threw down his gun and pulled his sword. At his back he felt a strange wave of warmth, as if the walls of the dead city wished to pour into him what remained of their ancient might. When the first jaeger came at him, Robert waited until the last moment: he felt the rush of air, breathed the sour, evil smell of the steed, practically saw the oblong head of the worm in the rider's visor. He jumped aside and with all his strength smote the horse. Out of the corner of his eye he glimpsed the descending ax of the second jaeger.

The troll rushing at Hardadian became a moving cliff. He grew, thickened, hardened. His arms and legs were hewn columns, his fingers lengthened into stalactites, and his eyes were two holes bored into the granite boulder of his head. He wielded no weapon but swung his mighty paws to hit and crush the elf. Hardadian dodged nimbly, struck with his sword, and once or twice cut the troll. But those wounds seemed not to concern his opponent, who kept charging, a bulldozer eager to level an ancestral home. When a jaeger chopped from behind, the troll only shook himself and with one swipe of a paw tore the jaeger's horse in two. Instead of finishing off the rider, who lay on the ground, the troll turned and again made for Hardadian.

The blade of the jaeger ax fell faster on Robert, who saw that he could not escape it. But in that moment Hardadian cast a liminal, which enveloped Robert. The ax skittered, missed. The ward burst under the force of the blow, but it had served its purpose. The momentum of the swing pulled the jaeger from his saddle. Robert struck with his sword at the outstretched arm and hewed it from its body. The howl of the jaeger rang among the walls of the towers, danced in the empty chancels, and returned to Robert like applause.

Hardadian's next thrust entered the troll's body, but Ha-hon didn't seem affected. He seized the sword, not caring that the blade was slicing off fingers, and pulled the elf to him. Intersecting fields throbbed, but the troll gave Hardadian no time to put together any complex spell; he gripped the elf, splayed his long fingers, and jabbed them into the elf's face.

Time slowed for Robert. He saw the last jaeger struggle to spit out yet more combat auxmorphs, saw the dying convulsions of the steeds, saw Hardadian drop to his knees.

He cut at the jaeger. The black head slid from the jaeger's shoulders, though its open mouth still spewed lumps of darkness. Robert rushed toward the elf—but he was held by one of the jaeger beasts, a brown, fish-shaped thing with three snouts. It would vanish with the death of its master, but until that moment it had substance enough to attack. The chimera flapped on the ground, beating at it furiously with its snouts and tail, coiling, snapping, and its teeth closed on Robert's thigh like knives. Robert fell to the ground with a scream.

He looked and saw five long claws stabbing the face of the elf, crushing the nose, piercing the eyes, entering the brain. He heard Hardadian's death rattle and Ha-hon's roar of victory.

And then: the dying elf, in a final spasm, reached out and tore the gray amulet from the troll's neck. Dead fingers closed around the key.

The sky turned blue again. The towers and the yellow earth disappeared. They were back in the forest clearing, among fallen trees, broken branches, the corpses of jaegers and their mounts. The troll—now in his usual shape—was bent over the dead elf, whose face had become a featureless mass of red.

Ha-hon fell upon Hardadian's body, grabbed at the key, babbling spells.

Robert tried to move toward him. He groaned with pain when he put weight on his damaged leg. The severed muscles would not hold, and he fell heavily. Touching his thigh, he felt the hot stickiness of blood. He tried to rise but rolled instead on moss, surprisingly soft now and fragrant. The pain blotted out everything for a second, then returned him to the world. He saw the troll writing in the air, with the key, the Sign of Opening, heard him utter the final formulas. Robert knew he wouldn't make it. Again the troll would flee into the Nonworld, this time using the elf's death for the ritual.

Suddenly the MP7 coughed. Its bullets flew through ordinary air, at their expected speed of a hundred meters a second. Not all found their target; many tore the leaves of surrounding trees, sent pieces of bark flying, sank into stumps, the earth, ferns. But some made a row of bloody holes across the troll's back, thudding into his body, throwing him into the jerking dance of a puppet gone berserk.

Ha-hon was silent, then dropped. The key of passage tumbled from his open palm and slid over grass.

With difficulty Robert turned. He saw a small, blond boy of maybe ten gripping in both hands the black automatic.

"That's for Dotty! For Dotty!" the boy shouted, and threw the gun to the ground. He knelt by the body of his sister but didn't touch her.

The boy's shout rang in Robert's ears as he crawled toward the corpse of Ha-hon, as he lifted the magic artifact from the earth, as he then crept to Hardadian and activated the rescue signal. The growl of the chopper later did not drown it out, or the loud voices of the command team landing, or the steady thump of the machine forcing oxygen into his lungs.

He lay on the floor of the helicopter and submitted to the medics. In his right hand he clutched the key of passage. With his left he stroked the head of the little boy still sobbing. When he finally fell asleep, he dreamed of beautiful Bess.

They flew east. Toward Poland.

A Cage Full of Angels

Andrzej Zimniak

I hawked a gob in his navel.

It takes aim, but I have aim too.

Spitting in one's bellybutton is an insult not punishable by law. The insulted party, as a consequence, gains the right to respond physically—i.e., his response also is not punishable by law. No legal code covers the escalation that ensues. A moral code maybe. I've always been careful about such details, and so far it has paid off.

Of late I had been visiting a number of colorful, so-so, and totally dead towns in search of the Big Bad Black Man. His fame had preceded him and followed him, but I was in no rush. I knew that sooner or later we would meet and that the meeting would be as amusing as it was of use. Definitely of use to me, possibly to him as well.

I had heard much about him. They said he could bang a woman for two days without getting off, kill a dog with two fingers, and remove a punk's head by karate chop with practically no room to swing. Even if only a tenth of that was true, he would make a nice coot.

So I find the guy finally in a resort town as bleached as a clam shell, where combed couples walk the boardwalk and available houris pose waiting on the beach. Half the people assembled in the evening at a dive where there were matches.

The Big Bad Black Man turned out to be white, with olive skin and a torso glistening with oil. He wore only a studded vest and high boots. Before him a row of beer bottles had been set up; these he sent flying at the delighted crowd with the aid of his gargantuan whang. Obviously getting your beer in midair like that cost more. The guy had a topless stacked chick helping him, to keep him inspired. Ridiculous.

"You publicly insult the young lady," I said quietly but loud enough to be heard. "Even for your type that's low."

The Big Bad Black Man stopped smiling, or rather, the grimace of a smile froze on his big-jawed boxer's face. His out-of-focus eyes showed the presence of drugs in the blood. Scarcely had I formed the thought that he would be of little value when he grabbed a bottle and hurled it at me. This time normally, by hand.

Just before the missile reached me, I bent back, caught the bottle by its bottom, and resumed a vertical position. I popped the cap, took a swallow, and flung the beer away. It bounced along the floor, leaving a trail of foam.

"I only need my hands," I said, raising them. They were small. I was in the form then of a slender Slavic youth with a misshapen nose, a nondescript face, and a shock of straw-colored hair.

That's when I went and hawked in his navel.

The Big Bad Black Man was not entirely without class, however. He didn't sputter or come at me with furious curses. I gave him a little show of my stuff, as a pro forma warning. A touch of sportsmanship doesn't hurt when one has attained a certain level.

My opponent now broke into a smile designed to raise goose bumps. It got so quiet in the place, you could hear the beer gurgling from the fallen bottle. With one hand he pushed aside the table that held the bottles, with the other the stool that held the topless stacked chick, who was afraid to move. The guy's whang still poked stubbornly, respectably, from between the tassels of his vest.

"Apologize, child, apologize, and I will spare your life," he said.

His voice was ragged; he clearly wasn't looking after himself. Well, that was his business. But why take me for some snot-nosed kid?

"Go lick your stupid ass if you are contortionist enough," I replied, too loud to leave him any choice. I was growing impatient.

He straightened his vest, not with his hands but with a shake of his shoulders and back, as if to feel the knife sheath sewn there.

You benighted fimp, I thought. What now? Either you're hopeless or trying to keep your nose clean. Can you be smarter than I think?

He stepped heavily, like a machine. When he came within striking distance, he lifted a leg, but so tentatively that anyone could have seen through it. I watched his arms raise, and then I received such a kick, it sent me sailing into a table, which broke into pieces.

I was in rapture! The Big Bad Black Man was a master of the multiple feint. It was more than worth all my tracking down to learn this new thing. Still in the air, I took careful note of his technique, recorded the moves, and practiced them in my mind. Excellent, excellent!

Meanwhile the massive torso was above me. The Big Bad Black Man didn't hurry, assuming his opponent was stunned. He assumed wrong, having no knowledge of the coots working full steam inside. I had twenty of the finest in me, and it was thanks to them that my mind was clear and muscles functional throughout. Thanks to them, I practically never tired and was faster than anyone.

He bent over, to deal his famous chop with no swing, but I was ahead of him. Like lightning I hit with fist and knee. Both connected, though the fist sank into chin a bit more solidly than the knee into crotch. He stepped back, and I walloped him also in the noggin, at a very specific spot. He should have been royally dazed, but this was a tough customer. He straightened, then crouched in a way that let him reach to his back. His free hand hung toward one of his high boots.

A true master of the multiple feint. I couldn't tell which move would be the real attack. I kicked the wrist of the hand reaching down, positioning myself also to parry a blow from the other. I did well, because a stiletto gleamed. It had been concealed not behind him but in the front of his vest, and was drawn out by one of the vest studs. I managed to duck under the blade, and I hit twice the hand that held it, not hard but with precision. Then I twisted the hand to his back until joints cracked, and jabbed him in the neck. Now I could apply the classic strangle. Yes, it had been an interesting fight.

"I will throttle you now, and no one will object," I said into his ear. "But you can save yourself, you still can."

He heaved twice, tried to use his legs as levers. None of that worked, it couldn't now. He rasped, and his eyes rolled up.

"It doesn't matter," I continued in a whisper only he could hear, "that you don't understand. Just think the thought that you agree to become my coot, and all will be well. I know how to do this. The free choice of a free member of a free society."

What had to happen happened. The thing that always took place. The body of the Big Bad Black Man lost its vigor and substance, shriveled, shrank, and its content departed from it. It dwindled to the size of a doll, of a smoke ring blown from a pipe, till it was a pink creature with no clear shape that jumped inside me. My head spun, and I felt a rush of strength. It was time for my next change.

I left the gaping crowd, their beers in their hands, and ran to the back. I burst through a door to the men's room. On the white tiles was the reflection of my face, but no longer my face, pulled and stretched by rippling convulsions. My whole body burned, hurt, something shifted within, overflowed, swelled, grew. I made the wish to be tall this time, lean, swarthy, with brown hair. I turned my jeans and T-shirt into a tweedy suit the color of steel. Added a worsted tie, blue: good. A gray shirt with a blue stripe: just right. I felt power; the twenty-one little guys had done the job well.

A few out-of-breath men came running in. They opened the doors to the stalls.

"You didn't see a blond kid in jeans, did you?" asked one of them.

"He looked in, but left when he saw me. He was in a hurry," I informed them in a warm baritone, and took my leave of the place at a comfortable saunter.

The knock at the door was cautious, therefore suspicious. It announced the arrival of weakness, which always complicates things unnecessarily.

I put the shiv in my collar, picked up the gat, stood in the far corner, and opened the door by remote.

The guy who entered was stocky and had furtive eyes. His left sleeve rode a little high, so he must have been carrying a sizable piece in a shoulder holster; the right pant leg hung a little low, so there was probably also something stuck in his belt.

Apparently I didn't seem the boy scout type, because he raised both hands and said, "Look, I don't want trouble."

"Beat it, Byron. You're still here at the count of ten, you'll have trouble."

I went and put down my gun. We were too close now for him to get the drop on me.

"You're Enkel. We know all about you." His voice was hesitant. Everything he did was hesitant.

That clarified much. The first person plural used to intimidate indicates a lack of confidence in oneself, the need to establish that one is part of a fearsome collective. My visitor was a low-ranking government official. To a likelihood of 99%.

I pretended to attack, went at him. In a blink I had my fingers around his fat neck. He reached for his armpit automatically, the overstuffed dope, because I could have knocked any weapon from his hands before he even thought of touching a trigger. But I was being too careful, it turned out. The guy's holster was empty.

Without unnecessary words I pointed to the belt weighted on the right. He opened his blazer and showed a ring of keys. Even the handcuffs had been left with his pals on the other side of the door.

157

"All right," I sighed and sat down. "Make it short, bureaucrat."

"Matthias, federal agent," he said, showing a badge. He smoothed his clothes and sat like a girl, crossing his legs. Bad enough he was a faggot; he had to be ugly too.

"What do you want?" I looked at my watch. I had it up to here with these nancies from the government and other terribly vital organizations. God knows how they found me, recognized me.

"I bring an offer of collaboration. It's very—"

"Don't tell me. A special assignment, dangerous but lucrative. With a monthly retainer equal to a prime minister's pension. And of course the most expensive broads free. What are you throwing in this time?"

"A villa by the sea, in the mountains, anywhere. You pick the spot, we do the rest."

"Retirement benefits and health care?"

"Goes without saying." His eyes gleamed; he was beginning to feel the possessor of the blank check that would tame this beast. Ridiculous.

"Scram." I got up and opened the door. "Now."

"But . . . I don't understand . . ."

"You don't understand scram? I'll explain it to you, my pet. In a way you'll remember for the rest of your wretched life."

I waded through the underbrush, to get away from the noise on the beach. Here, under the trees, not that long ago a little boy played and dreamed grand and lovely things. Except it turned out the world respected only the scum and the thugs.

Actually, it wasn't quite that way. The little boy dreamed only of stuffing himself and playing and maybe getting into a little trouble. He also wanted to be strong, strong enough not to be afraid. Fear, he remembered, was a stab of ice through the chest. To tell the truth, none of that had changed, one just might put it now in different words.

I went deeper into the woods. I was god-awful sober that day and didn't even want to get laid. Maybe that was the reason for this sentimental mood. I was always Mr. Tough as Nails in front of others, but here, in this isolated spot, I felt lonely, and safe.

Where were my friends, the companions of my childhood games? Well, they were with me; we worked together. When we grew up and became young men, I killed them all, but not all the way, because what would have been the point of that? After I learned the Major Secret, I knew I could make coots of them, so they were inside me now and followed all my orders. Coots have to obey. All they can say is "Yes sir!"

"Sultan, are you there?" I asked their leader.

"Yes sir!"

"Would you like to talk?"

"Yes sir!"

"I permit you to speak."

"Yes sir!"

From my height the coots were peabrains, highly useful taken together but still peabrains. I would need to release Sultan, my best friend, otherwise forget about conversation. Release him? No, better for me to drop in on them. Just for a minute.

It's easy to become a coot. I simply think I'd like to be one, and there I am, inside myself, packed into a sky-blue-pink landscape, surrounded by a cheering crowd of wheyey critters. I was semitransparent myself, but my body was elsewhere after all.

Sultan had become just a runt, but it was him all right! His villainous puss beamed with genuine joy when he took me in his arms and hugged me tight and tighter.

"Enough, old guy, you'll squeeze the life out of me," I said, moved, trying to extricate myself. I didn't remember such friendly hugs.

He loosened his hold, but only to hit—in the neck, in the temple. How could I have been so stupid! Dropping in on them like this, I was no longer their master. I had let myself be taken, like a total asshole.

I grew numb, though I could still see okay. Sultan put the strangle on me, and the world turned gray like cheap paper. The other coots jumped around and chanted, "Sul-tan, Sul-tan!"

He hissed in my ear, "If you can't speak, all you need do is think, `My power is yours.'" I had let the bastard speak, but there's no gratitude.

I didn't know if it was possible to choke to death a soul paying a visit to its own body, but I felt pretty dreadful, so I thought the thought that was required. He let me go then and grew, expanded out beyond the sky-blue-pink firmament, and was gone, and I saw that my body was coming to me inside. I had turned a wheyey color and was now an ordinary coot. I could say only "Yes sir!" and had to help my Master, whatever it took, but I could think what I liked, so I called myself every name in the book.

Sultan wasn't bright. The first evening he got riddled with so much lead that we really had to scramble to patch in time. The bullets for us were like watermelon seeds; we swallowed them. We filled the holes, no problem, because we were all geniuses at physiology and metabolism, though none of us had studied it. Does anyone teach a baby how to find the nipple?

Sultan finally put the strangle on the pie-eyed revolver wielder, but what kind of coot is it who only waves his hands and pretends to care? There are coots and there are coots, you armchair strategists.

Sultan was simply not up to it. A lousy leader, no ambition, or maybe he didn't set himself appropriate tasks because he was simply a coward, the garden variety. I was ashamed of him, my former best friend: he avoided encounters with the enemy—he would even turn tail and run. I was livid when I heard people saying that the Great Enkel was over the hill. After a while they didn't say anything at all, just spat with disgust; meanwhile Sultan made himself scarce, covered his tracks, and kept changing shape, strangling assorted mangy mugs who were even more craven than he. I had no choice but to always say "Yes sir!" and in all things subordinate myself to that pathetic hack. He got heavy on the lousiest beer, and got bags under his eyes from the cheapest whores. Ridiculous!

Although I sat deep in his belly, it didn't escape my notice that for a while now these shameful flights of Sultan had become more and more despairing and random. I realized that a tenacious someone was on his trail. My Master was running for his life.

Once, as he lay amid rubbish in an abandoned garret, wheezing from the dust and watching the road through a crack in the wall, he groaned:

"He's too fast!"

"Yes sir!" I replied, since the remark was addressed to me.

"Shut up, pig," he snapped. He was about to launch into the usual stream of obscenities, but stopped and thought. A pity, so late in the game. But now his mind was taking the right path, I was sure of it. I felt warm.

"We're friends, right, Enkel? Maybe you have an idea . . . Hsst!"

Down the road came a well-put-together man in a light-colored, pressed suit. He wore a bow tie with polka dots as red as drops of fresh blood. Bearded, tan, not in his first youth. He stopped and looked up in our direction.

"He knows," Sultan breathed, clenching his big sweaty fists.

The man walked off unhurriedly.

"He knows I'm here! What should I do? Tell me!"

"Yes sir!"

Sultan gave a roar of rage, then freed me. He had no option, the poor bastard. I climbed out of his neck in a pink bubble, hopped to the floor, and grew, assuming my original form of a redheaded Irishman somewhat the worse for wear.

"But no tricks," he cautioned with a raised pudgy finger. "I am thirty to your one."

"Ten of them you can stuff," I said through my teeth. "They were your brilliant contribution."

"Fine, fine, old buddy." He spread his ham hands like an angel's wings. "We'll take him together, Enkel, Otherwise we're both dead meat."

163

"None of that, chiseler. Your help here isn't worth a wet turd—you'll only get in the way. I'll handle this guy. On condition that you give me the coots."

He stepped back, wiped his dripping face.

"Never! Don't even try!"

"Very well. I'm leaving."

"I did not give you permission to go," he grated.

"You can give it now." I put out my hand. "You want to keep me, you hit first."

The stranger again appeared in the road, his bright suit quite visible under the street lamp. He was in no rush.

Sultan breathed heavily. He had chosen the form of a powerful peasant, a bear of a man, but a slow bear. More fat than muscle on him, however—layers of it, the sucker. He could still take care of me, though, with the high-caliber rod he carried in his jacket. He didn't do that, too afraid.

"Then I'll leave," he said hoarsely. "You give your word you won't go after me? I've had enough. I'd like to . . . set myself up, get an ordinary wife, enjoy a quiet fuck under the covers, a hot dinner every day, kids to yell at. You understand?"

"No problem. My word on it. Hand over the coots!"

The porch door creaked. Sultan lost no time: pink dolls jumped into me, a full dozen.

"All of them!"

"But . . ."

"He's on the stairs now."

The remaining bums crawled in clumsily, still under the influence although the party was over. The moment I had the lot in me, I seized Sultan, my closest friend.

"But you promised!" His face a blur with terror.

I wound up to deal him one in the head, so of course he obligingly lifted both hands. A sucker of suckers! I could now kick him easily and methodically in the groin and stomach, then apply the strangle. I counted to ten and asked pleasantly:

"Would you like to be my coot?"

He fizzled and was mine. I would find a use for him.

I kept my red hair but got a better build. I was now ready for action, a killing machine, a mountain of muscle ready to pounce.

"You wish to die?" I asked the stranger, who was standing in the doorway, slightly bent under the sloped ceiling. Having no weapon, I approached him, alert to his smallest movement.

"I'd prefer to talk," he said with a smile. "There's not a bad dive nearby."

It was a real smile, I swear, not any kind of teeth baring or idiot rictus. This character had to be a rare master of moves, so I thought to myself I'd try getting a thing or two out of him before I finished him off. We went for shots of vodka, but I was on my guard, doubly.

We took an alcove in the middle of a flight of steps. Every now and then a waiter would come up from the gray hole below us and hurry to the brightness of the higher floors, leaving behind the mingled stink of sweat and fries.

I was humming with energy; my crew of coots were at attention and waiting for their signal. Anger bubbled in me, at Sultan, at all best friends, at the whole world. At this dude too in the summer suit and the bow tie with the blood-red polka dots.

"You resemble a government faggot, but you smell different," I began. "You give off something that makes one shiver."

He held his shot glass elegantly, between two fingers. I imagined myself banging the table, not to break anything, just enough to send the clear liquid bouncing off the wall in a wide spray.

"Stop that," Gabe warned—he had told me his name was Gabe. What, for Gabriel? Ridiculous. Incredibly, this fancy Daniel dared to raise his voice to me. "Restrain yourself, Enkel. I have two trumps on you."

"You?" I snorted, still deliberating on the blow to deliver. It would have to be just right, not so strong that I would skin my knuckles, not so weak that the effect would be measly.

"First: it was I who freed you from Sultan."

My amazement exceeded even my anger.

"What are you saying?"

"I've been watching you for a long time. Your crew worked much worse under Sultan than under you, so I put a little fear into him. It wasn't difficult."

It fit, actually. If he had wanted to finish Sultan off, he could have done it much sooner. He was waiting—waiting for me. I have to admit, I was not unimpressed.

"So you've been grooming an opponent for yourself? Well, you have one now," I said, more as a ceremonial thing than a challenge, and flicked his glass. As I had calculated, it went flying against the wall and burst like a bomb.

"A waste of good liquor," Gabe remarked calmly. "Watch out next time, because up my sleeve is trump two."

I don't know how, but a fact is a fact: his hand held a switchblade. The silver-plated knife popped from its sheath.

I winced. "I prefer dealing with pure steel. Trinkets are for cunts and homos."

"Yes, I know you have an allergy to silver. Alas, it happens even in this day and age."

"You want to fight here?" I asked, uncertain. My anger had evaporated, and without anger it is not as easy to beat the shit out of an individual.

"I'm not here to fight. I have a proposition."

I broke into a grin, then burst into laughter. I had known hundreds of these pimps and their propositions: they all tried to pull me into filth that brought no benefit. I accepted none of it, so why should I go along with what this pimp wanted? Because he knew how to tie a bow tie?

He put aside the knife but kept it within reach. A quick move, beginning by overturning the table, would probably work. Depending, of course, on the opponent's reflexes.

"Look," he said, holding out to me a medallion on a chain. It was all silver, Jesus. "A present from me to you. You can put it around your neck."

"You're crazy," I croaked with difficulty. My throat was closing up, and my skin itched unbearably. I tried to pull away, but it was too late: such a quantity of silver at such close quarters was more immobilizing than two full nelsons.

So I had got mine. What entire bands of bad-ass pros with their heaters and razors and knucks and piano wire hadn't been able to accomplish, this fop in a polka-dot bow tie did in under one minute. And with what? A goddamn letter opener and an old necklace, son of a bitch.

"If you can't speak," Gabe said, bending over me and pouring his poison into my ear, "then just think: 'From today I fight under a different flag.' You don't need to change a thing, just the sign. You remain a free agent with free will."

It was over for me. My throat was one gummy blob, my stomach was a brimming cesspool, my brain crawled with maggots. Fire in my gut, the body spazzing as in the final throes. What had that peacock said? That I didn't need to change a thing? So be it!

The grip slowly relaxed, my starving lungs drew in their first sweet gulp of air, and the awful twitching subsided. After a while I straightened and knocked back a shot of vodka. The chain was still around my neck.

"Hand it back," Gabe said.

I touched my chest. "Why?"

"Oaths made under duress are not valid. At least not with us."

Again that first person plural. Did even this Dudley Do Right have to back himself with numbers? Ridiculous.

I took off the medallion and hefted it. I was holding a full ounce of silver without pain. Without feeling at all bad. This was very amusing. More: it gave me a delightful sense of security. No one now would be able to get me from that side!

"You were saying, I don't need to change a thing, I can go on as before? You don't want anything from me?"

"Live as you wish. Our accounting isn't done in this vale."

I closed and opened my hand. "In that case I'll keep it. I'll take the knife too, to complete the set."

"It's yours." He closed the switchblade and pushed it toward me.

I took the silver-plated handle gingerly, but nothing happened.

Then, between one passage of the waiter and the next, I smacked him in the face and applied the old strangle. He kicked a little, but in no time at all I made a nice little coot out of him. I changed into a dark, skinny guy and left. No one even turned to look at me. Which was fine.

I let him out on the street. I hadn't even fought with him, so to hell with the guy. He brushed off his suit, adjusted his bow tie, and said everything was in order. For that I was tempted to rough him up again, but I only asked:

"Why me?"

"Because you were the worst. And at the same time the best."

Past tense, ha. I shrugged and continued on my way. At the corner I let Sultan out. Well, I had promised him. Let the bastard set himself up with a lawful wedded wife. He was a coward and a sneak and a drip, but, then, so are most.

Just don't go thinking, you bunch of tight-assed twits, that I intend to change a thing in my life. There simply was no need to hold on to those two coots. I'm not settling down, no way, Gus. I still have my own fear to set on, though that can be put in a way that sounds better.

You can forget my little tale if you like, just remember this: As long as the might stays with me, so does the right. Ha!

170

The Iron General

Jacek Dukaj

The train stopped, and the General jumped out. Through the billowing steam from the engine he could see the squat form of the gnome engineer already fussing among the wheels, which were four times higher than he. For some reason the gnome was beating furiously at the dirty metal with a long-handled hammer.

The General gestured with his cane, keeping his aide from running up to the tracks; he approached the gnome.

"Is anything the matter?"

The engineer looked up, snorted, set down his hammer. In his face, black with soot, gleamed yellow eyes. The gnome's matted beard was the color of tar; no doubt you could have combed half a shovelful of coal from it. He groped beneath that wild scraggle, pulled out a cigarette and a matchbook, lit the cigarette, and took a deep drag.

"It's OK, General," he said, having steadied himself.

The General took his watch from the left pocket of his jacket and glanced at it. "A quarter to two. Two clocks better than you promised. Not bad."

The gnome blew out smoke; the cigarette, stuck in the black thicket of his beard, for a moment glowed a brighter red. "That's not the point. My assistant's for shit. But don't you worry, General, *Demon* will go like hell, even faster."

"I'd like to see more cars on the train."

"That too, no problem."

"Good. Wonderful. I am pleased." He clapped the gnome on the back with his left hand (gems flashed, metal gleamed), at which the gnome bared his crooked teeth in a broad smile. But the General was now looking elsewhere, at his aide, who had approached them nevertheless.

The General said good-bye to the engineer and stepped under the coal shed overhang, where a swinging kerosene lamp threw a pale light.

Major Croak stiffened and saluted as per regulations: heels together, jackboots polished, left hand on hilt of saber, right arm thrust forward and up.

"Come on, Croak. We're not on the parade ground."

"Yes sir, General sir."

And he assumed the regulation at-ease position.

The General couldn't do a thing with Croak. He didn't even try. The officer ways of the man would remain with him to the grave. As a teenage cadet in the Academy of War, Croak had gone with his squad to the Dun Mountains—they had a month's leave and wanted to check out the legend for themselves: it seemed an appropriate excursion-adventure for the army's future leaders. Of his squad, Croak alone survived: the Iron General, happening to pay a visit just then to an old necromancer friend, literally plucked the lad from the claws of the dragon. The General, who even before that had been a hero to all the thaum cadets, in the eyes of Croak advanced then to the rank of demigod if not higher. Croak grew up—he had hit thirty now—but in his private religion not a thing had changed.

"What is it?"

"Bad news, sir. The Crawler's illusionists have opened Frog Field over the city. The people are watching it. The Bird is letting the princes have both barrels."

"Vazhgrav was supposed to issue a decree."

"He didn't."

"Great thunder. Why not?"

"His Royal Highness says he will not stoop to cen-sorship," Croak recited with a stony face. "But you sir, General sir, should take your mirror with you, to stay abreast, the polters are never reliable."

"Let me guess who told him not to stoop. Birzinni?"

"The prime minister hasn't left the Castle for two days," said Croak.

The General smiled a grim smile.

"You have horses?"

"Behind the warehouse."

"Then off with us to the Castle."

173

Riding, he calculated how long it would take the different divisions to reach their positions. In theory, the variables could not be approximated: for example, Nux Vomica, as commander of the Southern Army, might delay the whole operation three, four days, on a whim. The railroad itself decided nothing; the time advantage it gave could be easily thrown away by one unfortunate conversation at the Castle.

They galloped through the Wood of Even and hit upon the King's Green. Before them stood, in panorama, Dzungoon, capital of the United Imperium, since antiquity the seat of the kings at Thorth. The glow of city lights blotted out the stars, which were mostly blocked anyway by Frog Field. The metropolis of two million snaked in dozens of arms along the tear-shaped bay. In the ocean's pure water the bloody defeat of the troops of the Princedom of Peace beheld itself. The General watched the image in the sky, trying despite the inconvenient foreshortening to follow the course of the battle. The perspective was of an eagle (a buzzard, rather) circling above Frog Field. Here and there close-up insets were screened, when some particularly fierce duel took place, or some particularly brutal bit of butchery, or some particularly cinematic clash of mages.

When the ad for Smith's Stores came on, the General asked Croak, "Who else is sponsoring this?"

"No secret there, sir: the Crawler's steady customers, Sumac, Davis, the Xe Brothers, Southern Holding,
JZL. But I don't know who's in it for political reasons—assuming there is anyone, because that might not have been
necessary."

"How many of the Crawler's staff are on this?"

"Oh, I'd say everyone, sir. They've been going at it
a good three clocks, and it's nonstop."

"They've even closed the genie traffic."

"Hmn?"

"Just look: not one chariot crosses the transmission.
A block must have been set up. Half the city will be suing
again. The Crawler was no doubt funded on the side. No
way could he have pulled off such a spectacle on ads alone."

"I don't know . . . You see the terraces, balconies,
rooftops, General sir. And the streets. Not many people
are in bed. This is not a battle for some cow town: the Bird
is mopping up the Princedom. And this is playing to a full
house. The Crawler for sure will milk it. In addition the
sons of bitches lucked out—both moons are below the
horizon, so the quality of the image is like looking into a
distance mirror."

They came to the city outskirts. Here they had to
crane their necks not to lose sight of the battle unfolding
in the night sky above. Hell poured across Frog Field: dragons blazed in flight, volcanoes opened in the earth, lava
spewed, people were thrown hundreds of cubits into the

air; the torn space twisted them into pretzels, then un-twisted, pulling them inside out; metamorphic beasts un-furled over the heads of infantry; Tatarean floodlights placed on the hills surrounding the field crisscrossed, fused, forked; the separate duels of thaums became mad displays of magic fireworks. Ur-thaums in the space of split clicks discharged in battle all the power, skill, and experi-ence they had spent their lives accumulating; they rose cloudward, sank lower than a blade of grass, belched fire, water, vapors, nothingness, threw at their foes a hail of sharp objects and an avalanche of fatal rays, at the same time parrying analogous attacks.

The poor in the slums, lying on the bare ground or on cots they had set up, exchanged comments on the duels and rewarded the victors and vanquished with whistles, ap-plause, curses.

The two riders came to Upper Villa, and the Gen-eral pointed right. They stopped their horses by the six-story González Posada. When a stabler took the steeds, they proceeded to the service area. An old man running a chariot business rapped his pipe on a sign showing night fares. The General nodded to Croak, who paid.

As it turned out, the posada had only one chariot available; the others either hadn't come back yet or were out of service.

"The Castle," said the General to the genie of the chariot after they sat and fastened their seat belts.

"Specifically?" asked the genie, from the mouth of the bas-relief placed on the dash, as it lifted the vehicle into the air.

"The top terrace of Hassan's Tower."

"That's closed to unauthorized—"

"We know."

"As you wish, gentlemen."

They shot above the low buildings of the periphery. The Castle loomed on the horizon as a black fist thrust into the firmament. Raised on a steeply arched column of rock, fired from a single mass of stone-unstone nearly four hundred years before, it stood above Dzungoon in all its immutability, serving the succeeding kings of the United Imperium as a home, fortress, palace, and administrative center. The General well remembered the day when Skrl finally activated the spell that had been years in the con-structing, pulling from the bowels of the planet the gigan-tic block of magma and shaping it amid flood and thunder, in clouds of steam that obscured all—shaping it into the nightmare dreamed of old: the Castle.

They dove toward Hassan's Tower, a black finger pointing at the heart of Frog Field. The beacons, streaming up from the tower on every side through windows small and large and other openings, created a kind of ladder of light. The chariot flew into one of this ladder's highest rungs, braked, and landed softly on the terrace, which was a jaw jutting over abyss.

"Here we are," said the genie. "Do I wait?"

"No," said Croak, reaching for his wallet. "How much?"

"Two eighty."

The General was in the vestibule before the major had finished paying. He looked up one more time at the sky. The infantry of the Bird Conquistador, shielded by the curve in space, was cutting off the last escape route for the troops of the Princedom of Peace.

"Supreme commander of the Zeroth Army, general of the thaums of the United Imperium, permanent member of the Crown's Council, permanent senator of the Grand Plenum, honorary member of the Board of Electors, adviser to the king, twice regent, Defender of the Blood Line, First Nimb, dean of the Academy of the Arts of War, knight of the order of the Honorable Ebon Dragon, seven times Keeper of the Sword, abayer of the Castle, Count of Cardlass and Phlon, Raymond Kaesil Maria Schwentitz of Vazhgravia!"

The General entered and looked at the doorman. The doorman blinked. The General did not lower his eyes. The doorman tried to smile, but his lower lip began to twitch. The General stood and glowered.

"Enough, enough, you'll annihilate the poor bastard," said the prime minister, Birzinni, leafing through the papers heaped on his desk.

"He announces you like that too?"

"Not being the Iron General, I'm not eight hundred years old and don't have quite as many titles."

"True, not quite as many."

"You saw that?" asked the king, who was sitting in an armchair that had been moved to the open window. He pointed with his beard at the sky above Dzungoon.

"I saw it, Your Highness," said the General, going to him.

Bogumil Vazhgrav was smoking a cigarette, tapping the ashes into a shell-shaped ashtray on his knee. On the parapet at his left elbow was a distance mirror that held an image of the Council Chamber of the palace of the Princeling of Peace in New Pershing; the mirror's sound ruby was pushed to OFF. The Chamber was no less a chaos than Frog Field.

"That whoreson Bird has the luck of a fruckin Gurlan." Vazhgrav crushed his cigarette, immediately took another from the pack and lit it. "Pike gets fruckin caught in a phase change, and the Bird hits precisely then, for a whole clock the thaums of the damn princeling had no backup, none, half of them died from no oxygen. I don't fruckin understand why that asspicker Pike didn't retreat. What, do they have gold buried under that eatshit Frog Field I ask you?"

It was no secret that the young king's mode of expression had departed somewhat from the standards of intercourse expected in aristocratic spheres, but this tendency of his to use gutter argot, which had intensified of late, indicated the poor, and worsening, state of the ruler's nerves.

"As I explained to Your Highness," said Nux Vomica above the three-dimensional projection of the field of battle, his back to the monarch, "they weren't able to open a channel to a new locus in time."

"But the Bird's thaums weren't either!" Vazhgrav snapped. "What's the diff?"

"The Bird has an army of a quarter of a million," the Iron General said quietly to the king. "He would like nothing better than to put all thaums out of combat. Then he could crush the princes by the sheer number of troops thrown into battle."

"How come Ferdinand and I don't have a quarter of a million soldiers?"

"It doesn't pay," sighed Birzinni, stamping a document.

"It sure pays for fartfruckin Bird, may he rot in two."

"It doesn't for him either. That's why he must invade, conquer, annex."

"I wouldn't be too sure," muttered the General.

"You don't know fruckshit yourselves, and you're making up stuff! Let's have a general conscription, OK? That'll show the bastard. He has a quarter million? I'll have a motherscritchin million! Huh! I mean, this is the Imperium here, not some hickhole in the north! Gustav, what was the last census?"

"A hundred twenty million, four hundred seven thousand, two hundred fifty-seven citizens of age, Your Highness," said Gustav Lambraux, the Council Secretary and Exchequer, not missing a beat, because five demons sat in his head.

"And how many does the Bird have, may his dick wither, in all?"

"He himself doesn't know, most likely. The inhabitants of the lands he has captured number from two hundred fifteen to two hundred eighty million."

"So many?" Vazhgrav blinked in surprise. "Where did all that vermin come from?"

"There is poverty in the north, Your Highness. The poor multiply quickly," replied Lambraux, suggesting the obvious connection between these two facts.

"The natural consequence of demographic pressure," said the General, taking a seat on the parapet before the king, resting his cane across a thigh, his left hand on its knob. "Sooner or later, a Bird must appear. He is carried by a wave of population growth; he is like the lightning bolt that releases the energy of the storm. It was your great-grandfather who issued a decree closing the borders of the Imperium to immigrants. A wealthy man is wealthy only when he has a beggar present to provide contrast. Thus the Bird's offensive, when one looks at the map, seems absurd: his lands, alongside those of the Imperium and its allies, if I may be allowed the comparison, are a flea to a leviathan. But that's not the way to look at it."

"And what, pray, is the scritchin way to look at it?"

"Almost seven hundred years ago all this Imperium was only Dzungoon, the bay, Lighthouse Island, which sank to the bottom during the Twelfth, and the surrounding villages. 'Twas in the midst of the Great Plague that Baron Anastasis Vazhgrav dared to foment rebellion. And Tsarina Yx looked upon the map, saw the flea beside the leviathan, and put off sending troops."

"What sort of half-assed analogy is this?" Birzinni was annoyed. He had completed a short call on his mirror. "That we're some kind of colossus with feet of clay? And that the Bird, with his band of rabble, is the next Imperium?"

"We can determine that in one way only," replied the General calmly. "By waiting. But do you really want to allow him to build his own imperium?"

Birzinni waved his deactivated mirror in the General's direction. "Your perspective on this is completely warped. It's from all those spells of yours: you live and live, and live, one century then another goes by, the history of whole nations is bracketed between your youth and old age. Even if you wanted to, you couldn't change that scale in your mind."

"For a king," said the General, looking straight into Vazhgrav's blue eyes, "that is the most appropriate scale, the most appropriate perspective. We should strike now, while the Bird is busy with the Princedom. Without sneaking up, without feeling out—with our full weight. Attack him by the Upper Pass and the Lower, attack from the west through the Fens and by the sea at K'd, Ozz, and both Frodgeries, and by air, cutting off his lines of supply. We should move now and at once."

Vazhgrav tossed away his cigarette and began to chew on a fingernail. "Attack him, just like that? With no reason?"

"You have a reason, the best possible."

"And what is that?"

"Today the Bird can be defeated."

"It's *war* you want?" cried Birzinni, throwing his arms above his head and waking with his cry Sasha Quezatl, Lord Treasurer-Comptroller, who had been nodding by the fireplace. "War?! Aggression against the League? Have you gone mad, Schwentitz?"

For a long, a very long time, no one had addressed him other than as "General" or maybe "My Count," not even his string of paramours. The Iron General glared with an icy eye at the irate prime minister.

Birzinni stepped back. "I am not a doorman!" he said. "Spare yourself those tricks! I have a demon—you won't ensorcell me!"

"Stuff it, both of you!" said Bogumil Vazhgrav, and an immediate silence fell. "You, General"—the king pointed—"I remember now: you've been egging me on against the Bird for some time. Even back in Oxfeld you tried to get me to agree to that gnome railway through the Passes. You've been making plans. I'm speaking!"—with a stab of the finger—"Don't interrupt, dammit, when the king speaks! I don't know what you were fruckin thinking! For years you haven't had a decent war, so you hope for a little fun, a little gore, is that it? Well, I don't intend to go down in history as the one who started a stupid, unnecessary, senseless, and totally unprovoked war! Do you hear me?"

"He built that railroad anyway," said Birzinni.

"What?"

"The gnome train."

"Out of my own pocket," murmured the General. "Not one red cent did I take from the state coffers."

"Great God, what's going on here?" roared Vazhgrav. "Is this some plot hatched by militarists gone mad?"

"I don't know whether it will happen tomorrow or a year from now, or in twenty years," said the General, rising from the parapet. "But I do know, for a certainty, that the Bird will eventually strike at us as well. And then, then it will be *his* decision, the choice of time and place that favors him. Let us defend ourselves while we still can, while the situation still favors us."

"You mean to say: favors you," gritted Birzinni.

The General leaned heavily on his cane and set his jaw. "You accuse me of treason?"

The prime minister showed confusion but in a controlled way. "I accuse you of nothing . . . How could I dare?"

The silver-haired minister of the treasury woke up completely. "Have you all taken leave of your senses?" he rasped. "Birzinni, you must have tripped down the stairs and fallen on your head. To suspect the Iron General of treason? The Iron General . . . ? He who has had more chances to take the crown of the Imperium than that crown has stars! Your great-grandparents were not a gleam in any eye when the Iron General was stringing up those who disobeyed and conspired against the king! Twice he was regent; did he delay even a day in turning over full power? Twice he himself was offered the throne, but he declined! Of the heads of traitors he chopped off I could raise a pile higher than Hassan's Tower! You haven't nicked yourself more times shaving than there were attempts made on his life, precisely for his fidelity to the crown! Two families he lost in uprisings! For almost a thousand years he has stood guard over the line of the Vazhgravs! That line would not exist today at all, Bogumil, if your forebears had not been personally saved by him. Rejoice that you have such a man at your side, for no other ruler on Earth can boast of so devoted a servant, of whose loyalty there can be no doubt. I would question myself sooner than question him!" Having spoken these words, Quezatl subsided and again dozed off.

To escape the sidelong glances occasioned by this embarrassingly outspoken peroration from the minister of finance, the General retreated to a dim corner of the chamber and sat in a black leather armchair that had been set beneath the statue of a griffin. He lay his cane across his thighs and rested his arms symetrically on the arm rests, though of course there could be no real symmetry here, for the eyes of anyone watching would invariably have been drawn to the General's left: the famous Iron Arm, the Hand of Magic Main.

For eight centuries, never ceasing to perfect himself in the arts thaumaturgic—even before the word thaum came into usage, even before he was a general and before he set into motion the secret devices of his longevity—even then, at the very beginning, he was known for his limb encrusted with metal and with gems. Legend had it that, surrendering himself to the dark knowledge (and in those days the dark knowledge was dark indeed), Schwentitz entered into a pact with Ineffables so powerful that he could no longer control them, and after one of his meetings with them, a quarrel ensued and the creatures attacked him. With tremendous exertion of will he defeated them and by a miracle survived, but in the struggle he lost the use of his left arm, never to regain it.

Quickly realizing that all existing forms of therapy would be futile, and having no wish to be a cripple for the rest of his life (which would be a very long time, after all), he decided to resort again to magic, thus implanting psychokinetic rubies in the appropriate places of his arm, hand, and fingers. Thereafter it was not muscles and nerves that moved and guided his inert appendage; motion was accom-

plished without their agency, by the pure power alone of
the mind of Schwentitz. In this way he had transformed a
part of his body into a de facto magical prosthesis. Always
hating half measures, this time too Schwentitz did not hes-
itate on the path opened to him by the operation. Other
implantations followed, other fay enhancements and exten-
sions that made his arm and hand ever more powerful and
complex, a multifunctioning quasi-organic magioconstruct.
For the process never ended; as century followed century,
it continued.

Now the hand of the General, showing from the shadowy
sleeve of his jacket, was a thing that pulsed with cold, inor-
ganic life, a fusion of metal, glass, wood, precious stones, of
gossamer harder than any stone—yet a thing of flesh as well.
Legend had it that a flick of the General's finger could level
an impregnable fortress; legend had it that his clenched fist
could stop the heart of his enemies and cause the blood in
their veins to congeal. But that was legend only—the General would admit to nothing.

His hand lay still on the arm rest. He said nothing.
There was nothing left for him to say. Having lived so very
long, he recognized at once the moments of triumph or defeat when they came, he weighed his chances with the utmost precision, and he never confused the highly unlikely
with the flat-out impossible. He sat and watched.

The king nervously lit another cigarette. Prime
Minister Birzinni, standing by the large roundtable in the

center of the room, conferred in whispers with his two secretaries, all the while tapping with a finger the long-distance mirror near him. Sasha Quezatl snored. The fire in the fireplace crackled. At the opposite wall, Nux Vomica and his staff officers, on the basis of recon reports coming in over the array of mirrors hung at an angle from the ceiling (twelve by twelve), followed the progress of the battle, which was depicted in a three-dimensional projection of the lands bordering the Princedom and the League. One of Orvid's people, responsible for the maintenance and manipulation of the illusion, dozed on the couch behind the mirrors; another, selecting and hooking into the audio channels as he was ordered, was stationed yawning beneath the bust of Anastasis Vazhgrav. The low murmurs from the prime minister and the secretaries, the mechanically muffled voices of the reconnoiterers, the monosyllabic grunts of the staff officers, the flapping of the fire, the roar of the night outside—all this made a person drowsy, so it was no surprise that old Quezatl nodded off again in earnest. The General, however, had gone four days without sleep and had no intention now of shutting down his magical stimulants. He glanced at his watch. It was almost three.

Orvid entered with Blodgett, chief of the teleseers.

Birzinni silenced his secretaries. "What is it?" he asked.

Orvid waved a hand. "No," he said, "it has nothing to do with the Bird."

"Then?"

"Something the General wanted to know."

"Since you've gone to the trouble of coming here . . ."

Blodgett smiled timidly at the General, who sat in shadow. "We found her, sir," he told him.

The king frowned. "Found whom?"

"The General's planet," Orvid explained, approaching. "Your Highness surely remembers. It was right after Your Highness ascended to the throne. The General insisted and had me dispatch people to search space."

"Ah, yes . . ." Vazhgrav rubbed the end of his prominent nose distractedly. "The Solar Curse. The Holocaust. The other Earth. Yes. So you actually found it?"

"We did, sire," said Blodgett with a nod. "To tell the truth, we had begun to doubt. The General presented such a nice argument: the statistics, the billions of stars, and so on. Not possible that there wouldn't be a single planet with parameters close to Earth's . . . And yet it seemed there wasn't. Only today—"

"Well, well," said the king, twisting his mouth at the General. "So you're right again, eh? And now what do we floppin do with this great discovery?"

"What do you mean, sire, what?" Orvid was excited. "It's clear. We fly there and take possession of the planet in the name of Your Highness, as part of the Imperium!"

"Where exactly is it?" asked the General.

"It's the second planet of system 583 in the Blind Hunter. You can't see it from this hemisphere. About twelve thousand farkls."

"Well, my dear General," said the prime minister, baring his teeth in a grin, "you're restless without a war, you need activity, some action—and here's a golden opportunity. Take a ship and go. What an adventure! General Discoverer! What will you name the planet? Wait, I'll make you— it won't take me but a click—Royal Envoy and Governor Plenipotentiary of Acquired Territories." He grabbed his mirror and barked the necessary orders into it.

The General lifted his eyes to the king. "Now hardly seems the time to set off on such expeditions," he said.

Orvid pulled an illusion prism from his pocket, placed it on the table, and muttered the code. In the air appeared a three-dimensional image of a planet. With a few words he enlarged and lifted the image.

"Pretty, no?" He walked around the planet, observing it with pride, as if by activating the prism he had in fact created the heavenly body. "You don't see them, because the illusionists took the picture too close up, but she has two moons, one large, three or four times the mass of our Collop, the other a mere wisp, hardly a moon at all. The continent at the terminator extends to the other pole. And look at that archipelago. Those mountains."

Even the king now was beguiled. Vazhgrav got up and, with a cigarette dangling from his mouth, went over to the illusion. The General did also. Even Vomica became interested. The planet—half white and sky-blue, half black—hung above them like the eye of a bashful deity peering out of a fifth dimension. The image was frozen, the prism retaining only one frame in its lens: the hurricanes were stopped in their spiral, the clouds were caught and fixed over a quarter of the ocean, the storms were stilled in the middle of their fury, the rotation of day and night was halted—but it sufficed.

"God," Vazhgrav whispered. "I wouldn't mind going myself."

Birzinni smirked.

The General put his right hand on the king's shoulder. "Your Highness, I beseech you . . ."

"Dammit, there will be no war!" yelled the monarch, spitting out his cigarette. He pulled away from Schwentitz. "What's your problem? What?! I tell you to go, and go you go!"

The General took a deep breath. "Sire," he said, "on this subject would you grant me a private audience, just the two of us, in the Quiet Chamber?"

"What are you up to now?" barked Birzinni. "What tricks? Do you think to intimidate the king? A private audience with the Iron General indeed . . . !"

"I am the king's adviser and Preserver of the Royal Line. It is proper for me to—"

"Out of the question!" The prime minister turned to Vazhgrav. "You have no idea, my lord, of what he is capable . . ."

"Did I give a fruckin order or did I give a fruckin order?" The king was livid. "Well? Well? Do it, then, without any more flapping of lips. OK? Enough!" He regarded the illusion, scratched his chin, looked around, and let the air out of his lungs. "I'm turning in. Goodnight." And he left.

"What happened?" asked the minister of finance.

"Nothing. Go back to sleep," said Birzinni with a wave.

The General went to retrieve his cane, bowed to the prime minister and Nux Vomica, and made for the door. Birzinni twisted an end of his mustache, and Vomica clicked the stem of his pipe against his front teeth, deep in thought . . . They watched the General's back until he was gone. Orvid didn't watch, playing with the turned-off prism. Blodgett averted his face as Schwentitz passed, so as not to make eye contact; only later did he sneak a glance. Gustav Lambraux, eyes shut, was communing with his demons.

The doorman shut the door.

"For God's sake," sputtered Sasha Quezatl, "what's going on here?"

"Nothing, nothing. Go back to sleep."

"What??"

"By royal command. I depart tomorrow morning,"

said the General, taking a seat on the bench by the phosphorescent wall of Croak's office.

"Birzinni?" croaked the major darkly. "It's his doing, isn't it?"

The General didn't bother to answer.

Croak got up from his desk and paced fretfully. He checked the room's main antisurveillance system charms, then burst out: "He's got him wrapped around his little finger! Doesn't even try to hide it! Anyone can see. Thunder and nails, does he think he can get away with this? . . . I just learned that re Dwin has taken controlling shares in Yax and Yax. Can you imagine, General sir? That's now two-thirds of the Royal Council! Birzinni has us by the throat!"

"Re Dwin? That was to be expected," mumbled the General, looking at the opposite wall, where a couple of invisible djinns were moving symbolic arrows, lines, triangles, and circles across a cartographic fresco. "Has he broken through?"

"What, the Bird?" The major stopped and regarded the map wall. "It's the same still. But nothing short of a miracle will keep him from finishing them off. I have here a one-way reflection from Pike's headquarters." He pointed at a desk mirror. "They're thinking already of ceding the Backwood and Right Port."

"Ferdinand is lying down," said the General. "Lying down and asking to be cut open. Withdrawing from a pact with the Princedom was Birzinni's biggest mistake. We will pay dearly for it. A sea of blood might have been avoided."

"Nothing you could have done, General sir." Croak returned to the desk, began tuning one of the mirrors. "Your dissenting vote at least made a few of them think. But Vazhgrav would have done what Birzinni wanted in any case, even if you had managed to convince the Council. Except there's no one now to convince, you know yourself the price of a vote from Spôt or Blummer. But the word of the Iron General still means something, yes, people are behind you sir, don't pretend to be surprised, the lowliest peons from the remotest jerkwaters know that the Iron General never breaks a promise and wouldn't besmirch his escutcheon with any treachery or fast dealing, and it's true sir, that they believe in you, not the king, the king's a puppy, you're a legend, the people know the difference . . . Here. How many men will you need?"

"I'll take the *John the Fourth* with a trio of kineticists. Let's put Gould in charge of them. A full thaum crew, with heavy armor, landing marines, as many supplies as we can take, rations . . . no, forget the rations, they'll be in stasis. You know the routine. We must be prepared for every eventuality, since I have no idea what we'll be facing out there."

"Did you get that, Archie?" Croak said into the mirror. "The General takes off tomorrow morning. I'll go wake people. You have room there?"

"The Old Hall is nearly empty, since we set up extra places for those fleeing Crater," replied the mirror. "In a few dozen clocks we should be able to quarter a division here. The *John the Fourth* is in mothballs, hasn't been out for years, and I'll have to scare up djinns. Are you packing people off right away, General, or will there be some briefing, training? We're dependent on Earth for food, and with an additional hundred mouths here . . ."

"At most, one meal," said the General.

"At most, one meal," Croak repeated. "Any signals from Crater, by the way? The princes aren't leaving? How many ships do they have?"

"Four or five, and three shuttles, but I imagine they've been destroyed, taken, or blocked, because thirty clocks have gone by now without anything of the Princedom leaving the atmosphere. It's all politics ultimately—the Bird's thaums did some ambushing here from Subbermayer back in the days of Old Luke, ghosts got in the woodwork, specters, no doubt undamped manifestations of bilocal feedback, of the fourth or fifth degree. You know about the attempt to land on Crow, General? They wanted to dig in fifty cubits and set up soulsuckers all around, I don't know why they pulled back, it would have given them a kind of jumping-off place; though, true, expensive as hell, everybody domed, the main construct all of living diamonds . . . But Crater won't surrender. And if the princelings were to evacuate the civilians out of simple fear . . ."

"I understand." The General went to the desk, entering the field of vision of mirrored Archie. Archie stiffened, bowed. The General nodded. "Whose order was it, about the Old Hall?"

"Oh, we figured that out ourselves, sir, when the announcement came about neutrality. It was clear there would be no order to go back, and when the Bird takes New Pershing, Crater will be, in all the universe, the last free scrap of the Princedom of Peace. All hell will break loose there in a little while. They're preparing to die."

"And in Pershing no one said a word about those civilians? They forgot about them? You say there are a few ships left . . . Let's think: the right of asylum, with us or in the Islands . . ."

"No kineticists. They have practically no one. Of the thaums maybe two people are left, the rest are ordinary soldiers. With their big mobilization a tock ago they pulled everyone down from the moon. The poor bastards are getting killed right now in Frog Field."

"We must enter Crater, then," said the General, his jaw set, leaning over the major's shoulder to the distance mirror. "Now is the best time: before Pershing surrenders, but after the defeat of the Princedom. Are you in a position to do that? You need to plant the flag of the Imperium there before the Bird's first ship shows."

Archie grimaced. "I don't like it . . ."

"Don't be stupid, Archie," snapped the General. "For what did you set up Old Hall? You'll be saving people, preserving buildings and equipment, because if the thaums charge, there won't be a thing standing, not one brick atop another. You know that. But the Bird cannot touch a base of the Imperium. Zero bloodshed."

"They won't surrender!"

"To the Bird, no; to us, yes. Believe me, they're praying for some honorable way out of this. No one really wants to die, no matter how glorious the death. I'll be there in the morning; in the meantime do this: make the proposal in my name. The terms of the surrender as honorable as can be: I'll accept it myself, in person. My word on it. You understand? No humiliation. We can even call it a temporary protectorate."

"You're serious, General?"

"Don't be an idiot," bellowed Croak.

"All right. I'll try."

Captain Archie saluted and switched off. The mirror showed the faces of the General and the major.

The General straightened, smiled.

Croak shook his head. "I can see the look on Birzinni's face. He'll crap in his pants when he hears this. Now everything depends on whether or not the son of a bitch has spies planted on Collop. Because afterward he won't be able to hand Crater over to the Bird, even the king wouldn't go along with that. And when the Bird's thaums get itchy, you may finally have your war, General sir . . ."

Cold rage welled in the General. With a single thought he turned Croak and the armchair around to face him and aimed a finger sheathed in glass and metal at the major.

"You insult me, Croak," he said through clenched teeth. "The king and Birzinni don't understand, because they don't want to, but do you think, even you, that I require this war as an amusement or a kind of exercise?"

"General sir, forgive me. I didn't mean it in that way . . ."

The General's wrath passed as quickly as it had come. "It doesn't matter," Schwentitz said, waving his cane. He turned and left.

The genie set down the General's personal chariot on the roof of his villa several dozen cubits from the chaise longue where Qasmina slept. She had sunk into slumber while watching the battle on Frog Field. In her fallen hand was a glass that still held a little wine. The General approached, stood over her, gazed upon her. She wore a white silk peignoir; its belt had come undone; white silk flowed over the woman's even whiter skin. The General looked: the head resting on a shoulder, the lowered eyelids, the half-open mouth, the loose hair covering half her face, the cheek with a reddish mark—she had obviously just moved her head to the other side as she slept. He watched her breathe, her breasts moving up and down, their nipples taut from the night chill. He put his right palm to Qasmina's parted lips. Her hot breath burned his skin. He saw her eyes move beneath her lids. She had three-quarters elf in her, so it was not impossible that she could be watching him even through the lids. He bent and kissed her. Still asleep, eyes closed, she opened her arms and drew him to her.

"Old men, such as I," he whispered, "believe only such declarations: made unconsciously, spontaneously."

"How can you be sure who I was dreaming of?"

"Of me."

"Of you. You looked inside?"

"No. I saw you smile, and I know that smile." He took her glass and drank. "Did you like it?" he asked, gesturing with the glass at the sky.

She rubbed her ear, stretched, tied the belt of her peignoir. "Children, such as I," she hummed, "love shows bright and colorful. An invitation came for a banquet at Ozrab. Should we go?"

"No."

"You didn't even ask when it is."

"Tomorrow, the day after, it doesn't matter."

"You're off again?"

"Politics, Qas, politics."

She got up with such force, the hammock turned over. "Screw politics," she said under her breath.

He laughed, embraced her, squeezed her. "I had no idea you were such a rebel. Come inside, come; it's always coldest before sunrise."

They went down to the third floor. The poltergeists drew a hot tub for the General, but Qasmina said no, pretending she was offended, and went to gossip by mirror with her girlchums.

Half a clock soaking in piping hot water allowed the General to relax completely. He stirred from his drowse and made several calls, using the ceiling mirror, which he hexed for the purpose, clearing it of condensation and hooking into the municipal net of distance mirrors. Then the polters rubbed Schwentitz down with big fluffy towels and wrapped him in his three-ply robe. He went to his office. No point wasting time on a meal: he took his energy directly from his hand, thrusting it into the roaring flame of the fireplace.

Sitting in his armchair, he activated his visispex: the most comprehensive of the standard charms of visualization. The spex had a built-in decoder, to circumvent the blocking spells that kept magic hidden to outsider eyes; one had only to know the password, for all this was Schwentitz's work. But there are spells and there are spells, passwords and passwords, different levels of secrecy and different kinds of spex.

Like gaudy flowers the constructs shot from the walls, from the artifacts lying on the desk, from the cabinet shelves, and from the desk itself, and the left hand of the General burst into a giant particolored bouquet that nearly filled the room. Cutting off the other visuals, the General focused on that. He calibrated and expanded the branches that were of interest to him, pushing back inside the other symbolic manifestations of sorcery. Three constructs remained: one counterspell, a wavering black twister with purple bands, went from index finger to door; the second, a lush rainbow, flowed from the wrist to the General's knees and the rug beneath his feet; the third, a spiderweb of stiff decision algorithms, grew from forearm to ceiling and settled over the General in a coverlet of dense smoke. Schwentitz in a reflex side thought called forth quasi-illusional operators in the form of pliers, a knife, needles, and a silver spool of ribbon whose color, unique, couldn't appear in any spex display. He opened an orb of duration and set to work. The flame in the fireplace crept in slo-mo, like glass that has not yet hardened as it issues from a zero-g furnace.

It took him eighteen clocks, yet the sun was only just beginning to rise when he closed the orb. He put on his field coat. The mirror reflected several dozen incantatory ornaments, but he selected none of those. The poltergeists packed the papers he needed, the artifacts, the clothes, and carried the suitcase to the chariot.

Passing the bedroom, he looked inside. He shouldn't have. For the second time he saw Qasmina sleeping, her defenseless beauty, trusting nakedness, the tranquil breath through parted lips. He was enchanted totally by the whiteness of her feet. He warded off, had to ward off a second time, and only then was he able to take his leave of her.

When he stepped out onto the roof, there was not a trace of Frog Field in the sky, which meant the end of Ferdinand.

"The Academy of War, at Baurabiss," the General said to his genie.

A cold wind blew through the open roof of the hangar. Ugly clouds sailed across the gray rectangle of sky. A vile morning.

"How many?" the General asked Croak.

"Seventy-two," replied the major, looking through the office pane at a couple of magtechs who were giving the shuttle a last scan for flight.

"We did two runs, with the *Blue* and the *Black and the Red*," said Thule, the bosun of Baurabiss. "Fifteen men each time. Now's the last."

"Gould?"

"He's already on Collop."

"Captain Boulder reporting," spoke the demon of the operational crystal that sat at a corner of Thule's desk.

The General glanced at his watch. "Half a clock," he said. "We should go. Was there confirmation from Archie?"

"Yes."

"Birzinni sent the papers?"

"Last night."

The General got up, stretched, fixed his eyes on the ceiling, and smiled a sad smile. "Croak," he said. "You're coming with me."

The major looked at him with surprise. "But General sir, here I—"

"You're coming with me," Schwentitz repeated, and Croak shrugged, knowing that tone: his fate had been decided.

"There's room," sighed Thule, with a crystal throwing a schematic on the wall opposite the pane: a sketch of the *Black and the Red*. "In the last one, only thirteen are going. With the rest of the equipment."

The General went to the crystal, placed his hand on it, and stood sightless for a moment. "Good," he murmured, removing his hand.

The bosun shook his head with displeasure. "You might have done that with more finesse, General; my demons grow stupid after such vivisection."

"Sorry. I haven't the time." The General leaned across Thule's pile of documents and shook the bosun's hand. "May God..."

"May God," said Thule with a wave, and then he was conversing with someone in one of the distance mirrors on his desk.

The major and the General went down the iron steps to the floor level of the hangar; the office door was slammed behind them by the building genie.

Croak hunted for a cigarette, lit one, inhaled. "Why?" he asked, automatically shielding them both with a quick anti-eavesdrop charm.

"Because there is more going on here than meets the eye."

"What more?"

"You're coming with me."

"Yes, of course, sir. It's an order. But the demon in my intuition tells me to watch out."

"You have a smart demon," laughed the General. "You should always watch out."

"You won't tell me?"

"Later."

"Yes . . . ," sighed Croak and removed the charm.

They proceeded to the *Black and the Red*. The shuttle ship floated twenty cubits above the floor. It had the shape of a swollen cigar and was made of oak, much varnished and highly polished. At either end was a large symmetrical rose window composed of numerous crystals. The General squinted to see through his spex the visualization: the customized fourfold hermetic Labunski-Kraft spells that wrapped the hull tightly. He found no gap in them. Not that he expected to, knowing the exactitude of Thule's magtechs—in any case he'd have to trust in them, there was no way to check every detail himself, the constructs of a spaceship were among the most far-reaching and complex. But he had had more than one close call with suprastratospheric flight. Once, the ship he was on, in orbit, suddenly lost its seal; only the instantaneous artifactual reflex of his hand saved him from death by freezing and suffocation.

Since then—and this took place eleven years ago—he never left the planet without repeated application of his personal safety hexes. Since he didn't encode these, the thaums accompanying him had occasion to admire his virtuosity: scaling down Labunski-Kraft to a thousandth of its original wattage and toxicity. No one could duplicate that feat. Such examples were the best proof that magic was not a science but an art, and that the Iron General was the undisputed master of the art.

At the levitation column of the *Black and the Red*, marked by a tube of green gas, with which one of the ship's djinns drew passengers on board, they met the pilot.

"This is an honor, General," said the kineticist, hastily swallowing the last bite of a sandwich.

"Your own?" asked the General, looking at the holstered sidearm on the pilot's belt. The handle of the pistol, seen through the lens of the spex, blossomed gold and black.

"Oh, that," said the kineticist, the green parting around him. "Rumors have started circulating in Baurabiss. Crater is only seven versts from the Monk, and there's a war on, after all. You understand, General. But what can such a peashooter do, in any case? It's psychological, a crutch," he added, sailing toward the dark belly of the shuttle, which, obedient to the djinn's will, opened in a six-lobed hatch.

The major and the General flew after the pilot. Inside, the walls glowed orange; it was even brighter here than in the hangar. The *Black and the Red*, like all shuttles, was really only a solidly built box used to convey people and packages into orbit and back. It was smaller than it seemed from outside, comprising two rooms: the pilot's cabin in front and the rest of the cigar, where passenger seats and freight hooks were bolted to the walls. To maximize space, that part of the shuttle was covered with a glamour that temporarily deformed gravity: "down" was always beneath your feet, wherever a foot touched the craft's glowing wood. The diameter of the cigar was more than twelve cubits, so your head wouldn't bump the heads of those walking on the "ceiling"—provided of course you didn't get too close to the rose window, where the walls of the *Black and the Red* converged.

Strapped to a seat, one of the assigned thaums was already sleeping, in half-battle uniform, in a cocoon of defensive black magic.

The pilot, flying in, disappeared immediately into the cabin. Croak and the General sat near the rose window; through its panes they saw, from above, the slightly distorted hangar, the slightly distorted sky.

"I'm out until we reach Collop," Schwentitz informed the major, changing into a tar-black statue. Croak only raised his eyebrows a little. He took out his pocket mirror and entered into a long conversation with headquarters at the Castle, whose staff officers were analyzing the data that had just come in from the surviving spy specters.

The Bird's block was tighter than anticipated, so there was not a great deal of information. The Bird was headed for Pershing. He was throwing his main forces at Tchatarakka, having vaporized Poison Lakes, the Big and the Little both. Panic among the populace of the Princedom had reached such proportions that no one now could control border crossings. Bogumil Vazhgrav faced the dilemma of, Let them in or keep them out? There seemed no solution: immigration quotas against the League would only increase the pressure of refugees from the other side. At the guild in Thorth the price of gold and diamonds had skyrocketed, also the price of land in the Islands.

Soon the other eleven thaums showed up. Croak knew one of them, Ensign Yung; he got into a discussion with him on the subject of the new entrance requirements at the Academy, which for the first time was allowing women to become thaum cadets. Yung disapproved, Croak disapproved, and they seconded each other in their indignation. Meanwhile the kineticist had lifted the shuttle above the city and was climbing through clouds toward the stars. Faint in daylight, the stars shone brighter and brighter as the *Black and the Red* rose; the antifriction and clarifying spells made the view mirror-sharp.

The horizon darkened to the deep black of frigid space as they went into orbit. The few unfastened objects inside the shuttle began to float. In a wink the thaums pulled them down by kinesis.

The *Black and the Red*, changing course, began to chase the moon. The passengers didn't see Collop until the landing maneuvers—docking maneuvers, rather, since Collop, although the largest of the planet's natural satellites, was little more than a big spherical rock. Its gravity was hardly noticeable; those coming to its surface had to wear special boots enchanted by molecular artisans so that they didn't accidentally "jump off" into space. The thaums, of course, had charmed their own footwear in advance.

No sooner did the shuttle settle into the deep lunar hangar than the General emerged from null time.

Captain Archie bilocated himself inside the vessel as the pressurization dome closed over it and locked. He reported to the General: "In one clock, we rendezvous at the halfway point. Re Kwäz will be there in person. I agreed to transmission to Crater; I trust you have no objection to that, General."

"None. Have the Bird's people shown?"

"Not yet. But we're up to our ass in specters; they're getting into everything like roaches, we're blanket-exorcising them."

"They're the Bird's?"

"Who else's? The League was never subtle in its recon."

"Where are you?"

"I'm waiting here at my post, that's why I couldn't come in person . . . You're taking off now, General?"

"Yes. You have the papers?"

"Following Major Croak's suggestion, I based the text on the surrender of the Sixty-Seventh Arcadian; demons copied it from the archive."

"Phantax it to me here."

Archie reached out a hand, and a file appeared in it. The General touched it with his left hand.

"Thank you," he said. "I'll peruse it en route. Were there any orders from the Castle?"

"Only confirmation by harmonogram."

The captain vanished.

The *Black and the Red* had come to a stop, and the thaums began to jump out. The General, Croak, and the pilot were the last to leave. They floated down to the hangar door. The entire military base was under a hermetic hex of the type Kraft III, which maintained an Earth atmosphere; the temperature was stabilized by a construct of living diamonds, which was double-feedback-spliced into the sixth dimension to channel heat directly from the sun.

The officer on duty had the General and Croak sign the arrival book and gave them directions to the chariot terminal—unnecessary, as both the General and the major knew their way around the buildings of the Monk as well as the officer on duty did. The name "Monk" came from the shape of the rock that loomed above the base: a cowled, bent figure. At a certain hour of the Collopian day it covered the entire base with its shadow.

The General and Croak didn't proceed immediately to the chariots; first they entered one of the nearby hangars, which was filled completely with the hull of the *John the Fourth*. The ship was not remotely similar to a *Black and the Red*–class shuttle; it was more than ten times larger. As for shape, it was difficult to speak of any: the *John the Fourth* seemed a random assortment of structures, several dozen, that had been erected by untested spells and then pulled in all directions without regard for gravity and attached here and there with no plan. From this riot of wood, metal, stone, fabric, and glass, jutted every which way great masts and sails made of a strange, iridescent material, crooked spires, dented domes and spheres, even things like plants: leafless little white-barked trees growing on the sides, below, above, and at angles.

The *John the Fourth* had been built at the order of Lucius, the father of Bogumil Vazhgrav, for the purpose of exploring the other planets of this system and neighboring systems. It had been given an independent network of living crystals so there would be no limit to the energy it drew upon in its magioconstructing. It was a self-sufficient habitat for more than a hundred people, who could live in it indefinitely, travel in it to the most remote spots of the universe, and in it face any enemy. An uncrackable nut of life in an ocean of icy death. The magninimb who had built the *John the Fourth*, on the vessel's maiden voyage, tested it—rather, he demonstrated the perfection of his work—by sailing through the

core of the sun: the vessel, its living diamonds pumping energy in the opposite direction, deflected the heat.

"Stay here," the General said to Croak. "See to
everything. Load the people and matériel. Check the
provender. The moment I return, we take off. Muffle our
link with the Castle. The order was public?"

"No. I recruited without telling; otherwise people
would have enlisted in droves, hearing your name, because
you're a legend, General sir."

"Enough of that. The destination coordinates go
only to Gould. I'll tell the others myself when we're out of
mirror range."

"Yes sir."

"For God's sake, stop clicking your heels!"

"As you wish."

"Can't teach an old dog," mumbled the General
under his breath, shaking his head as he made his way to
the chariots. Shadows followed him along the rock, from
Earthlight—a rusty green in Collop's starry sky—and from
the innumerable ignes fatui that hovered desultorily over
the base's hermetic dome.

The genie of the chariot was in fettle. "The Iron
General himself, my, my, the honor is too great."

"Shut up and fly."

They shot above the dome, and the chariot
wrapped itself in a Kraft II bubble. At the same time it covered itself with a camouflaging mirror, the same sort that

the base used: spy specters were everywhere, and there was no point handing them information on a platter about who was on Collop and what exactly people were up to.

For the first time in a long time, Schwentitz was swathed in weightlessness. His artifactual hand injected into his organism a series of quick physiological charms to neutralize the unpleasant side effects of gravitational discontinuity.

The chariot now flew just above the ground, leaping in unpredictable jerks to clear each rise and falling like a stone into each depression. The shadow thrown by Earth slid along the rock like a faithful dog, a wavelet of night. The great planet, hanging over the head of the General like a balloon lantern, gave the scene an unreal quality: an illustration from a fairy tale.

The chariot plunged into the next pseudocanyon of Collop. A translucent bubble, three-quarters of it in shadow, glowed there with doubly reflected light. "Stop," said the General, and the chariot, guided by the anticipating genie, dropped to the bubble and pierced the silver hemisphere with no problem, for the camouflaging hexes of both stationary object and flying vehicle recognized each other's identifying friend-or-foe codes.

Inside the bubble were several dozen people, gathered around two groups of chariots. The genie landed by the group of Captain Archie.

The General jumped out. The captain went to him quickly.

"I've read it," said Schwentitz. "I like it. I have a few quibbles, minor points, but a quick decision is more important now than legalistic details, so I accept the document in toto. Re Kwäz is ready?"

"Uh . . . yes."

The two of them approached the Princedom's group. The imperial thaums turned to watch. When the General lifted his magic hand in greeting, they answered with salutes.

"How is their mood?" he asked the captain telepathically, under a mind lock, which made Archie blanch a little and miss a step.

"The princelings? They're not happy. No one would be. They insisted on consulting with Pershing."

"And?"

"You have to realize, General, that, for the Bird, New Pershing is like glass, his specters pass through it at will . . ."

"So?"

"I had a mute clamped on them," Archie admitted after a moment, reluctantly adding his lock to the General's.

"Very good," praised the General, sending him also by thought a half smile and gesture-expression indicating satisfaction.

"They think it's the Bird. I told them they could keep trying to reach Pershing until you arrived. We've been keeping the mute on."

"Don't remove it until this matter is settled. After evacuation they can use our bands."

"That's not altogether fair," Archie squirmed in his thoughts.

"What can I tell you? Thinking is painful. Above a certain level in the hierarchy a man no longer has the comfort of simply carrying out an order . . . Major Archie."

"Mmn. Thank you."

"I hope that your people have also run thorough exorcisms, because I wouldn't want to be in your shoes if even a single specter from the Bird or, worse, from Birzinni gets in here."

Re Kwäz came toward them. He was accompanied by a black-skinned aide with one or two regenerated eyes, which you could tell by the difference in their color.

The General shook re Kwäz's hand; in that same moment he saw, through the visispex, a side ribbon emerging from the aide's left eyesocket.

"Who is securing this transmission," he asked Captain (still Captain) Archie by telepathy, "we or they?"

"They are."

"Cripes."

"A shame, that when we finally meet, it is under such circumstances," re Kwäz began. "History—well, it's history . . ." He curled a mustache, winked, put his hands behind his back. "Yes. So, then, General, are you prepared to guarantee, with your word, that the terms of our agreement will be kept?" He didn't call it surrendering, since the Princedom was not at war with the Imperium. The arrangement therefore preserved the appearance of a contingent collaboration between neighboring outposts of friendly nations—it did not, strictly speaking, affect the division of territory on Collop, nor did it raise any political issue: it was a voluntary declaration by a certain number of subjects of Prince Ferdinand regarding the receipt by them, on a temporary basis, of the Imperium's protection, extending unto their chattel and possessions. Actually, the arrangement had all the earmarks of high treason and could well have been interpreted thus by the prince's casuists. Those present were aware, however, that such a turn of events was unlikely: the Princedom of Peace existed de jure but no longer de facto.

"I am" was the Iron General's unequivocal answer to re Kwäz.

"Excellent, excellent." Re Kwäz nodded to his aide. The aide handed him a file with the document, and Archie took out his copy. As there was no surface to write on, with a quick spell the General produced a mahogany desk whose top was fixed at a convenient level by kinetic hex. They spread out the papers on this virtual piece of furniture, they produced their pens, and in the celadon light of the globe orbiting swiftly above them they signed the agreement. The different-eyed aide peered over their shoulders.

Dotting the last *i*, Schwentitz straightened. From the direction of the chariots that had come from the Monk, a little tentative applause was heard. Re Kwäz cast a melancholy look at the imperialists. "Would that I could peek into a history textbook published a hundred years from now," he said.

"I never peek in the book of history," stated the General, and snapped his pen in two for good luck.

The General had begun his search in space for a second Earth in response to the Armageddon Spell invented by Innistrounce of the Islands, an elfin master of the arcane arts. Innistrounce, doing research for the Southern Company on the commercial use of living diamonds for the safe and affordable transmission of energy taken from the sun, had developed a blueprint for a magiconstruct that, when applied to the diamonds, would lead inescapably to the explosion of the star, whose core was accessible to the quasibilocated biocrystals via a higher-than-seventh dimension. The full Armageddon or End of the World Spell—also called the Solar Curse—required, true, two arrays of diamonds and two stars (in order to pump energy from one into the other in real time), but the cost of that was nothing in comparison with the result: the total annihilation of Earth! Innistrounce left the Company and went public with his discovery. Many criticized him, but the General felt they had no reason: sooner or later someone would have hit upon this. Whatever was possible invariably tended toward self-fulfillment; whatever did not yet exist had the will to; and once a thing was imagined, it was nine-tenths along the road to being. So grinds the mill of history.

The General didn't blame Innistrounce, but he immediately began to consider a shield that might counter so great a sword. In this way was born the idea of seeking out and colonizing a twin Earth. But the General found it difficult to move his project through the army bureaucracy, since the farseers, under Colonel Orvid, the chief of the section of operational services of the General Staff (read: military intelligence), took their orders directly from the Staff and so were not part of the chain of command in Schwentitz's thaumic Zeroth Army. Moreover, besides the count no one seemed to believe that someday someone would be mad enough to activate the Armageddon Spell—inasmuch as he would be thereby causing his own demise as well. Some even said that the availability of a second Earth could actually encourage an enemy to work the Solar Curse, since the possibility would then exist for said enemy to survive the sun's destruction. The General pointed out that the United Imperium should therefore be the first to find an Earth prime, precisely to avoid becoming the target of such cosmic sabotage. The Staff gave up, finally.

The *John the Fourth* had not yet left the range of the distance mirrors and artifactual telepathy when the news came of the Bird's general assault on New Pershing and Ferdinand's flight to the Castle in Dzungoon, teleported there by his thaums. This development was final confirmation of the fall of the Princedom. The thaums of the League evidently had broken the defense and set up blocking spells; otherwise Ferdinand would not have agreed to be teleported, for that was still a risky operation: despite the labors of the nimbs and mages over many years, at best only every other sendee reached his destination, the rest perishing somewhere among alien mindscapes. Prince Ferdinand made it. He asked for asylum. Even by the time communication ceased between the *John the Fourth* and Earth-Collop, Bogumil had not reached a decision in this matter. His hesitation caused much dismay on board the ship.

"You don't think he's frightened?" Lieutenant Gould asked the General when the General joined the kineticists in the cupola.

"It's politics, Max, politics," Schwentitz said, taking an unoccupied seat. "I imagine that Birzinni, as always, is trying with his slippery little ways to gain some advantage."

"On the other hand," put in a kineticist, not visible because he was mostly buried in the sculptured chair of the first pilot, "giving Ferdinand asylum might be taken by the Bird as a declaration of war against the League."

"You be quiet," Gould told him as he filled his pipe. "Watch out instead that we don't run into a star."

"You could put a troll in this seat. The probability of hitting a star is less than your setting fire to your beard with that stupid pipe," retorted the subordinate.

Gould cocked his head, used pyrokinesis to start a few sparks, took a pull, and blew out dark smoke. Leaning toward the General, he pointed with his eyes through the transparent dome. "Will this be an invasion?" he asked.

"Invasion?"

"You expect resistance from the locals? On that planet."

Schwentitz shrugged. "I don't even know if there are any 'locals' there."

"Blodgett didn't have a look?"

"You saw the images the illusionists took from the farseers. This whole thing was done in haste. Of course Blodgett should have provided me with a complete report on the planet, terrain, landing site; simple logic would require first that cautious reconnaissance be done . . . There was no time. Birzinni pulled the king's strings, and before I could turn around, the order was given. So I must be doubly on my guard."

"Politics in this too? Unbelievable. It's a plague."

"An obsession, rather. A pixie crosses Birzinni's path, and it's a political problem for him."

"A problem for the pixie?" said the invisible pilot with a laugh.

They turned to him.

"Doesn't this come under lack of respect shown to a superior?"

"You told him to shut up. It's insubordination."

219

"He disobeyed an order. I'll cut off his head and demote him."

"Right. Let the rank and file learn a little discipline."

"Then I'll cut it off again . . ."

The General had known Gould even longer than Croak; they could joke in this way, in front of others, with complete ease. But tension was building in the men wreathed by the smoke from Gould's pipe. Gould read that tension also in the calm in the General's dark eyes. The General clearly expected—sensed—danger. The old lieutenant tried to penetrate the depths—was it a matter of politics? or locals?—but with no success. Possibly Schwentitz himself didn't know what he feared. Gould sucked thoughtfully on the stem of his pipe. At a certain age, premonitions took on the certainty of deductions, and the General was beyond any human age.

Soon they would see the planet with their own eyes; soon it would be reached by the recon subspells of the *John the Fourth's* construct. This was their fifth day out. The ship's light funnels collected stray rays from space and with them painted both the translucent and nontranslucent walls. The crew watched the constellation of the Blind Hunter part before their prow. Points of light ran away from the axis of the *John the Fourth*, which was aimed at the sun designated 583 in *Uttley's Atlas*, the differences in their relative velocity enormous, and the constellation quickly lost all resemblance to what the crew knew from the sky maps on Earth.

The cupola of the piloting kineticists, as indeed the whole interior of the *John the Fourth*, was appointed with truly royal luxury: gildings, carvings, panelings, silks, tapestries, rugs, mosaics, frescoes, intaglios, coffered alcoves, paintings, busts. Only the "lower" part of the ship, which held the armaments, larders, the conservatory of living crystals, and the sleeping quarters, preserved a certain show of functionality, though Schwentitz would have loved to sweep from there a hundred ridiculous knickknacks. But that would have accomplished nothing: the *John the Fourth* had been designed for old Lucius Vazhgrav as a pleasure sloop. Any changes in decor now would prove more disadvantageous esthetically than advantageous ergonomically.

When the construct announced that a planet had hove within range, Gould and the General went to the upper mess hall. As this area was gravitationally opposite the cupola of the kineticists, along the way they came to a bend in the field and the tobacco spilled from the lieutenant's pipe. He had to collect it flake by flake, mentally, and was muttering oaths when he entered the hall.

The planet, the size of a dragon's egg, spun slowly in the middle of the room. A still-sleepy Croak stood by it, a cup of hot quok in his hand; he was whispering to a trio of thaums who sat rigid, their eyes rolled back, on chairs moved away from the table. Two other thaums were working on an operational crystal that hung above their heads, and four at a side table were summoning a cohort of wraiths whose aura was not human.

"A little mobilization here, I see," said the General, eyebrows raised.

Croak took a sip of his quok and waved a hand. "I sent a polter to you, General sir."

"It must have got lost. Report."

"Aye aye, sir. We dispatched a low-energy Follinger." The major pointed his mug at a color image of the planet. "Lieutenant Dram, on watch, put it on crystal and has assigned a man to analyze it. The demons wanted to do a multidimensional scope, which would give them full topology below the cloud cover. But the Follinger dissolved. The construct went into alarm mode, the needle tipped to 3.8. Dram sent me a polter and had all stations manned. I ordered the active subcurses and all interfering charms to be put under. We're now going at maximum passive McDowell-Karlinsky, recursively pleated and quadruply muffled. This"—he again indicated the illusion—"is a loop of archived images. The demons are now sorting through the data collected and trying despite everything to cobble together a map, and these three men here have been sorcelled as farseers with the help of the living diamonds."

"And the wraiths?"

"I intend to release them, blind, at a tenth of a fint."

"Whose are they?"

"I don't know. Whose?" he asked the four summoners.

"We passed a system of gas giants," replied one of them. "Devil take the ugly bastards. Can't understand a thing from them without demons, and I'm not sure we will even then."

"Shit."

"What do you conclude?" asked the General.

"It's plain," burst out Croak. "The Follinger crashed from a counterspell."

"So it's locals after all," said Gould, nodding.

"The demons took a profile of their magic?"

"Nothing to take it from, no data; the Follinger was cut off instantly."

"Any attempt made to probe our ship?"

"We have registered nothing like that."

"And they?" Schwentitz jutted his chin at the sleeping thaums. "Have they found anything?"

"They found someone," Gould murmured as he watched the illusion of the planet spin. "Not something, someone."

Croak made a face. "I can't extract boo from them. It's a block for sure."

"The construct, is it shunting them?" asked the General.

"It should be," admitted the major and went quickly to the thaums working the crystal. "Give me all three," he said, pointing to the left of the planet, where the ceiling and the wall met.

"Coming up."

After a moment three knots of darkness roiled in that spot.

"Blast."

The General quickly went to the unseeing thaums and with his left hand touched the head of each. They slumped out of their chairs, unconscious. The clouds of darkness disappeared.

"Someone should have been put here to monitor them," he said. "They fell into a spiral. They would have pulled free if you hadn't given them the help. The diamonds could have pumped half a galaxy into them, it's a geometric progression, and the resonance would have turned us into plasma. Why didn't you think of that, Croak? Three-quarters of the cities in the Imperium have similar traps for farseers, it's the Privacy Ordinance."

"My mistake," said the major. "But how could I have known? The last thing I would have expected is another Imperium."

"Major, sir . . . ," called one of the thaums engaged with the crystal.

"Yes?"

"We have a complete map."

"And?"

"Nothing. A wilderness, a desert. Throw it on visual?"

"No cities? No . . . beings?"

"Nothing. You want to see?"

They took a long look. Gould tapped his teeth with the stem of his pipe. "Nice work," he finally said. "A total fake. At such a distance and for the whole planet . . . a masterpiece. With an illusion like that"—he regarded the phantom orb—"the Crawler had better look to his laurels. Ah, this will be a tough one, General, a tough one."

Since they had mastered the wraiths only at the last moment, there was no time for any real reconnaissance, so the General had them verify a few places chosen at random: each turned out to be in conformity with the map drawn under the subspell of the *John the Fourth's* construct. Which came as no surprise, since falsity was not anticipated in every detail. Anticipated were a few lies submerged in a sea of truth.

As the ship entered the planet's gravity, its glamour scanned the moons. The demons made a multiscale map of the system: six planets. The four more distant were frozen rock, the one closer to the sun was molten rock.

The four thaums who had been cursed into telepassives eavesdropped on the minds of the locals. They in turn were monitored by both men and demons, and when the foursome encountered the first threads of the Brain Spider, the connection was immediately severed. The Spider was powerful, its net covering every continent. The reverse spells sent along those threads of might looped at the first nodes. It had been brilliantly designed: by spinning its web spherically, the Spider concealed the source of the curse, which lay inside, either above or below the planet's surface. The thing could not be tampered with.

A landing site had to be chosen. The General asked Gould, Croak, also a damnèd shade, a medium modality that was an almost pure vortex of thought, this to introduce a more rigorous element of necrompiricism. They played a three-dimensional obi mumba drum. The crystal transposed its results to a map of the planet's surface. It pointed to a promontory on the largest continent, near the equator: a tropical savannah broken by groves of something like trees, with shores on a shallow gulf. Right at the terminator. The *John the Fourth* pierced the night.

Charms were activated to counter air resistance. The explorers entered the atmosphere in a protective field produced by the ship's construct; the living diamonds pulsed at an ultrahigh frequency of energy consumption. The crew felt no g's, because the inertial deformation enchantment was still in place. Neither did they feel, for that reason, the braking of the *John the Fourth*, which was executed only fifty cubits above the ground, with monstrous deceleration. The ship hung over a sea of red grass.

The Iron General, who had hooked himself into the main system through an operational crystal, now released a hundred thoughts that had been previously primed and aimed. Observed through spex, it would have looked like an explosion. Spells sped in every direction. The power gauge climbed eight units as the *John the Fourth* raised around itself battlements of magic.

A split click later, at a telepathic nod from the General, the thaums activated the temporal thrusters of their suits and in streams of accelerated time fell to the planet's surface through holes that the *John the Fourth* opened in the highest dimension. The constructs of their armor maintained reduced Labunski-Kraft fields in readiness, to snap shut around them at the first whiff of danger.

This landing too was like an explosion. With the thaums burst forth hundreds upon thousands of charms and curses and nimbic runes, until the whole area throbbed with a wild tangle of interfolding, interpenetrating pneumas, glamours, and astral weirds. The thaums, still on their thrusters, carried by teams of djinns and their own psychokinetic rubies, flew to their prearranged positions. A few rose vertically, straight as a candle, to seal the top of the protecting dome.

Meanwhile the demons of the crystal analyzed the information taken directly from the surroundings and announced that they could find nothing off or bogus in the earlier image obtained by magiorecon. Schwentitz therefore advised that the level of combat alert be lowered a notch, and he sent spirits to do a regular scope of the vicinity, in an expanding spiral. Then he himself emerged.

Croak, in full battle gear, stood at the base of the levitator column. He resembled a petrified insect. His codestruct familiar turned slowly above his head, baring its fangs of mortal curses at unseen foes.

The decisional lethals, fully autonomous, released from the merlons of the *John the Fourth*, swarmed in the quickly darkening air like carrion birds above a future battlefield; seen through the visispex, they were blazing diamond hearts, from which issued spherical waves of ectoplasmic poison.

The General landed in the grass and stood on legs spread wide. He stamped the ground as one tests the integrity of a floor in an old building.

"So, it has come to pass."

Croak, deep in a conversation with his demon, through which he was supervising the actions of the thaums, answered Schwentitz with some vague thought.

The General inhaled; the air smelled of fresh paint and the stink of an extinguished campfire. He looked around him through his spex. Spells obscured the horizon; the poltergeists tearing through the grass, the artifacts of defense and attack spreading everywhere made one dizzy. He seized time-space in his left hand, tore it, and rode a wave two versts to a grove by the gulf. A thaum who had levitated atop a cliff, seeing Schwentitz, flew down.

"General."

"I only wanted to have a look at the water."

The sea was like any sea on Earth: the same billows, the same roar, the same limitlessness and might of nature.

"Do you have an idea who they are?" asked the thaum, clearing his visored helmet. He was young, blond, with a hooked nose and red eyebrows.

"Who?"

"They."

"They are the enemy."

"I mean, what they look like, what kind of creatures they are . . ."

"No."

The General visited a few more outposts and returned finally to where the *John the Fourth* stood.

The sun had set; everyone had switched to infrared. The thaums who weren't serving in the cordon of sentries had spread out in the area. In the blue light of the phosphorescent belly of the ship a table and several chairs had been set up. Someone had started a campfire. Farther off, they were showing, by illusion prism, the last episode of *Ajarvina*. A half-naked fairy was singing, under alien stars, an incomprehensible song in a dying tongue.

The General sat down beside Gould.

"Croak permitted this picnic?" he muttered. "Doesn't make sense. It's dangerous to relax in the middle of a military operation."

"You exaggerate." The kineticist waved his pipe. "You can see for yourself how surrounded with charms we are. The Bird with his whole army couldn't get in here."

"The Bird could."

Gould looked askance at the count. "What's eating you? Why are you so low? You found your planet! Have you decided what to name it?"

"I haven't given thought to that," the General lied.

Poltergeists brought supper from the ship's kitchen. The culinary genie had made, for the occasion, a savory game dish. Croak turned a blind eye to the keg of ale that had been smuggled in.

Ajarvina was no longer singing—she was in tears. Someone clapped. Someone else began humming "The Lot of a Thaum." All this increasingly annoyed the General. He flexed his magic hand, setting up a rhythmic spasm in that gleaming hex machine. "For God's sake, these are soldiers, the veterans of many battles!" he growled. "No one yet has declared victory. We haven't even seen the enemy! We're on territory that couldn't be more alien, farkls from home—and they are having a party!"

Gould gave him a look. "Qasmina, I see, hasn't helped you. Those eight hundred years are a weight."

Schwentitz glared at the lieutenant much as a graybeard glares at a tot, with stern eyes and a raised finger.

Gould winced. "Tell me instead what your plan is."

"The plan is simple," said the General. "We find the origin of all these snares and blocks. Then we'll see."

"Simple, yes. And how do you intend to find the origin?"

"It's only a matter of time. The ghosts will hit a wall somewhere, and there we strike."

"You're prepared to start an interstellar war with a hundred men?"

The General didn't reply to that. He finished his ale, took another bite of smoked ham, and walked away into the darkness.

He disconnected his spex and shut down all the nonvital functions of his magic senses. Now he could hear the whisper of the high grasses that brushed his legs like faithful dogs. He broke off one blade of grass. It shriveled in his hand: in a few clicks the blade had blackened and shrunk into a tight coil. He threw it away. He walked on, and from the ground the whispering continued. Sh, tsh, shhh. Above a hill he saw a flat shadow against the sky. He put the light eater on his eyes. The shadow was a tree. That is, not a tree but its counterpart here. The crown was leafless, a pink cotton ball all of breathing pulp. Nothing there moved in the wind—the throb only of a dense rose. The General drew closer to the plant. Was it a plant? With his magic hand he touched the trunk. He felt life. He felt thought. The deep overhang of quivering fluff dipped even more over Schwentitz. The General released a demon.

The demon gave a mental shrug: smoke through one's fingers. The pseudotree breathed. The General stepped back. Not my life, not my death. It withdrew too, a fold of its pink. Did you wish, as I did, only to touch the unknown thing? Or did you come to kill me, swallow me, destroy me? Are you my enemy? Well? He smiled; the pulp pulsed. The General switched off the light eater, and night again dimmed his vision. A few dozen cubits from the thick trunk, he sat down on the warm earth, the sharp grass. The breeze washed his face with an unpleasant odor. The clenched fist of the silhouette shook at the sky. You hate me, eh? But what does your hate signify, if you are only a tree?

It was a massacre: the way a bug is crushed between finger and thumb. A massacre until the beginning of the second quarter of the click, when the Iron General stepped in. The killing continued, but the vector of deaths was reversed.

For that first quarter of a click, the defeat seemed total. The power of the magic unleashed on the *John the Fourth's* shields was so enormous, all four operational crystals on the ship shattered. Their demons, unexpectedly freed, only added to the confusion.

Fifteen of the eighteen thaums standing watch just then at the edge of the protective bubble were vaporized to free plasma before they had any inkling. The enemy's battle djinns entered in wedges of multilevel retrocurses amplified by three equidistant independent arrays of living diamonds that without letup sucked from the heart of neighboring stars their burning blood. A fourth diamond array suspended its thermodynamic function to point-place through the breaches that had been made the undiluted fury of solar fire.

Against such an attack the thaums should have been protected by the reflex-rebound algorithms of their armor, algorithms that automatically entered the mode of maximum time acceleration and bilocated their possessors over a probabilistic smear in space double curved to allow their immediate escape. They should have been; they were not. The invasion constructs, pulled in after the djinns, struck with eight-dimensional chaos fields, developing these with power witched by living gems into narrow entropic matrices. The charms of the thaums all fizzled. Some thaums, already in the plasma state, bilocated their scattered ions over the horizon. The djinns on their wedges of burning constructs passed through the defense envelope of the ship as if it were not adamantine but butter.

At that moment all the countercurses of the *John the Fourth* construct were working at the highest pitch—that is, all those that did not require the constant monitoring of operational crystals. It was magic against magic. The infernal ovens of stars, turned into cold-steel energy, coursed across the battlefield in ripping torrents. The tension jumped the N'Zell-Mâ Barrier; the living diamonds were twisted in their settings. Their resonance opened above the peninsula hundreds of so-called damaged spells, which arose from the mindless permutation-recombination of formula fragments. Thus colors began to reverse in land and sky—the clouds and sun became negatives of themselves. One looked at one's outstretched hand as if through the wrong end of a telescope, its thick lens marred by an overwhelming defect. Winds arose; hurricanes tore the pink trees from the ground, roots and all. Through the air came the scream of changing frequencies from barometric plunges where the interstitial seams were ripped asunder and gravitation crushed stone. Two thaums perished thus, torn to pieces barometrically.

The response of the other defenders was perforce slower than that of the *John the Fourth* construct—even with their tempo pushed to the limit. There was little they could do. The battle scopes showed such almighty pandemonium to their senses, such a tangle of spells from the enemy, the ship, the lethals, with a mass of nested obicadabras, magivariations autonomously generated on the theme of Annihilate—that they simply were unable to plug themselves into the fight. Without the help of the demons of the operational crystals, they had to fall back on their genies and analytic amulets, their personal artifactual shielding. Moreover, the entropic matrices unfolded by the invasion constructs ate into the most fundamental structures of the spells inadequately fortified against them, and now these eroded curses only added to the confusion. Some presented to the thaums their comrades as the foe. In fractions of a click, fratricidal duels flared and died. Another seven corpses. The lethals began to malfunction; because not one genuine, physical enemy had yet shown himself, the only objects recognized by their algorithms as living were the bodies of the imperial thaums, so the lethals attacked them instead. Another twelve thaums expired, therefore, from the sudden turning of their blood to dust, from the freezing of their brains, from the infusion of toxic doses of hormones, from the instant rot of liver and heart.

At the moment when the Iron General entered the fray, only those thaums lived who had been quartered for the night inside the *John the Fourth*. But in that same moment the pikes of the intrusion phalanx had already reached the ship's last integument, and even the soldiers within had only split clicks left to live. The sword is invariably mightier than the shield.

With his first thought the General activated the entire artifactium of his corporeal persona. For his hand was only the most visible part of the transformation that had perfected his panoplied organism. What people saw, even seasoned thaums, even Croak—the Count of Cardlass and Phlon in the field dress of the leader of the Zeroth Army—was the head of the dragon only, raised above the mirror of the lake, above its wavering, flat reflection in flowing water.

At times something glimmered there below the surface, an enormous dark monstrous shape—but they forgot it instantly, put it out of their mind, because it was unlike anything, it could not be named, could not be compared, a strain on the imagination. They went no further than the legend: the deathless Iron General, the archetypal thaum. But the legend was but a fraction of the reality.

He bent time and space. He entered the chronosphere of maxtempo. Again he bent the continuum, creating a second chronosphere. Four times he repeated this. At last, enfolded in a temporal onion, he was so in advance of the rest of the ether that only a handful of photons reached his eyes. In the outer shielding he relied on the algorithms of his hand's hard curses and opened for them a path to his living-diamond tetradon. This was a quintuple infinite series of crystals connected in phase, each up one dimension. It ended and began in the "finger bones" of the General's left hand, except for the thumb, which played another role. Inert, the tetradon, as a closed system, was completely hidden. Engaged, it could implode quasars, explode pulsars.

The General flexed his left hand: the *John the Fourth* coiled into a torus, spun, shrank to a grain of sand, and disappeared. The General unflexed his left hand: the first layer of the temporal onion was blown away, along with all the other chronal and entropic charms. He made a fist: the environs, to the horizon, were reflected hemispherically on Schwentitz's body and thrown to the other side. Thousands of tons of earth, air, water, plants he crushed in his clenched hand. He stabbed with his thumb, and they were consumed by the black hole of a galactic core.

He stood now at the bottom of a vast crater of destruction, a black saucer of the planet's interior brutally scalped of its biosphere. Rubble trickled, rocks fell, sand flowed, lava rumbled. The rays of the rising sun pierced with difficulty the dust and ash that hung in the air. If not for the whirlwind produced by the sudden hole in the air, he would not have seen the sky. Through his spex he observed the cold flame of the tetradon pulsing at an undreamed-of frequency, brighter than forked lightning, brighter than a naked star.

Before the first of the broken rocks reached in its fall the bottom of the crater—so slowly, slowly did it fall—the General spread across the entire planet, enclosing it in the mirror of his temporal onion. He was now all-time, the clepsydra of all clepsydras. In the palm of his hand turned with wormlike sluggishness the life of the planet. He saw everything. Gigaspex revealed to his eyes the lines of power. He observed and made another fist. The planet imploded. Before he had removed the last layer of his temporal onion, the black hole had evaporated.

The General opened his hand. The *John the Fourth* was spat out. He folded himself to enter it.

At the sight of him, Gould yelped, "Arrr! What—?!"

The General quickly assumed the illusion of his normal shape.

"Ah . . . it's you," said the lieutenant with relief. "Good God, Schwentitz, what's been happening is—"

"I know. How many on board?"

"We're in space!" exclaimed the kineticist from the seat of the first pilot. "Autoherm! Purple alert! Evasive maneuvers, lieutenant?! Do we . . . ?"

"Right. And full throttle." Gould gave the orders, then turned again to the General. "You have no idea what—"

Croak bilocated himself into the control room.

"You're alive, General sir!" gasped the aide-de-camp. "The crystals all cracked, and—"

"Eleven," Schwentitz told them.

"What?"

"I counted. We have eleven thaums with us on board. That's how many survived."

"Lieutenant, the planet has imploded!" cried someone outside the room, possibly by phonic hex.

"What planet?" snapped Gould, disoriented, patting his pockets for his pipe.

"The planet Treason," said the Iron General.

"There's no doubt. Consider, gentlemen. They were waiting for us."

"Who? But you collapsed that globe, General."

"Not a living soul is left," said Gould. "Yes, treachery, of course, it's obvious. But now all the evidence has been destroyed, and we're nowhere."

"If not a living soul, then a dead one," said the General, and he opened his arms to summon. The others quickly shut their minds. Schwentitz spread the net of his thoughts, luring ghosts into it. "We're sufficiently close," he explained, "and not enough time has passed for them to lose their identities."

"But this is dangerous," Croak put in. "Because if they aren't human, and if it wasn't treachery . . ."

Just then Ensign Yung materialized between the arms of Schwentitz.

"Not you," the General whispered. "Go, forget, go."

"Hurts hurts oh it hurts," sobbed Yung.

Schwentitz clapped, and the specter vanished. Again he stretched forth his arms and repeated the summoning.

They waited long. Finally a few shadows churned and solidified into the silhouette of a man. The face did not belong to any of the fallen thaums of the Imperium.

"You are mine!" the General shouted at the ghost. "Serve me!"

The veins stood out on the neck and temples of the specter, but he bent over in a bow.

"Who are you?" asked Gould.

"I . . . am Haasir Trvak, Blue Company, Assagon . . . Let me go."

"You were a thaum of the Bird?"

"I am . . . was . . . yes."

"The Bird sent you here?"

"We lay in wait . . . those were the orders. To kill everyone. That there should be no trace left, no witness escaped. We . . . carried out our orders . . . God's punishment on you . . . Let me go!"

"How did you know we were coming? Who sent that information?"

"I don't know . . . don't! It came directly from the Leader's office. We trained . . . then were teleported . . . eleven hundred didn't make it. We were to wait and . . . Those were the orders, I know nothing."

"A suicide mission," mused Croak. "The Bird doesn't have interstellar ships, so he resorts to the crapshoot of teleporting. They would have lost plenty coming back too. But no, there were no plans for their return: no witnesses means no witnesses. Most likely they would have been teleported afterward into the heart of a star."

Schwentitz clapped; the spirit disappeared.

"So?"

"Treason."

"Treason."

"Who?"

"Blodgett. Or Orvid," said Croak. "It's clear. Orvid was the one who announced that they found a planet. And the Bird's thaums even had time to train for this."

"A setup, the whole thing," agreed Gould.

"An attempt to assassinate you, sir," said the major, nodding. "I see no other explanation. None of us is important enough to warrant such costly measures for liquidation. Whereas killing the Iron General, that is no little thing. They laid their trap with care. Cut off from the Imperium, without communications, taken completely by surprise . . . we really hadn't a prayer. Their scheme should not have failed."

"And yet," said Gould, looking over his pipe at the silent General, "and yet it failed. What are you, Raymond?"

"What I must be to survive," replied the count. "Nothing less. And it is growing harder to have my successive assassins take me for a doddering old man. Next time, they'll blow up the sun to kill me."

"What do we do, General sir?" Croak quickly asked, to change a subject that was clearly painful for Schwentitz.

"What else? We fly to the contact point with full masking, and we listen in. And then we see."

Gould, puffing serenely on his pipe, had opened a telepathic canal to the General. Securing it with a heavy mental block, he asked:

"See what? You know it's a plot. The Bird in cahoots with the Castle. I'll bet you anything that Bogumil no longer lives. You really shouldn't have allowed them to horn in like this."

"There was a royal order."

"I know there was a royal order. But on whose initiative? Not the king's. I can guess: Birzinni. Well? You think I'm mistaken?"

"I must be sure."

"Sure? It's all so plain. How could they have been so stupid?"

"You suggest a plot behind the plot?"

"I suggest nothing. I simply know the legend of you, and they do also. If Bogumil is not alive . . ."

"Then what?"

"May it be on their heads!"

"Come in, Archie."

"Where are you?"

"Close enough to converse. Speak."

Major Archie on the large distance mirror in the mess hall of the *John the Fourth* wiped the sweat from his forehead. He was in his office on Collop. The ugly rock of the Monk, visible in the window behind him, stretched the gnarled claws of its shadow across lawns of gray.

"A coup, General. Birzinni has crowned himself. He has the backing of the Bird. He gave the Bird the Hills and all of Twa. And Magura with the neighboring islands. The Bird will secure the new borders. They signed a treaty. In the armies now people either take the new oath or they're out on their ass."

"All have sworn allegiance?"

"Some have."

"The Zeroth Army?"

"No."

"And what of Bogumil?"

"Birzinni denies it. But no one has seen the king since the assumption of power. Most likely the Bird's thaums teleported him to his death."

"How is it for you at Collop?"

"They've just reminded themselves of us. We have seven clocks, no more, to submit. Then . . . God knows, they'll grind us, to dust no doubt."

The General turned to Gould. "How soon can we be there, at top speed?"

"Top speed?" The lieutenant laughed. "This ship has been tested often, but its limit is determined, each time, only by the timidity of its testers."

"The diamonds were dislocated during the attack on planet Treason," said one of the thaums.

"Undislocate them."

"Hang on, Archie," the Iron General said to the mirror.

"Yes. If I only knew what to hang on to," said the captain gloomily.

"To me, Archie, to me."

They arrived in the nick of time. Hardly had the Labun-ski-Kraft field of the Monk closed around the *John the Fourth* when a mighty soulsucker clamped shut on Collop. Archie's spy shades retreated along the giant's lines of force and reached Grough, one of the main cities of the League—a good sign, because Collop had not been mentioned in the treaty signed by Birzinni (evidently the usurper didn't have many thaums of his own and needed to use the Bird's); in that way he had incurred a debt, revealed his weakness, and lost his equal footing.

The soulsucker, an automated invoker of all souls in living bodies, made it impossible for anyone to leave the moon alive, but it also made invasion impossible: only polters, demons, djinns could pass through it—either lower creatures or, as people put it, spirits already liberated from the flesh.

"Although . . . we can go around it," said the Iron General during a council quickly convened after his arrival. Besides him, at the table were Gould, Croak, Archie, and the small staff, subordinate to Archie, of the moon's imperial outpost of the Zeroth Army. Also attending were two of the crew of Crater, a protectorate now of the Monk: re Kwäz and a woman civilian called Magdalene

Lubicz-Ankh, supposedly a blood relative of Ferdinand himself.

They represented the 280 former subjects of the Princedom of Peace who now found themselves in this fatal trap—thanks to the Iron General.

"And if they start tightening it . . . ?" asked Lubicz-Ankh, clearly occupied with her own thoughts.

"Our diamonds should be able to handle that," said Archie with a shrug.

"Can't they block our diamonds' access to solar energy?"

"Too many variables," the captain said, turning his head. "We can dodge their blocking, without even a noticeable pause in power."

"The General was saying," Croak interrupted, raising his voice, "that he knows a way around the soulsucker."

"Really?" Re Kwäz raised his eyebrows.

"It's simple," said Schwentitz. "Teleportation."

"Uh . . ."

"Playing roulette with death."

"Is there another suggestion?"

"We can wait."

"At least we're still alive. They aren't exterminating us quite yet. Why put our head in the noose?"

The General loosed a short acoustic charm. When the gong died to silence, he said, "I will do the teleporting."

"You mean, you guarantee it?" asked re Kwäz.

"Yes."

That made an impression.

Lubicz-Ankh leaned over the table. "You guarantee, a hundred percent, that we will survive teleportation?"

"That is correct."

In a single moment the mood changed from grim fatalism to guarded optimism.

"Is that . . . the plan?" asked Croak. "Flight?"

"Plan for what?" shot re Kwäz.

Not answering that, Croak turned directly to Schwentitz. "Are you giving up, then, General sir?"

The Iron General smiled, for Croak's response was exactly as he had foreseen: Croak alone never lost faith in his god.

"This is not a matter to discuss in such large company. How many thaums do we have on Collop?"

"Thirty-two, counting ours and the moon's," answered Archie.

"That will do."

Re Kwäz guffawed. "With such a handful you would take on the Imperium?!"

"Don't forget all the thaums, below, who haven't sworn allegiance to Birzinni."

"How do you know? Perhaps they have by now, or else are dead. We have no communications, no idea what's going on there, all transmissions are scrambled, and the spirits too have been taken care of."

"We'll find out. Where should we place you? On the Islands?"

"I suppose."

"Good. In that case . . . we'll see you in hangar 4 in two clocks."

Re Kwäz and Lubicz-Ankh bowed and left.

Archie locked the door and turned on the room's antibug construct.

"You can do this, General? So many people, individually?"

"I have teleported whole armies, son."

They recalled the legends.

"So—what is the plan?" repeated Croak.

"I move everyone here to Earth. There we take stock of the situation. I might mobilize the Zeroth Army, what remains of it, and launch a surprise attack from Baurabiss. As this is only an initial stage of the coup, the organizational structures are not yet in place, things still depend on a few dozen traitors. Before the attack, I take out Birzinni and his band. Then the thaums occupy the Castle and the key positions in Dzungoon. It might also be a good idea to make the Crawler provide us with direct transmissions."

"You make it sound so simple."

"Basically everything hinges on our removing Birzinni and the cabal. The Bird's troops are far from the capital. People will need to take the lead from someone.

The Castle is the easiest: its bureaucratic inertia will serve us as it has served Birzinni. As for the rabble, one can never be certain there, but I doubt that the populace burns with love for Birzinni. Bogumil has not yet managed to offend his subjects, whereas Birzinni undoubtedly had to act decisively during the takeover, so we can expect a certain number of new corpses. And even if not, the Crawler should be able to handle that. When they see Birzinni in the sky as a prisoner, humbled . . . it will suffice."

"Still, so horribly simple," said Archie, shaking his head but grinning.

"They didn't exaggerate," remarked Gould. "They ought to have blown up the star of planet Treason. And even that would have been a cheap price to pay for your demise."

Birzinni was just leaving the bathroom on the royal floor of the Castle when from a wall mirror with a gold frame the Iron General stepped out and blocked his way.

"A phantom," Birzinni thought.

"No phantom," said Schwentitz, whereupon he grabbed him with his left hand, squeezed him, tossed him in his mouth, and swallowed him. Then he went back into the mirror.

A click later he burst into his office in Baurabiss. Croak was waiting for him there, with practically the entire staff of the Zeroth Army. The Iron General emerged from a point of light, in a thunderclap of expanding air.

Exchanging bows with his men, he checked the constructs of the tower. They were untouched. He could feel safe here: for several centuries he had been continually building and perfecting them.

"Bad news, General," said Colonel Tube.

"Speak."

"You may already know. Birzinni had Qasmina far Nagla killed, her body incinerated, her ashes scattered across several planes, and her spirit cursed with summary and irreversible depersonalization."

"Yes, I know."

"He apparently did the same with a few hundred others."

"Yes." He spat. "Here is Birzinni." He spat. "Here is Orvid." He continued spitting. They popped open three-dimensionally and fell senseless. The thaums blocked all five senses of each. "Keep them alive. They may be of use."

The thaums saluted.

"Croak explained the plan to you?"

"Aye aye sir."

"There are no changes; everything according to the harmonogram. The clock is thirty-seven and a half. The djinns and polters are in harness?"

"Aye aye sir."

"Where is the Crawler?"

One of the thaums gave a telepathic order.

"He'll be here in two trices."

"Good."

"Count." General Wiggins came forward, after Schwentitz the oldest and highest-ranking thaum. "You know about Bogumil. You know about Anna and the little Urmatrix. They too were on the list. We have confirmation from the High Invisibles. All are dead and unresurrectible."

"And so?"

"Birzinni is finished—that is good. But what will follow him, seeing as he has severed the dynastic line so thoroughly? Who comes after, who? The Bird is at our doorstep. He may remember his collaborator when the throne of Thorth is empty."

"And so?"

"In your veins, Count sir," Croak put in, coming to the aid of Wiggins, "flows the blood of the Vazhgravs. True, the point of consanguinity goes back hundreds of years—but for that the blood is all the more noble."

In my veins, thought Schwentitz, amused despite himself. In my veins. They are not veins, nor is there blood in them, and certainly nothing of the Vazhgravs.

"The major is right—he has convinced us all." General Wiggins bent at the waist, in a bow reserved for the monarch. The others without hesitation made like obeisance. "For the third time the people put the crown on your head, and this time you may not, you do not have the right, to refuse it."

"Croak, Croak," sighed Schwentitz. "What have you cooked up? I should have collapsed you when I collapsed planet Treason."

"You may collapse me at any time, sire," said Croak. "But first accept the crown."

The Iron General waved a hand. "Not now, not now, it's too early for this. Let us not divide up the treasure of a dragon that still lives."

"There may not be time later."

"We have little time now. End of the meeting! To your places!"

The thaums departed. But as they left, they exchanged a secret smile: He didn't say no.

In the office doorway the Crawler passed Birzinni being removed by the polters. His face showed nothing. But entering, he practically stood at attention, silent and unmoving until Schwentitz spoke first.

"I have reason to believe that you were in on this."

The old kobold blinked. "I wasn't," he said.

"I'll give you a chance to prove it."

A flutter of the eyelids. "Thank you."

"I want the best that you and your illusionists can do."

"Over all Dzungoon?"

"Over all the Imperium. Every shrop and shire."

"It's not possible."

"It is possible."

"Yes, of course. When?"

"Tonight."

"Of course. May I go?"

"My demons will go with you."

The night went on and on. From the passage of the terminator through Dzungoon, at which instant the General
commenced a series of quick teleportations, until two
clocks before dawn, when the sky blazed up with the
Crawler's illusion, the capital's ordinary night life filled the
streets, alleys, parks, port, and buildings. The inhabitants
took in their stride the change that had occurred at the top
floor of the Castle, showing the aplomb of those accustomed to eating the daily bread of politics. An outside observer would not have guessed, from their behavior, what
had transpired over the last few days—or what was tran-
spiring now, since none of the persons teleported from Collop manifested themselves on the street until Operation
Flash Flood began, and the operation itself lasted no more
than several clicks and there were hardly any eyewitnesses
to what the thaums did. The thaums preferred on principle
to act in a sudden and covert manner; moreover, their actions were by and large unobservable by nonthaums or people without artifactual implants or aids like spex.

In the moment the Iron General appeared with his
division from Collop, there were almost a thousand thaums

within the walls of Baurabiss who had not yet sworn fealty to Birzinni. In the neighboring encampments as well as in their homes downtown there were another five thousand. All in all, over a third of the Zeroth Army—the branch of the Imperium's thaum forces that from its inception had been led directly by the Iron General. For that reason, could he count on each and every thaum? Of course not. But with a respectable degree of probability he could count on them as a group: tradition, of which the Iron General constituted an indispensable part, formed the image and concept of a thaum every bit as much as did the ability the work martial magic. Trampling on that tradition, a thaum would have to trample on himself.

Until the Iron General's appearance, negotiations between Birzinni and the staff of the Zeroth Army had reached an impasse, the point when the word "unacceptable" is used, each side feeling that it will gain nothing by changing its position, and that the least concession for diplomacy, even one step, will lead to its destruction.

Birzinni knew that he lacked the wherewithal to crush the thaums: sending ordinary troops against them made no sense, and the trained thaums who stood behind the usurper numbered no more than a couple of dozen. They were mainly recon people, taken from the Zeroth and placed under the command of the General Staff, people not as influenced by the Iron General—more theoreticians, more technicians than your basic thaum.

Whereas in Baurabiss there was the realization that any radical move against the power structure at Thorth was pointless, inasmuch as in the present geopolitical context no such enterprise could possibly succeed for more than a week or two: the Bird was at the border, the Bird was crossing the border, and the Bird—as had become abundantly clear in the light of the most recent communiqué—was hand in glove with Birzinni and without a doubt had at his disposal more than enough battle-ready thaums. Prospects were therefore not promising, in the view of Wiggins and his subordinates: time was against them. The Bird would eventually send the traitors reinforcements; and that could happen sooner than Birzinni expected or, indeed, wished, because in the end it would occur to the Dictator, given the persistent weakness of his partner, that in one move he could have it all—ordering his thaums to take Dzungoon to "secure" the city against the rebels in Baurabiss.

Did Birzinni too feel the knife at his throat? And if so, what more could he do, what concessions could he make, if in the negotiations with Wiggins his back was already to the wall . . . ?

The Iron General's arrival on the scene changed the situation to a degree that astonished even Croak and Gould. For in one way or another the thaums would have to include the return of Schwentitz in their calculations. True, rumors were circulating about his death (rumors no doubt begun at the behest of Birzinni), but such rumors had accompanied every disappearance of the General. It was evident, in any case, that if the *John the Fourth* had gone outside the range of the mirrors, all such information was unreliable.

Still, the return of the Iron General made such an impression, it was as if Lucius Vazhgrav himself had risen from the dead. No sooner had the news spread than the thaums of Baurabiss began to gird for battle. It was obvious to everyone that at the present pass there was no point in waiting, that whatever had to be done should be done quickly, because Schwentitz's presence would not remain a secret for long and then they would lose the trump card of surprise. Accordingly, the Iron General set the attack for that very night. No one protested.

"They needed only a leader, a name, a flag," Croak said later. "The General restored their faith in a future, offered them an alternative to Birzinni and the Bird. Legends don't die, Impossible, We'll manage, It'll all work out, He can't lose. That was how they thought."

So there was no hesitation, and no elaborate preparation. It would not be a long campaign but precisely a blitzthaum raid: Operation Flash Flood. At the synchronized signal the divisions moved out. Everyone in full battle gear, everyone with a temporal afterburner, in spheres of invisibility maintained by demons, in camouflage clouds of microlethals, in cryosnake array. Tens of thousands of djinns and polters had already risen from Baurabiss.

"The city will be ours tonight," the Iron General told his army by telepathy.

Not one inhabitant of Dzungoon saw the thaums threading their way across the starry sky among the chariots, tearing through the night like ultrasonic comets, tails braided with enchantments. No one happened to look in the right direction through spex or some artifactual equivalent, and no wizards were on their guard.

Schwentitz went with the division assigned to the storming of the Castle. Storming—too strong a word. The whole idea was surprise and taking out those few thaums and merlinists who had sided with Birzinni. The rest was a matter of striking fear into hearts—at which the thaums were uncommonly good.

Those victims tracked down by the djinns in their homes, most of them asleep, were killed or frozen before they could even form the thought of defending themselves. Only in the rooms of the General Staff was there combat. Its few witnesses, nonthaums, heard no more than a cry cut off, saw no more than a sudden jerk or two. A blink, and it was over: everywhere blood, bodies, ashes. Gradually on the field of battle, stepping from illusion, appeared the thaums in their armor. The bat swarms of the lethals flitted over the parquet floor from room to room, down corridors and stairwells, seeking persons who fit the image given them. Death rattles were heard. Around the captives taken blue cryosnakes writhed, the chill from them freezing and cracking the blood that had flowed. Some of the thaums, still temporally onioned, flashed past in colors as they sped to their destinations, shielded by polters from obstacles moving and nonmoving.

"Aargh!" aarghed Lambraux when the Iron General plucked from his head, one by one, all five demons.

Nux Vomica in his chambers on the highest level of Ivo Tower tried to commit suicide, but the microlethals found him and covered him like flies. They burned out the nerves in the muscles of his arms and legs, then the personal polter of Schwentitz brought a cryosnake and iced Vomica.

Several people jumped from the castle windows, but the djinns caught them in midair. One of the jumpers, a thaum, rocketed toward the sea. Chase was given by two thaums of the Iron General, and over the bay filled with ships a brief battle ensued, of curse and countercurse, lost by the one pursued before it was begun, for he wore no armor and, unaccessoried, fought at a significantly slower tempo than the pair in full gear. They turned him inside out through his backbone, and he fell to the water like a bloody octopus of bone, vein, tendon, and flesh. They sent a pneumolytic after the traitor, to dissect and disentitize his soul.

"The city is ours," said the Iron General when he received reports from all divisions. "Now, administration." He turned to Croak. "Communications. Intelligence. We have a hole here: what the Bird is doing. A second loyalty oath from the troops. Mobilization. Keep an eye on the

Crawler. Also, have him calibrate this balcony. Staff the castle. And so on. Where is Wiggins?"

"He flew off to talk with the regulars."

"Good. Find re Kwäz, let him know what happened and let him tell Ferdinand. The offer to negotiate remains open. I give my word. He knows, after Collop he'll have no qualms, he'll vouch for me, that Lubicz-Ankh woman may also. Let the prince come out of hiding. This is his country, after all. There's an alliance to repulse. If that doesn't interest him, nothing will."

"Yes sir. One of Orvid's men requests an audience, General. He gave the password."

"Who?"

"Blodgett."

"Send him up."

The Iron General went to the adjoining room and shut the door after him. From the balcony wafted a nocturnal breeze. The General was still in full gear, which, though fundamentally different from the standard-issue suit of a thaum, made a similar impression: the asymmetry of the weaponry; its stems, spouts, sprouts, tentacles, nozzles; its tiny wings made of unknown material and serving no obvious function; the body hidden in wart-covered armor—a two-legged insect. The General took off his helmet and set it on the table. With creaking and crunching he eased himself into a chair, and the chair too creaked and crunched. Through the open door to the balcony he could see the sky over Dzungoon, the stars, the clouds veiling the stars as they scudded inland.

Blodgett entered.

"Close the door."

Blodgett closed the door.

Schwentitz activated the antisnoop.

"Did you plan all this, General?" asked Blodgett. Having crossed the threshold and taken two short steps, he stood motionless, separated from Schwentitz by half the empty room, by light and shadow, his sullen gaze on the count, who sat by the table piled with papers and whose face held absolutely no expression as he watched the dark clouds cross the night.

"Did you? I must know!"

"Why must you?"

Blodgett clenched his fists. "Traitor!" he rasped in a strangled whisper at the back of his throat. He cocked his head, glared at the calm General with half-closed eyes of rage under raven-black brows, his face swollen and flushed.

"What do you want, Blodgett?"

"You knew everything! I was your informant for a year. You knew all Orvid's plans, knew that we found that 583B in the Blind Hunter months before and that Orvid was only waiting for the word from Birzinni. You knew, you knew it was a trap, a plot hatched by Birzinni and his cabal. And what did you do? Nothing! Spurring them on by doing nothing. You didn't warn Bogumil. You didn't warn anyone. If that is not treason, what is?!"

"And had I warned people—and I tried, God knows I tried—what would that have accomplished?"

"Bogumil would be alive!" Blodgett spat. "Do you think I don't see what is going on here? Do you think I don't hear what people are saying? In their hearts they have already crowned you!"

"Ah, so I did it for the crown, is that it? To exalt myself?"

"You deny it?"

"God, Blodgett, you amuse me."

"You mock me!"

The General for the first time turned toward the farseer. He crooked a finger, and the space between them folded: Blodgett suddenly found himself within arm's reach of Schwentitz.

"And if Bogumil were alive," said the count between his teeth, "what would that accomplish? Would he remove the danger? Would he destroy Birzinni, crush the conspirators? Move against the Bird? You know he wouldn't do any of those things. He was a weak ruler. A bad king, because he feared to use his own power. With his every word, his every decision, he asked to be betrayed—if not Birzinni, it would have been another; if not the Bird and the League, someone else would have attacked. This is a matter not of persons but of moment and circumstance. The realm now finds itself in a period of feeble senility. And Bogumil's reign marked its death, the death of the kingdom. We are food for political predators, who even now tear pieces of quivering flesh from the body of the Imperium."

"So the scepter must pass into the hands of the Iron General, who alone can save the country."

"Yes. Yes. I couldn't wait any longer. Bogumil with Birzinni—both fruits of the same tree, the same time— would have destroyed, squandered the heritage of dozens of generations of Thorthians."

"Then death to them, and for you the crown."

"Can't you understand? For hundreds of years I served this nation, did everything so it would grow in strength and prosperity, protected it from misfortune, guided it to still waters, led it in war, sustained it in times of woe. The people believe in me, in their Iron General; I am their talisman, banner, hymn. How could I let them down, let them fall into ruin?"

"The people?" Blodgett laughed. "And you say that, eight-hundred-year magus? And what sort of people are they? Thorthians? Think back to the beginning, remind yourself. What do the millions who inhabit the lands of the Imperium today have in common with the tribe by the bay that gave its name to the realm? Language? Religion? Tradition? Culture? An ideology or worldview? Nothing, nothing is the same. To whom did you swear loyalty, to what? To the Vazhgravs, the blood line! Not to any abstraction, which you cannot even define and in relation to which such things as love, fidelity, and treason have no meaning. One can be faithful only to individuals, and you pledged yourself to serve individuals. To serve the dynasty! That is your faith and your motto: Defender of the Line. It is a truth that has been held to, unshakably, by beggar and baron alike; it has been taught to each successive heir, from earliest childhood repeated: This is your shield, your shelter, true since time immemorial and for all time, he will lay down his life for you, trust him, trust him. They saw your face above the cradle, and you taught them, wiped their noses when they wept; and Bogumil too, who as you say was a weak and bad king. He fell asleep in your lap—I saw it myself. And you, Iron General, what did you do?" Blodgett sneered. "You betrayed him, turned him over to his killers. For the realm, for the people—for your power! Knowing you could not survive the defeat of a land with which you are so bound, whose might is your might. The Imperium and the Iron General, they are one and the same.

"So it was out of pride, self-worship. We, the short-lived, had to dip our hands in blood, wield the sword, while you simply waited: eventually everything would come to you. It was a matter of probability, the calculation of chances, and even if a given circumstance was unlikely, you had time, it would come to pass, and did. Because you were not interested in a coup in the style of Birzinni, you didn't want the crown by force or intrigue, no, you aimed higher, you wanted the crown without having to pay for it. You wanted to betray the king, seize power, and all with your honor intact, the loyalty, the patriotism, the reputation of the Iron General unsullied. Could anything be more monstrous? . . .

"The people! Yes, they are born, they multiply, live, die. In this nation or another, under this rule or another, and there are more and more of them. Do you really consider them? No, what you see is a multitude: faceless millions. The people! How could you"—he cried in sudden despair—"how could have have trampled on such a lovely legend?! What are you anyway? A man? I doubt it. I remember what you said to me. In the beginning it was the hand, but the centuries passed and you kept improving yourself. I tried looking at you through spex: I was blocked. For tocks and tocks I built a powerful metavisi with dozens of deciphering gems; I came with Orvid and the ring ready—and beheld you as you left the room. Spells, spells, nothing but spells. Your body a knot of psychokinetic and sensorial hexes, your thoughts a roil of demons, you are one great walking curse, a homeostatic vortex of magic! Yes! Stop laughing! I spit upon you, monster!

"First the hand, then the arm, then the whole body was redone, then the mind. The bones are weak? Replace them with gravitational cryos. The thoughts slow? Accelerate them with crystal operators, fortify them with demons, and with more, and more again, and arrange all this in a hierarchic logical megametamagioconstruct. The heart is unreliable? Let corpuscular nanopolters move the blood in your veins. But veins age—so let us assist them with directional runes. But why even blood, when one can find a better, eldritch substitute? What then was left of the original? The basic instincts, the spectral dominants written into the algorithms of operational enchantments. The thirst for power. Pride. The name: the Iron General. An analogue of a man. An illusion. That is what you are, a self-maintaining illusion, for those around you as well as for yourself, since you continue to believe—rather, it still seems to you that you believe—that you are human. But it is not you, not you. Raymond Schwentitz no longer lives, he died, dissolved, dwindled to zero after the nth spell cast upon himself, not even noticing his disappearance, his melting away in that thaumatorium of thaumatoria. Whom do I accuse, whom do I blame? How can I demand decency from you, when a conscience is not compatible with a calculator demon? Upon what do I spit? The wind, an apparition, a mirage. Avaunt, begone! Tfu tfu tfu!"

The Iron General tightened his left hand, and Blodgett shrank to the size of a speck of dirt. Schwentitz extracted his soul and tossed the rest into the sun's core. The ghost inveighed and imprecated in his mind. The General spread out before him Blodgett's personhood, analyzed his memory for potential threats and wiped it completely clean, after which he released the empty spirit over Thorth. He then wove a five-sense illusion of Blodgett's body, placed a demon in it, instructed the demon how to act and respond as Blodgett, added an antispex block—and ordered the illusion to leave the room, leave the Castle, and drown itself in the bay. The illusion departed.

Through the door left open by it, Croak peered. "May I?"

"What is it?"

"Ferdinand has replied. He is ready to parlay, re Kwäz has vouched for you. He wishes to know what the status is of the succession."

"Which means?"

"You know, General sir, what it means. He inquires about the crown."

"Ah Croak, Croak, you will never give me peace."

"Never, Your Highness," said the major with a happy grin.

"Tell him whatever will make him agree."

"So, yes?"

"Has Wiggins laid the ground?"

"After the official proclamation, there should be no problem. The sooner you do it, the better."

"Don't rush me. The Crawler opened the links to his mirrors?"

"Yes, it's now under his icon."

"Contact my railroad gnomes and have them start sending matériel and provender across the Pass."

"For how many men?"

"For an army, Croak, for an army."

"So there will be a counterattack."

"Of course there will. The Bird won't keep one inch of Imperial soil, of that you can be sure. I understand that Birzinni has already called for mobilization; we'll continue that. Start thinking about the concentration of forces, the deployment of people and demons, logistics. I want us to move like lightning."

"Yes sir—sire! Highness!"

"You may go, count."

Croak blinked to hide his emotion, bowed low, and left.

Croak, Croak, Schwentitz sang sadly in his heart, what would I do without you? Of whom else could I be so certain that he would instantly recall my blood connection to the Vazhgravs and start agitating for the throne for me, before I breathed one word on the subject? And of course I may not breathe that word. Truly, you have placed the crown on my head, you, major, now count, soon senator and then High Chamberlain. You had to live, you were as indispensable to me as Birzinni, maybe even more so. A pity, though, that I couldn't hide Qasmina or take her with me on board the *John the Fourth*. Her little childish pouts, her whims . . . If her soul at least . . . But no, Birzinni was thorough there; it was to be expected. Unavoidable losses. Blodgett too. A pity, a real pity, a truly honest man, sterling, it didn't even enter his mind that I would obliterate him, so he hadn't protected himself with any afterlife backup.

Through a wall mirror the Iron General opened his connection to the Crawler.

"Track this form." Schwentitz pointed at himself. "Begin when I step out. Don't wait for a sign."

"General," said the obeisant Crawler. "You wish more than the picture, I gather."

"Exactly. I would handle the sound myself, but I can hardly multiply my person and reach all the towns simultaneously, whereas you have ether links practically everywhere."

"It's night. This will wake people. There will be confusion. To cover such space I must use a strong wave. There may be damage."

"Don't worry about it," Schwentitz said, ending the conversation. "I take full responsibility."

Closing the connection, the General removed for a moment the mental block from the room and gave a brief thought command for Birzinni to be brought in. Shortly the door opened, and the usurper flew in headfirst. Schwentitz dismissed the polters and took direct control of the paralyzed prisoner. He unlocked his vision and hearing, returned the power of movement to the muscles of his face. Birzinni batted his eyes furiously, bobbing in the air at the height of the General's shoulders, and tears began to flow.

"Ach," he groaned. He looked up, made a face. "And what now?"

The General crooked a finger, and on the table materialized the crown of the Imperium and the red-gold ceremonial robe of the kings of Thorth.

Birzinni swore.

"Glutted on triumph, are you? The Bird didn't get you. Ha. Vazhgrav, Vazhgrav. And what next? You'll strike at him now, start a war? Yes, of course you will . . ." He turned his head, a bitter smile twisting his mouth. "There will be a trial? You'll condemn the traitor? Let me tell you . . . You people are the traitors! Imperialists from the time of Lucius, Xavier, the Antoniuses. Don't you see where all this is leading? Self-destruction! I had to remove Bogumil, because he never would have understood; he grew up in your shadow, he thought in your categories, and even when he went against you, he did it sullenly, always in reference to you. I never would have been able to control him completely. It would have ended, that way too, in disaster. Now the disaster is certain. You'll unleash a war we cannot win. Even you, the Iron General, will not win it, for that is impossible. If there were more continents on Earth . . . but there is only this one. What will you do? Level everything that lies beyond the borders of the Imperium? You'll need to exterminate four-fifths of humanity. Will you do that? Yes, I believe you are capable of such a thing.

"But even then, even then you cannot maintain the status quo. Because this is a completely different Earth. Can't you grasp that? How can you be so blind? These are no longer the days of imperial expansion, of annexation and discovery, of the politics of struggle for land, privileges, prestige. That epoch has passed. We have reached limits in our development, horizons have closed, the whole planet lies in the palm of our hand; we are now—humanity, civilization—a closed system that no new variable can enter. There is no longer any elsewhere. No more others, no aliens. An empire now cannot be self-sufficient, independent. Famine in the Princedom, plague among the peoples of the League—they affect us as much as if we too were the victims. If only you had studied a little economics! But that was always beneath you: numbers, papers, bookkeeping, miserable commerce, let the peons and the gnomes see to that. Another conceptual archaism, another inanity of the old time. War, it must be war!

"What world are you living in? Now I, and those like me, the aristocracy of money, the CEOs, we are waging war in the name of the Imperium, we and not those thaums of yours. If you had spent even a moment thinking about the economy . . . An agricultural collapse awaits us, a pit we will not climb out of. It is impossible to keep running the Imperium in the form that you nurture so fondly in your heart, impossible for us to close ourselves off like a single organism that eats its own excrement. We need precisely to experience a Bird, the League, a powerful League, the hungry mouths for our surplus and the cheap-labor workforce of hundreds of millions and the secondary markets and the economic enclaves on their lands.

Jacek Dukaj

"And what do you do? Start a crusade to defend the
values of feudalism! You would make slaves of them? Slaves?
That will kill us! For two generations now the Imperium
has been rotting like a corpse. It *is* a corpse. For God's sake,
General, think for a moment! We need the Bird, the
League! Give them land, access to raw materials, open lines
of credit! . . . No, I waste my time. You are deaf to me. No
new idea can reach you. You reason in the same rigid formulas of yore. You are old, I know, old, yet old age need not
mean stupidity, especially as you do not actually age—but
then why can't you revise your views a little, allow a new era
to influence you? When you created the Zeroth Army, after
all, you showed enough flexibility to adapt to the new
strategies of thaumic war. Though true, that was centuries
ago. After, it's been as if someone froze your mind in place.
You can only pile curse on top of curse, improve those spells
of yours. Yet to see what's going on in the world, that exceeds your ability!

"General, make an effort, at least once! Don't destroy the Imperium! But I see I am talking to a wall, such
an unyielding wall. So rejoice, you bastard, you've caught
the traitors, yes, yet another triumph for the unsinkable
Iron General, for honor and the blood line, the banners
wave, hymns resound, hurrah thaums, God will bless us,
ever onward, in the name of the General, for the Imperium,
honor above all"—Birzinni frothed—"you idiots, morons,
benighted retarded dense—"

"We are all heroes and martyrs here, I see," muttered the Iron General, then numbed Birzinni's throat.

He rose. He counted to three. He went out on the balcony.

The sky boomed with the General. His person had swept aside the stars, moons, clouds. There was only he. An enormous, angular form in quasithaumic armor, an effigy of metal and glass that covered the cosmos. When he opened his mouth, the force of his words tore leaves off the trees.

"Thorthians! Citizens of the Imperium! The rule of the traitors is at an end! The conspirators have fallen into the hands of justice, and their punishment will be swift!"

Birzinni, bent in half by psychokinetic field, on his knees, his arms pulled before him, crawled out on the balcony. The Iron General grabbed him by the hair and jerked the head up, to show, in the sky above the city, the face of the former prime minister. Birzinni grimaced and writhed in helpless fury, bared his clenched teeth, batted wolfish eyes.

Schwentitz waited for the streets to fill with people. He waited a moment more in case some were late in other cities, cities whose inhabitants' responses he did not know.

"Behold the traitor! The murderer of King Bogumil!"

The people roared.

"What am I to do with the regicide? Should his life be spared?"

The people roared. Words could not be distinguished, but the sentiment was unmistakable.

271

The General lifted his left hand. A sword of blinding white shot from it—the sky blazed brighter than the sun, Dzungoon was transformed into a maze of light and shadow. The General swung his arm and cut off Birzinni's head. The sword vanished. Dazzled, the spectators saw only after a moment or two the head held high in the right hand of Schwentitz. Though the cut had been cauterized by the fire of the magic blade, blood flowed. The Iron General stood motionless, his arm raised. A gray statue. Blood dripped.

Again the people roared.

"Death to all enemies of the Imperium!" cried Schwentitz.

"Deeath!!"

"Death to the Bird!"

"Deeeeath!!"

"Lo, I am the Iron General, the last of the Vazhgravs!" He cast away the head of Birzinni. From his room fluttered the crown and the ceremonial red-gold robe. The crown alit slowly on Schwentitz's brow, the robe buttoned itself around his armor, flapping in soft folds across the horizon. "I will wipe away your foes, regain your lands! I will return to you the days of ancient glory! On my honor I do swear this!!"

The people roared.

Acknowledgments

The translation of Huberath's "Yoo Retoont" ("Wróciees Sneogg, wiedziaam . . ." [1987]), appeared in the online journal *Words without Borders* (2004), where it has been archived; it also appeared in the anthology *The SFWA European Hall of Fame*, edited by James Morrow and Kathryn Morrow (Tor Books, 2007). Sapkowski's "Spellmaker" ("Wiedźmin" [1986]) is also available in the English of Danusia Stok in a collection titled *The Last Wish* (Gollancz, 2007). A selection from Kołodziejczak's "Key of Passage" ("Klucz przejścia" [2004]) was read on the radio, in Jim Freund's *Hour of the Wolf* (WBAI, 2005), and appeared in an issue of *Words without Borders* (2009), where it is archived. Dukaj's "Iron General" is a translation of "Ruch generała" (1997), and Zimniak's "A Cage Full of Angels" is a translation of "Klatka pełna aniołów" (1994).

273

CPSIA information can be obtained at www.ICGtesting.com
Printed in the USA
BVOW08s0741040515

398709BV00001B/22/P